CRIMEU

G000162796

Careless Love

A Murderous Ink Press Anthology

****

Murderous-Ink Press

CRIMEUCOPIA

Careless Love
First published by
Murderous-Ink Press
Crowland
LINCOLNSHIRE
England
www.murderousinkpress.co.uk

Editorial Copyright © Murderous Ink Press 2021
Base photo image © Bob Matze (www.unsplash.com)
Photo manipulation, texts and graphics © Willie Chob-Chob
Producktions 2021
All rights are retained by the respective authors & artists
on publication
Paperback Edition ISBN: 9781909498303
eBook Edition ISBN: 9781909498310

Acknowledgements

To those writers and artists who helped make this anthology what it is, I can only say a heartfelt Thank You!

And to Den, as always.

Contents

*First published in a slightly different form in the Bryn Fortey collection of short stories and poetry, *Compromising The Truth* (Alchemy Press 2018)

Oh Baby, Baby,
How Was I Supposed To Know...
(An Editorial of Sorts)

The logs settled noisily in the hearth, and the rekindled firelight made new-born shadows dance around the open plan room. Three fingers of something amber and smooth in a whiskey tumbler rested comfortably in my hand. As Lonnie Tewkes' slow trumpet flowed like warm, rich chocolate from the stereo, I told myself that it was time to move on.

Plenty more fish in the sea...

Plenty more pebbles on the beach...

Plenty more frogs in the pond...

Ah, who was I kidding?

Being dumped sucked.

Big time. [Extract from California Twist]

Is Love ever perfect? Or is it an obsession that remains rather than just a passing phase? And who's to say that Revenge isn't, in fact, a dish best served hot from the flames of passion?

The late Steve Sneyd gives you one perspective by opening the collection with **Careless Love**, which then allows a mixture of characters fall where they will.

Ange Morrissey's Crimeucopia debut presents us with **Point Taken** which, along with James Roth's **A Career Killing**, and Michael Wiley's **Where There's Love**, take us down different, albeit sometimes humour-tinged paths. As does Gustavo Bondoni's **Secrets of the Inner Ring**, and both Matthew Wilson's **The Happy Next of Kin** and Peter W. J.

Hayes' **The Wait** prove that writing from a different gender perspective can have very impressive results.

Wil A. Emerson also flips the gender in **The Driver**, and shows that sometimes love can have more than one agenda – before Brandon Barrows (**Night After Night**) and Bern Sy Moss (**Just a Shadow**) show that love isn't always about manipulation when there's a woman involved.

Does Love conquer all? Michael Anthony Dioguardi's **Ariadne's Skein of Thread** seems to suggest as much, as does Russell Richardson's **Woman Lost** – though Robert Petyo's **Love and Divorce** may well differ on that.

Finally, the second newcomer, Sam Westcott, with his **One Night in a Barn in Montana**, shows that sometimes Love is blind – well, metaphorically speaking.

And that just leaves Bryn Fortey, a Welshman who has been writing and publishing, off and on, since the 1960s, to close out this collection with his **Oh Babylon.** He's someone we're very pleased to see back in action behind a pen once more.

So, while the jury's out regarding Love's guilt or innocence, we hope you'll find something or someone that you immediately like, as well as something that takes you out of your comfort zone – and puts you into a new one.

In the spirit of the *Murderous Ink Press* motto: *You never know what you like until you read it.*

[Sadly Bryn passed away 21st July 2021 due to kidney failure and sepsis.]

Careless Love

Steve Sneyd

(1941 – 2018)

Over his ninth pint the little unlovely man

in the dark corner of the *Crested Vulture*

confides furtively to me, half-

listening,

as I watch the door for

the girl who so far has

failed to turn up.

"I've realised at long last," he says watching

for the effect of his words,

a little spittle dribbling from the corner of his mouth.

"I am a circle of self-hatred, complete in myself –

like the looped Abyssinian snake

in the Bible somewhere it says rolled along

a wheel with its tail in its mouth ...

I inject my own venom into myself, continuously,

& live in frenzy,

feverish with my own poison."

Careless Love / Steve Sneyd

"Yeah," I say, watching the clock,

& move to buy myself another drink.

Disappointed he says venomously,

"You're all alike, care for nobody but yourselves.

To think we fought the war for

the likes of you." And then,

coward again, "I'm sorry, I shouldn't have said

that. Goodnight." And scuttles out,

uncomforted.

She never does turn up.

And on the way home, stumbling just the slightest bit,

I realised to my surprised

annoyance

just how much of what that fellow said I could

apply just as well to myself.

And change the subject by singing *Careless Love* off key

the whole rest of the way uphill

past the new playground towards

home & bed & unconsciousness.

"I'll shoot you 5 or 6 times

stand over you to make sure you're dying …

O Love, O Love, O Careless Love,

O Careless Love, what have you done to me."

The Driver
Wil A. Emerson

The woman with the red-brown hair, in a black shiny trench coat to ward off the misty rain, hid her face behind wide, dark sunglasses even though clouds lingered overhead. She slid across the cordovan leather seat of my limo without saying a word. Her sigh, or was it a groan, was audible as she dug into her red, brown and black tote bag.

I walked around to the driver's door, sat in my designated place and adjusted the mirrors. First the sides and then the rear view. No hurry, an old habit. By the time I'd eased into the traffic lane, the woman had thrown her stiletto heels into the tote and applied a menthol-type ointment to one foot, then the other. After the ritual, about the time I'd gone three blocks, she put on a pair of dark brown, orthopedic style shoes. The kind she wouldn't be caught dead in if cameras were near. I'd seen enough television shots to know her style; more so, know the attention derived from how she presented herself. Youthful, indestructible, always in those suggestive, sexual charged high heels. A woman with power. Everything centered on image.

Hot and Spicy, so said the foot ointment label. Red, yellow and white label catches attention, too. I didn't have a total view of the tube and wasn't about to ask if I guessed the right brand. I liked being right. Forever observant, not one to miss small or large innuendoes about a person's life, persona.

At the next light, I used my handkerchief to dab my nose,

than a quick blow. Soft, not to be gross. The stuff she used made my nostrils drip like a water faucet. Great if you had sinus issues. A friend suggested I take an antihistamine on the day I drove for her but I was concerned about side effects. Groggy or not? Would it show up in the blood test I submitted to each month? A requirement for the job: no drugs. Monthly tests to prove it. Over the counter, essential or not, I didn't take chances. I liked my job. Liked it immensely on bonus days.

I never knew when a bonus day would fall in my lap because it was all a matter of timing and opportunity. It usually took this woman about four blocks to make up her mind if this would be a quick trip to her apartment at Watergate or a round-about excursion which would net me a bonus. Sometimes on a round-about she met up with someone, sometimes she directed me to a secluded placed and walked or sat on a park bench. If she asked to go to a specific restaurant or bar, it might or might not be a lengthy distance from the Capitol. I'd watched her order a large martini with three olives on a few occasions at a swank place near Baltimore Harbor. Alone, reflecting no doubt on her position in life. On occasion, she stuck close to the Capitol for a meeting. Not quite as relaxing I figured, because at a well-known eatery or bar it was probably a political encounter. A message to the public. Full light of day and on equal terms with the masses.

As a matter of record, I drive for a profit organization that caters to high ranking government officials. Elected or appointed. The job hadn't been a lifelong goal, but it serves me well. It came about in a circuitous way. After graduating from the University of Virginia with a four year degree in criminal justice, I joined the military. Officer training and anticipating a three year stint to repay my country for the privilege of freedom and then, I'd be free to pursue my dreams. But the U.S. government only kept me under her thumb for all of twenty-one months. Embarrassing, I didn't follow my younger brother into a war zone where he earned military honors. Instead I'd been relegated to stateside duty in the logistics branch. Important, you say. Supplies for frontline soldiers a dire necessity. Keep them clothed, fed and well equipped with super weapons to get their job done. As a 1st. Lieutenant, I ran my unit like a well-oiled engine. My Captain gave me rave reviews.

"Michael Lafferty, the higher ups want you to make a career out of the Army. They'll push you through the Lieutenant phase. In no time a Captain. A Major, birds on your shoulders."

On and on, they said. Not my intention. I'd do my duty and get on with goals. Police officer of the finest order. Maybe one day Chief or Commissioner in a large city.

During an inspection at Fort Briggs, I encountered a setback. Plans sideswiped. A truck load of explosive material, driven by a punk, cowboy Corporal, collided with a brick wall. Going thirty-five miles an hour in a restricted zone, the fool thought he could prove his capability at maneuvering a large cargo truck. I happened to be standing in formation with the brick wall at my back. Four soldiers lost their lives, two were severely injured and, several suffered multiple broken bones. The driver disappeared in the dust. Homeland terrorist? Speculations abound, no proof.

All things considered, that was a lucky day. As a survivor,

I received immediate care at Fort Briggs' trauma unit and then got transferred to Walter Reed where I lingered in an out of a coma for three months. Then months of re-hab, voc-hab, psych-hab, elevations included, and finally honorably discharged to focus on the future.

A Cochlear implant helped the hearing deficit, my vision improved over time from laser surgery and implanted contacts. Facial features returned to a ruddy, masculine appearance with help from a skilled plastic surgeon. Quite handsome said a few.

By the time, I got my act together emotionally there were a variety of reasons a law and order organization considered my employment a risk. Eyes, ears, bones, a string of glued and stapled parts, even though efficiently healed according to medical records, on paper I looked like a jig saw puzzle with pieces missing. Sure, I could pass a physical, run a mile without breaking a hard sweat, fire a weapon and guzzle beer with the best of them but damaged neurons for sight, sound, and a heavy dose of shell shock were hard to overlook. Also, a fractured attitude provided another edge to this new way of life.

The dole from the Government paid bills but increases would always be far and few. I wanted more than an opportunity to exist. On a lark, I applied for a commercial driver's license to keep me busy. Drive a giant mother f'er truck back and forth across the country. To my great surprise, I landed the license with hardly a squeak. One thing led to another. While I waited for a long haul assignment, a co-worker asked me to fill in one night for a limo driver. One thing led to another. I never got into that shiny heavy-duty

Peterbilt with 430 horsepower. Instead I bought a remote control model to play with at home. One thing led to another.

I had to be vetted to drive VIPs. That's where my military creds came in handy. This choir boy had been severely damaged, survived and proved to be loyal, too.

Black shiny suit, white shirt, black bow tie; on occasion a standard red or blue tie to please the biased passenger. A few people requested the full regalia for special events. For those formal occasions, I kept a black cap on the front seat. Didn't like the heat it generated. Headaches from nerve injuries. Grin and bear it. That's when nice bonuses came my way.

The limo service charged a fixed rate for service within a certain mileage range. When a client deviated from the initial request, management billed them separately with a hefty off-contract fee or they paid the driver under the cuff. No money or credits cards handled by the driver. Unless it was a bonus.

I juggled my schedule for the highest anti by learning when to accept a side contract. Turf off a short drive for a low ranking VIP to a beginner, one trying to build up his own contact list, as I waited for the golden ride. Decisions. My motto: Bide your time. Wait till the last minute. Be the last driver for select customers always and take the unexpected if they show promise.

Woman with the red/brown hair and menthol foot ointment had become an excellent client. Her moods and demeanor were so erratic I could count on her at least three times a month to ask, "Sir, do you mind…." And then the venture would begin.

That's why my income grew to the mid six figures and my

1040 tax return reflected a working man's wage. That's why I didn't pine over not being a police officer. And that's why I drove this woman with the red/brown hair and menthol foot ointment over to Foggy Bottom, Hay-Adams Hotel, Baltimore or wherever she wanted to go. Yes, I slyly watched as she pulled a blond/gray wig out of her tote bag, stuff her tailored suit jacket back in and struggled into a shaggy sweater that looked as if it had been picked up at Goodwill for a buck or so. That's why I did my job with a smile each and every day. That was then. Now I'm a driver, just doing a job.

One important lesson learned on the curve of low to high maintenance VIP life is never become a Congressional *servant* whether in the House or Senate. The expectations are killers, the secrets, the lies, the indiscretion and fear of being caught in the backdoor life is a sure route to insanity. And the second job never to desire is the *journalist* who spies on these people. They pay twice as much for dirt as an elected official pays for secrets.

It's necessary to go light on the servant description, too. Very light. From my view, these various lawmakers are also lawbreakers. They focus on one job and one job only. Self-satisfaction. Whether it be power or gluttony, they indulge to the maximum and expect the subservient in the world to keep their mouths shut. Shut tight.

Dollars do the trick.

"Sir, do you mind? A little deviation." An early spring diversion.

"No problem, Ma'am. An address? Or would you rather I GPS a location?"

"No, not necessary. I'm meeting a friend near Dupont Circle. Drop me off in front of St. Matthew's Cathedral. I expect a pick up from you at exactly seven-thirty. Not one minute later. Please."

A new destination. A few minutes before I pulled in front of the Cathedral, she did the switch. A new disguise, darker blonde wig, longer variety, a green jacket and clear, wire rim glasses. "I trust you'll take care of my personal belongings."

"Yes, Ma'am." I motioned toward the trunk. The standard operation. Out of sight, locked.

As she stepped out of the car, she slipped money in my hand. "Seven-thirty exactly."

Who could say she wasn't going to Mass? However, midway in the block, she got into a light gray, four door sedan, front passenger seat. Foreign made but not German. Honda or Toyota? Non-government. Perhaps a male driver but behind sunglasses and the awning of branches from oaks and maples, it was hard to make out distinct features.

I opened my fist at the stop light to check the folded cash. Five hundred. Not bad for the first half of the evening. On my non-work phone, I keyed in the location of the drop off. I had a memory for license plates, like the way some people remember every house address they've lived in. A skill the coma didn't take away. Then I set the alarm on my wrist watch and drove to a nearby restaurant for dinner.

It was unlikely I'd run into a customer where I ate but I wouldn't take a huge risk. Never eat near their meeting place. I had a switch for those occasions, too. I kept a sweater or jacket, depending on weather, baseball caps and sneakers in the trunk. Sometimes, I changed my hair with a sweep of the hand, Brad Pitt style, or a quick dab of moisturizer to smooth it down. Glasses helped. A variety of eye pieces, classic, hip, dowdy. Whatever worked without too much effort. Warning to the public—a nerd out alone. I wanted to eat or sit with a book and not be harassed for a ride. It wasn't a game.

When woman with the red/brown hair walked into Farragut Grill at P St and 16th, I almost choked on my cheeseburger. The place wasn't a dive but it wasn't where a high ranking member of the House of Representatives would slink up to the bar and order a vodka martini with blue cheese in the olives. Beer on tap and house wine type of joint. It suited the younger crowd who could handle an eight dollar burger. Prices kept away the riffraff looking for McDonald's. Way below her pay grade and expectations.

I squirmed for a second as I watched her covertly survey the room. And then I managed my own scan of her escort or companion who was dressed in classy jeans, a dark turtleneck and a black leather sport coat. Definitely high end. They took a table in the back, away from foot traffic, her back to the crowd. Too near the kitchen door for easy conversations but I wasn't the person out on the sly.

Not intentionally spying, yet, unable to ignore this clandestine meeting, I took quick opportunities to gaze through the bar mirror as I munched on truffle fries and finished off the burger.

It seemed obvious they enjoyed each other's company. Hands touching, heads close together, eye contact. Not necessarily lovers but one might consider the possibility. A mid to late thirties guy attracted to a good-looking cougar.

Money, status, why not? Thing was, the woman with the red/brown hair had a husband. A well-known husband often seen in her political/social circle. Numerous pictures of them in the Post and also, reports of the same in west coast papers where she performed for voters.

I knew a couple of journalist who would pay rocket prices for this scoop. My monthly driver salary would instantly double with just one picture. If something nefarious had drawn them together, a lobbyist courting a congresswoman, money under the table, the anti would triple.

But it could also be the end of my driving career. At this point, I could be the only one who knew the high ranking congresswoman was in Farragut Grill. If she had spotted me under my make shift disguise, the rat would be obvious.

I sipped the last of my diet coke, pulled out a twenty and a five and laid it on the counter. Nodded my head to the bartender and left. A nice two block stroll, with my eye on my watch. When the bing bing of the watch alarm went off, I went back to the limo and drove to St. Matthew's Cathedral.

Five minutes early per my routine, I waited fifteen minutes more and got nervous. A first. This woman always stuck to her rule. Never strayed from the designated time. I imagined those who worked for her had conflicts about her promptness. Rigidity can be annoying, too, if it leaves no margin of error for mortal humans. Anxious, I checked my watch again. It didn't tell lies; it synced with the satellite car data. Sixteens minutes. Knowing what I knew about her, I toyed with the idea she could be in danger. Look for her, or wait it out. Knowing what I knew, should I notify the police? Twenty-two minutes past due, sweat pearled down my back. I got out of the car, walked around it, looked up and down the street and then, took out my cell. One minute more I'd call the cops.

Peripheral vision caught movement near the evergreens. Close to a walkway by the side entrance of the stone-walled cathedral. Voices and then two people. Woman with the red/brown hair, wigged to the darker blonde. Man in priestly black garbs. She had a tissue to her face. He had his hand on her shoulder. Who could say she hadn't gone to mass?

I hustled to the driver's seat, put the car in gear and slowly eased up to the walk-way. At the end of the church path, she turned and shook the priest's hand. I opened the back passenger door for her and she nearly dived in the seat. Tears on her cheeks were as noticeable as the fake hair.

"Get me back as fast as you can." She checked her watch, as if she needed confirmation. "Is your dash clock correct?"

"Yes, Ma'am, it is."

We'd gone two blocks before she spoke again, more of a shout. "Stop, stop now."

I eyed the traffic and signaled for a right turn where I could pull to the curb.

"My tote bag. I must have my tote bag. I'm going to be very late for a meeting. Get it now."

Obviously, she was more rattled than me. My mind had her kidnapped or dead. She had a case of nerves over being late and looking like a drab, house mouse.

"Yes, Ma'am," I replied.

When I lifted the tote into the car, she grabbed it like it was a lost child.

"Are you being especially slow tonight?"

I didn't expect a thank you for the bag of clothes but I wasn't the one who caused the tardiness.

"The traffic is a little heavy, Ma'am." In fact, it couldn't have been better. A lot of white lies were passed back and forth in this business.

During the remainder of the drive, she dipped low, changed out her hair piece, brushed the real stuff and dabbed make-up on her cheeks and gloss on her pouted lips.

I pulled in front of the regular Capital building spot, the closest pick-up area for taxis and limos, and stepped out to open her door. I decided to say my piece as I reached out to help her.

"Ma'am, I was concerned. My next step would have been to call for assistant. Your security detail, the police."

"That would have been very foolish, young man. A deal breaker." She slid her hand into mine as though we were parting with a greeting. "I do appreciate the concern, though." And off she went, as fast as possible in her high heels and red/brown hair flying in the wind. Cash went to my pocket.

With nothing else on my plate, I took a slow drive to my apartment in Georgetown. Kicked back to watch Netflix. No date, no desire. I had pocketed a thousand dollars on that one pick-up and delivery. A hefty price for secrets. Why should I ever be concerned about what motivated those secrets and the means taken to cover them up. I did write down the license number of the gray sedan and added it to her file. It took a few minutes to decide to call a cop friend who'd gladly run the plates for me without any questions.

The Driver

For three weeks, four days a week, I encountered the usual mix of urgent meetings, late dinner dates and, the unexpected arrivals in town. The regular paying drives and several out of pocket deals kept me busy. VIPs acted like fools when they met a girlfriend, boyfriend, dealer, lobbyist, huckster and tried to keep it all under wraps. As if limo drivers were invisible people, no names, no eyes, no ears, but essential in their secretive world. They paid money for tight lips. That's why I left Friday for unexpected day assignments and her.

Pictures of woman with the red/brown hair were in and out of the Post and NY Times over those weeks. I noticed the articles more often and read them with renewed interest. She had a reputation as a bull dog taking chunks of flesh from the opposition which seemed more evident as I read in depth. Was this woman driven to be vengeful or had some misfired gene left her incapable of working with those who didn't agree with her?

The biggest piece of the puzzle was how she had acquired all the power she wielded over other congressional members. If I dwelled on her too much, it would interfere with my vow to never take politicians seriously. Like or dislike, they for the most part, kept me in a comfortable lifestyle. I'd even planned to take the month of April off and rent a luxury house in the Virgin Islands and forget everything about Washington, D.C. Heal some love wounds and forget about money under the table.

But curiosity can lead to trouble and plans can go astray.

*****

Another week passed and no calls from woman with the red/brown hair. Not far from thought, her call did surprise me, though. Five p.m. on a Friday. A really bad time since I lingered three Fridays waiting for her requests and decided to book a couple promising rides. So I had to make a serious decision. Was guilt money being thrown away? Worth cancelling a connected, on the rise public employee in the Federal building with a bundle of extra side-girlfriend money? A guy who was blatant about it, spent bucks to impress. Red/brown hair did try to mask whatever sense of joy she went after. One situation seemed more honest. Fractured logic, you might say.

A quick call to a fledgling driver and off to the pick-up line at the Capitol building. I couldn't help but admire the striking figure approach my car. Her posture, that straight, confident back, the elegant business outfit. A model's stride in black stiletto heels, broad smile for those passing by. In gold framed sunglasses that looked like a Prada brand, I could see why a thirty-something guy might be attracted to her. Personality unknown, one assumed the best.

This time, she carried a brief case and an extra-large gray/black tote bag. Stylish to the max. In my suspicious but creative mind, it looked as if she might be heading off for a weekend tryst.

When she settled on the bag seat, she broke the routine. "Thank you for the last minute trip. I hope it wasn't too inconvenient."

"Not at all, "Ma'am." At the end of the block, I asked, "GPS an address, Ma'am?"

She actually chuckled, "Of course not. I'll give you an address in a moment. Go towards St. Mathews Cathedral, please." Her hand was deep into the gray/black tote. When it came out, she held up a small piece of paper. "Read this, follow the instructions."

I held it at the steering wheel. An address near 16th and P. "I know the area, Ma'am."

At least, I could grab dinner again. Farragut wasn't a bad place to hang out for an hour or so. Maybe try their Fish Fry. My Irish Lafferty's taste buds needed an unhealthy fix.

Another surprise came from the woman with red/brown hair when she didn't apply her god awful foot ointment. Going to a meeting that necessitated a professional look. My curiosity was on high drive. If this were an official outing, a dinner event, wouldn't she go in a government service car? Probably with extra security, too. But it was a plus for me. I could at least eat battered cod without the lingering effect of menthol in my nostrils.

"As you will see when we get closer, I've given you a name of a restaurant. I'll leave my bag with you. But I'm taking the brief case." She talked as she slipped a band on her loose hair and secured it at the nape of her neck. Then she took off her high heels and replaced them with a pair of black flats. Respectable heel, easy walkers. Out for a stroll? I wouldn't ask.

As I neared, P St. I glanced at the street numbers. Very close to Farragut Grill. Two more blocks and we were in front of where I planned to eat battered cod. No indulgence for me. The gray sedan idled at the curb.

"I need to pull ahead to drop you off, Ma'am."

As I maneuvered, the gray sedan made a quick U-turn and pulled into a parking space on the other side of the street. The same guy she'd met before jumped out of his car, waved and dashed across the street. He was suddenly at her side.

"Pick up time, Ma'am?" Asked as I closed her door.

"I'll have to call. Can you set aside two hours?"

"Of course," I nodded and went back to the driver's seat. A re-adjust, mirrors side and review.

She kept distance between her and the guy, no embrace or polite hand shake. If I had to describe her reaction, I would say it wasn't favorable. However, I'd never seen any latch on, hook-up between them in the past. I could only guess she hadn't broken a pattern.

With one hour and fifty minutes to spare, I considered whether it would be food or a nap in the car. Curiosity won out. Would woman with the red/brown hair actually eat in Farragut, in public, with no disguise except her hair pulled back and Prada sunglasses? The spiffy glasses would draw attention if she ate and drank with them on.

Like a cat with nine lives, or a limo driver thinking the flow of cold cash from VIP's might not last forever, I decided to eat at a joint three doors from Farragut's. Chinese. High on my list of food choices when I had a couple days off. Too many carbs in a full meal to keep me alert during work hours. The distance gave me the opportunity to walk past Farragut, see if the two trysters were enjoying a glass of beer and, slip my cell out for a quick picture if the scene looked good enough.

Geared in an old college baseball jacket and New York Yankees ball cap turned brim-side to the nape tourist style, I slunk by the grill's broad window. Not good visibility but enough to see shadows of two people deep in a conversation. Heads together, at least.

Playing it smart, at Ben Wei's I ordered a bowl of hot and sour soup and one spring roll. Enough to tide me for a few hours. Half way through the hot and sour my cell rang.

"I'm ready. Pick me up now."

"Yes, Ma'am. But I'm not close to the drop off. Will take a few minutes." Shit, I thought. Three blocks away and if I walked by Farragut again, I'd be spotted. At the checkout, I asked if they had a back door.

"Not for customers. Use front only."

"It's an emergency." I laid twenty bucks on the counter.

"No, not for customers."

I eyed the guy. He wasn't asking for trouble, just following rules. That was his problem. I turned and walked passed the seated customers, into the kitchen. A few gasps and a 'no, no' and I spotted the open door where one fellow stood smoking a cigarette. I didn't expect a fight and size worked in my favor so I pushed past the smoker and stepped into the alley. Several cats were rummaging through the garbage. A scurry of rats had me thinking twice about the hot and sour soup. A bigger problem would be if I had to climb a fence at the end of the festering alley.

No fence. A quick run left me sweating. I pulled off the jacket and threw it and the cap in the trunk. Took out the woman's tote bag to place it in the back seat. Fingers slippery or just too hasty, the bag fell out of my hand. 'Shit' didn't help. I bent to pick up the fallen items and placed them back in the tote. General stuff, tissues, lipstick, a wallet, folded note paper. Probably not in any particular order. As I put them back in, time wasting as it was, I felt a hard object. Familiar hard object.

A congresswoman shouldn't be carrying in D.C. This woman didn't look like Annie Oakley, but gals can fool you. A permit to carry? Very unlikely as the fair city had strict laws against firearm possession. Only the bad guys and police were allowed to defend themselves. I reserved the questions I had, then decided 'none of my business' had to suffice.

My cell rang as I sat the tote on the passenger floor. Out of sight but within reach as she entered the car.

"Where are you?"

"Three blocks, Ma'am."

"Please, get here."

"Yes, Ma'am." The tone left no doubt the woman was crying.

When I pulled around the corner, the gray sedan with a driver at the wheel had moved again to the front of Farragut's. Near the awning, the drop off for diners if it were raining. Cloudy but no rain in sight. Why block the drive up? Woman with the red/brown hair stood with one shoulder against the restaurant brick wall a couple of feet from the entrance. She had her head turned away from the driver in the sedan, her brief case in her hand with the latches undone. Even with her sunglasses in place and her hair still pulled back, I doubted if she had too many drinks. Yet, her posture suggested she needed support.

Without care for double parking, I stopped the limo, essentially blocking the gray sedan and jumped out. At her side, "Ma'am," I reached out my hand.

"Please, get me the hell out of here." She stumbled, her face red and tears on her cheeks.

A horn blared but I waved the driver off as I helped her in and buckled the seat belt.

With the limo in gear, I crossed the center line and drove away which angered a few more people. Horns out of control, a couple of middle fingers thrust at me.

"Sorry, Ma'am."

*****

A few moments passed before she responded. "No apology necessary. The problem is all mine."

"Back to the Capitol Building."

"God no. I dread that place on Friday evening. Just drive. Will you?"

"I've set aside two hours, Ma'am."

"A drive along Rock Creek Parkway or George Washington Memorial, please."

"Of course, Ma'am." I juggled in my mind which round-about I'd take if I crossed the Arlington Memorial Bridge to pick up GW parkway. Traffic would still be bustling in the Capitol area.

Either route would be a quiet, scenic drive. Peaceful.

Not far into the drive, I took a double glance at the rearview. A gray sedan three car lengths behind me. How many were in the area? Half, no doubt, government cars. I maneuvered into Dupont Circle to work my way west to Teddy Roosevelt Memorial Bridge. By the time I reached Washington Circle, the gray sedan was two cars behind. Still not convinced it was a coincidence and with an active imagination on overload, I decided to circle twice. A real test.

I don't know if I failed or the driver passed. The same gray sedan made the circle twice and then eased back on my tail as the traffic thinned. Across the Teddy, I knew the tail was the woman's Farragut hook-up. Would I tell my passenger or ride it out?

"Michael...may I call you Michael?"

"Yes, Ma'am. Of course. What can I do for you?"

"If you drive me to my apartment, will you walk me to the door and check out the interior?"

"Of course, Ma'am. Anything to help out."

"Good, thank you. I'm sure it's just nerves. Read too much in the paper, you know how it goes these days."

"Yes, Ma'am. Things happen. Better to be safe." I eyed the rearview again. He was about four car lengths behind. Dusk taking over the better part of my view but enough light to confirm it was a male driver and same stature as the male my passenger had met.

"Do you want to go back now, Ma'am?"

"Not necessary," she looked at her watch, "let's give it a little more time. The ride is relaxing."

I'm sure if I told her we had a tail and it was probably the man she'd met a Farragut's her comfort level would take a nose dive. Not knowing her intentions or the tail's motive, I decided to watch and wait. We weren't in harm's way, where we? Why call the tail dangerous if by sheer coincidence he tagged along on the same road. While I didn't like the situation, I decided to let a cool head prevail.

Several minutes passed in silence.

"Lights from Lincoln Memorial are outstanding."

"They are indeed, Ma'am." We were heading south east on George Washington Memorial Parkway.

"I've never seen them from this view," she said with a sigh. Then she turned to look as the Memorial left our immediate view. Her head jerked, to me and then behind her again.

Waiting to hear her say she'd sighted the gray sedan, I didn't react. High hopes that she didn't. High hopes that at the next turn, the sedan would go another route.

"Do you mind a drive over to the Tidal Basin?" She spoke with ease, a gentleness that revealed her appealing side. "Perhaps take the water route and then catch Rock Creek Parkway?"

"No problem, Ma'am. Would you like a little soft music, too?"

"Not necessary. I need to concentrate."

I knew the roads like the back of my hand and took exit 10 to cross the Potomac. The gray sedan followed as though we were a caravan. Lucky me. What did the guy have up his sleeve? So I slowed down for a test. How close would he get?

I didn't wait long to find out.

With a hard jolt, his bumper hit the rear end of my limo. No time to prepare my passenger, I watched in the rearview as her head plunged forward. Her eyes went owl wide and she gasped, then howled as if she'd been hit in the back of the head.

"Ma'am, down, get down on the floor." I pressed the accelerator, cleared the bridge and made a sharp turn onto Ohio Drive, sped past the Roosevelt Memorial and onto the Parkway Drive. It was one hell of a tour for the casual drive but my VIP passenger might well be on the ride for her life. Danger had become a key word. What else could it be? I dodged a few oncoming cars, cut in front of another limo and hightailed it up Rock Creek.

The bastard, for whatever reason, stayed right on my bumper. High beam head lights glaring, no other intention but to cause trouble.

"He's been blackmailing me." She cried out. "What can you do to get away from him?"

"I'm calling security, Ma'am." With better control now that the road had less traffic ahead, I reached for my cell attached to the dashboard. So she had spotted the gray sedan. Knew who drove it.

"Don't you dare. No, no. Don't," she shouted. "He's after money. Just money. More than I've got with me."

"He's dangerous. Rammed us, no telling what he has planned."

"Lose him. No matter how long it takes. Please, don't call anyone." Her voice shook, her sobs convinced me to take a risk. I could ditch him. It would take a little time. I eyed my passenger who had released her seatbelt and turned to look fully at the car behind. When she turned again I saw her stark congressional determination, her gritted teeth and, that stern squint of her eyes. I had a vague notion, I'd made the wrong decision. Then again, the customer is always right so I let bravado, my warrior skills and, macho instincts control my actions.

Save the damsel in distress. Prove I could outsmart the jerk behind me with dirty deeds on his mind.

We sped along the twisting road as though it were the Gran Prix. My foot stayed heavy on the gas pedal, my eyes going to the mirror, to the road ahead like watching a tennis match. The gasps and groans from my passenger was enough to make me want to shout 'shut up'. I couldn't. Too much at stake.

I took a sharp turn, heard a thump in the back. Not his car on the bumper, but her being tossed toward the door. Maybe she was safer sitting with the seat belt on.

"What the hell," she shouted. "Enough. Pull over where it's safe. Let me settle this once and for all."

"Ma'am, I'm not sure it's safe. I have no idea what this guy might do."

"Damn it, I said pull over. I'm done with his cat and mouse game."

There weren't many options along the wooded, curved parkway but I remembered a trail with parking space near Kalorama Heights. In my youthful days, it was a good place to go for a variety of reasons. Girls, guys out for a hike, girls. A few problems had occurred in the area, some had made the newspapers. Some were crime related.

"Just stay down, Ma'am, until I assess the situation. I suggest again, one call and we have backup."

"Definitely not. This is nonsense. And I'm not going to put up with it any longer."

I pulled into the dark area. Even darker and more dangerous with a cloudy sky and a canopy of oaks, beech trees and maples. The gray sedan pulled up about ten feet from my driver's side. Too close for comfort in my book.

"Stay in your seat, Ma'am, and no matter what, do not get

out of the car." I held the key fob in my hand.

With the sedan headlights off now, the dim interior light illuminated the man as he opened the driver's door. I stood with my back toward my door, not completely shut but enough so the light remained off. Why give him an easy target.

"What the hell do you want," I asked. A tone as tough as any uncertain guy could make it. Was he out to kill or just scare the shit out of her? I wasn't totally fearless, either. My pockets were empty when it came to a weapon of defense. What would happen to those fragile fractured parts if I got into a real struggle? Or would a flair up of PSTD at any moment have me crying like a baby again. It wasn't my cowardly nature, it might be that I'd literally fall apart at the seams.

"She knows what I want. We had a deal. She reneged. Offered crumbs, not the whole loaf. Get out of the car, bitch."

"Hey, take it easy. The police are on their way. Capitol security. You know you're playing with fire." In my mind, it sounded ominous.

"Don't make me laugh. She'll do anything to protect her reputation. No one's coming. This is between me and her. You're in the way."

I couldn't see much of his face but felt the heat of anger by his tone. A deep, almost guttural grind of words.

"You'll have to go through me to get to her. She is not getting out of the car." I took a couple of steps forward. My plan was to get to the passenger's side and block the entrance.

"Do you have any idea what she's hiding? A bold faced liar and cheater. She'd throw her own kid under the bus to keep her congressional seat. Move or you're going to be sorry."

His hands were in his pockets so I figured he had a weapon. But why hadn't he shown it by now? Maybe if I rushed him, he'd cave in, give up. Save us both from physical contact. He looked heavier than me, maybe two or three inches taller. But I'd always been fast, could think on my feet. On second thought, if I ran at him, I'd leave my passenger unprotected. Better to be a shield than risk failure.

"Is there some way we can resolve this issue? You obviously were tailing us for good reason. What can we do to settle this? Go back to the city and talk. Let's do that." Stalling, wishful thinking, whatever worked to de-escalate the situation.

"Talking's over. She's coming back with me and we are going to a reporter who's going to take pictures and she'll declare to the world I'm the son she gave up for adoption. What a tramp. Ashamed of a wild affair…tossed me out like stall bread."

I heard the creak of the car door and turned my head. At the same time, the guy rushed forward and pushed me against the car. I stumbled back, regained footage and plunged forward again. Fists raised, ready to slam the assailant with the full weight of my body.

"Count yourself lucky. I didn't seek an abortion. My mistake."

Red/brown hair woman had the tote-bag pistol aimed our way. Hopefully at the bad guy.

The thought barely crossed my mind by the time she pulled the trigger. I felt hot air by my head. Too close. Then another blast from the gun. The third shot caused the accuser to fall like a sack of potatoes. A loud thump. I leaned against the car and waited for the next shot.

She stood about ten feet from me. The gun aimed at my

chest.

"Body mass. They teach you to go for the largest area. I say I've got about a ninety-nine per cent chance of changing your life permanently."

"Ma'am, I don't know what's going on but we need help here. I've got to call the police." For those few seconds, I knew this wouldn't end well.

But why kill me? If she did, would she just get in my limo and drive herself back into D.C., back to her apartment at the Watergate? Call for a driver the next morning? Sit in the House of Representatives and talk about the next tax hike?

I moved closer. Fear no longer a factor. I could die trying to disarm this crazed woman or let her slaughter me like a helpless lamb.

"Give me the gun. Don't be foolish. You acted in self-defense. There's nothing to worry about." I inched closer.

"He's been after me for months. Every day a text, a phone call. Different places, untraceable cell phones. More and more money. Then these last few weeks, he changed course. Said he wanted to be part of my life. Can you imagine that? Taking him in as one of my own. Under the family folds? Using my name? I didn't raise this monster. His father was the shyster. Bastard. I would never have that kind of character in my life."

Her face flooded with tears.

I moved cautiously forward and then she feebly let the gun fall limp in her hand. The nine millimeter was mine to take. I grasped it and pointed it at her.

"You knew he was following us all along."

"Of course, I did." She wiped her cheeks. "Do you think a

stupid woman gets as far as I have? From the second meeting on, I knew he was out to damage my reputation. And one little mistake set the stage for him."

"His father told him about you?"

"No, he's gone. An early demise. My mistake. I left my jacket on the chair and used the rest room. Hair samples were all he needed. No telling. Maybe he slipped a fork in his pocket. Bastard went so far as to get DNA and then messenger RNA for confirmation. No question about it, he said, and waved those damn papers in front of my face tonight. Once too often. Wouldn't take my final buy out. Enough money for him to start a new career. Prepared as I was, something had to be done."

"Something?" My mind raced with the revelation. "It's a criminal offense to blackmail. Why not have him arrested?"

"Why would I want this creature, this mistake of nature, to haunt me for the rest of my life? I had to take action. End it once and for all."

Like a bolt of lightning, it came to me. "You planned this?" I nodded toward the dead guy on the ground between us.

"He made his decision. You both were so helpful in the execution of my plan. I appreciate your input." She wiped her face again and smiled.

"Helpful? With all due respect, you shot this man."

"And it won't be my Waterloo."

"You claimed he blackmailed you. Facts are he followed my limo. Yes, confronted us. Perhaps, you acted in self-defense." I felt in control now. Weapon in my hand, I had witnessed a murder and that was my legal defense.

"Way too messy. No, you'll have to clean this up."

"Forgive me, Ma'am, but that's not my roll. I'm a driver, not an accomplice to murder."

"Oh, you're more than that. You've taken cash from me. An accomplice to blackmail. I do have bank records and reliable history on my side. So, you will get rid of this clutter."

I pulled out my cell and snapped a picture. "This picture goes directly to my cloud." I snapped another for security. "My involvement is limited to being a paid limo driver."

"Limited? Why are you holding that pistol? Your finger prints are all over it. I'll push the panic number on my cell." She held it in her gloved hand. "Security will know exactly where I am in a matter of seconds." She raised it higher. "One picture. One gentle touch. I'd call this is a Mexican standoff."

The faint sound of her cell, click, click and she turned the screen around. I saw the faint replication of me holding a trim, black nine-millimeter. A perfect match for her image.

The clearing I'd pulled into was bordered by thick brush. No marked trails for hikers, only a path made by foraging deer. Their narrow lane made it convenient to drag her neglected offspring's body far into the woods. I used his belt to secure his arms behind his back for easier portage. After rummaging through his pockets for his I D, credit cards and pocket change, I covered him with dead leaves and loose brush.

Back at the car, the woman with red/brown hair had disassembled the nine millimeter. Her expertise came as a surprise, but at this point, I should have known she had the required skills to manage the care of the weapon.

"You'll throw his car keys in the Potomac as we cross the

Washington Memorial Bridge. Leave the back window open. I'll disperse the gun parts as we continue this relaxing, scenic drive. It's a perfect night for an escape from hard work."

I took several days off after that eventful evening. Not the sunny southern vacation I'd anticipated. My head not right for the road. Not right for anything, it seemed. The angry and self-loathing inner man left me in moral conflict. I'd been played to the max. Fight city hall? If I did, I'd face the most powerful woman in Washington, D.C. politics. A fate hard to embrace. I woke up at night with the image of his body, her son, in the bushes. Cold, wet, dead. Most nights, my face replaced his.

Then, on the next Friday, I got a call for a VIP pick up. I told dispatch I'd take the gig.

She sauntered up to the limo. Black suit, a new tote bag, red, blue and white. Ready for Memorial Day celebration. Heels stiletto, killer style. The swagger stopped any casual observer.

Even though it felt like I'd put one foot in the grave, I jumped out, "Ma'am, at your service."

She slipped the folded money in my hand and, as requested, I drove her to the Willard Hotel. She didn't change into the blond wig or the trashy sweater on the short drive. The swank hotel was an established meeting ground where monster deals were made. Very public for high ranking government officials. Those that wanted, needed to be seen were often at the bar. The bartender had a reputation for the best martinis in town. I figured she'd have at least one.

When I got back to my apartment that evening. I unfolded the money wad. A thousand dollars. And a post-it note. "From now until re-election, I'll need a nice drive every week."

The Happy Next of Kin
Matthew Wilson

They say most people need money to be happy, and if that is the case then it's no wonder why I haven't smiled for years. Of course, initially I was happy to leave that orphanage and be adopted by the lonely old man. But he took over my life, trying to mould me into a pious, sober nun.

Instead, I spent my teenage years drinking and partying away his money and my twenties in sleeping around.

Still the old man thought he would have the last laugh, he changed his will, ensuring that I would only inherit on his death should I turn over a new leaf. If I turned into the good little daughter he had always dreamed of.

Instead, I was determined to kill him before the new clause in his will came into effect.

It was not hard to flutter my eyelashes and talk my latest sweetheart into doing the deed. The old fellow said ladies didn't get their hands dirty but if someone was arrested, then I would rather it was someone else who met the hangman.

My patsy's name was Patrick Something - I never cared to learn his surname but after a few rolls in the hay, he was willing to do anything and even though he had butter for brains, my plan stuck in his head.

All he had to do was shoot my benefactor in the heart when he came home, take some silver away and stash them for later retrieval.

The police would think that robbery was the motive for who could possibly blame Patrick Whatever when he didn't even know the old man?

The changing of the will was coming and my anxiety threatened to be the death of me so with one more kiss I told Patrick that it had to be tonight.

Until he confessed that he didn't have the fire for it.

I admit that my blood burned, I struck at the coward with my nails but then fought to regain myself - I still needed a Patsy if my deceitful webs were ever undone and the police needed someone to hang.

I treated his cuts with kisses and bandaged his worst wounds. I told him I understood his pacifism and would do the deed myself.

But of course he was late, two hours of nail biting and constant checking at the window until there came a twist of the door knob, a cry of surprise at another man in his house and the old man cried out, clutching his chest as I raised the revolver's and sent him crashing back out into the rain.

One bullet was sufficient, there was some struggle, a strangling noise but then the light left his eyes and he was dead.

Which meant I was rich.

All that remained was for my patsy to scoop up the old man's coin collection and bury them near a recognizable tree in the woods beside the house for later exhumation.

Then my fake smile threatened to rip my cheeks apart when of course they sent William Purvis to oversee the case. I long ago earned his ire by rejecting his advances and he had sworn to get even with me for laughing at his ginger mutton chops.

"Emily Marnett," he beamed when he stepped over the dead man and peeked inside. He shot forward and embraced me with a greater kindness than I had expected. I almost felt sorry for pretending to have forgotten him.

Selective amnesia is a fine tool in a murderer's arsenal.

Not wishing to bring up bad memories in the man's head, I merely blamed the fog of time.

"Oh, never mind," he said, ushering me to a seat as if stress had made me forget how to use a chair. "This must be quite a shock."

"Y-yes," I stuttered. Would it help the act if I had started crying? But again I found myself staring at the silly ginger hairstyle fluttering out around William's ears and struggled not to burst out laughing.

Hardly the reaction of a broken hearted relative.

"Now the old man was *not* your father, I gather," William flipped open an ear dogged notepad and rechecked page 9.

"Er, he may as well have been," I corrected. "He was *very* dear to me."

William nodded and made a note that it seemed he did not wish me to see.

"And you told the first officer that you've been in the house all night?"

I dabbed my eyes but could summon no tears forward. "Yes, I gave my statement."

"Oh, it's just best to go over these things more than once because in the excitement of the evening, people's minds can slip. They can forget or misremember things, like your boots."

I forgot my grieving daughter role and almost dropped my hanky. "My-"

"Your boots," William jabbed a pen at them like a knight's sword before a dragon. "They seem muddy. It strikes me as funny that in a house as clean as this that the old man would let you tread muck around. So you must have -"

"Oh, y-yes," I stammered. "Of course I had to rush out to check if he was okay and then I ran to the phone box at the end of the street."

William made a note. "No phone in so big a house," he smiled in an effort to lift my spirits but there was a nasty light of suspicion there that I liked as much as his egregious hairstyle. "I thought with you in one wing and he in another-"

"I just forgot," I said too quickly and then blew the fire from my breath. "My mind was playing tricks."

William closed his book with a snap. "Yes, funny thing the mind," he agreed and then insisted I get some sleep.

I would need to be well hydrated and rest.

"Oh, there — there needs to be more?" I said with alarm.

"Nothing too taxing, just standard questions. When you're ready, could you write me a list of items you believe were taken?"

"Of course."

We shook hands, parting on good terms but when he reached the policeman posted to the door, I heard him say he was going for a walk.

He was going to see if there was a working pay phone at the corner of my street after all.

*****

Of course I burnt all the letters that Patrick Whatshisname posted me every time the coast was clear. He said he needed to talk, that he couldn't sleep now the weight of guilt was pressing on him.

There was some red headed officer that kept asking him questions. Many people had seen him necking me at parties and kissing quite brazenly down the pub so many thought we were a couple.

If we were such sweethearts then of course William had questions for him.

What kind of person was I?

Did I have a good relationship with the murder victim?

Patrick said he needed to hold me, for me to explain our next step when it already seemed clear.

Keep your mouth shut, stay away from me until the heat dies down and *don't* write any more letters!

"Emily," William cheered when I finally awoke and headed downstairs and I was so surprised that I thought him and a robber and almost tripped down the steps.

In his hand he held a letter with Patrick's handwriting.

"Sorry I'm early," he smiled. "I've come to finish our

interview - I thought I'd pick these up off the mat for you."

I had to stop myself from snatching my mail from his hand.

"Can the law just walk in like they own the place?" I quizzed, hoping my question came off as humorous rather than aggressive. I would blame the lack of caffeine if I failed in that regard.

"No," William said, reluctantly letting go of the letter. "But this is a crime scene and we are old friends, right? I did have your permission, right?" he smiled again with awful eyes.

Did I have a reason to keep him out of the house?

"Of course," I said. "And as promised, I have your list - can I interest you in a coffee?"

"That would be wonderful," he said. "We have so much to talk about."

*****

Murder is a ghastly business, so when I was forced to do it a second time, I enjoyed it even less.

Since I had returned none of Patrick's correspondence, he didn't get the message about holding off on his pen.

Accomplices had to keep their heads down and not make waves. All these notes passed to me like a lovesick school boy would bring notice and I had not done everything just to have a noose around my neck.

So I decided to visit him at night, at such an ungodly hour that I was sure I would not be seen by neighbors or spotted by ginger haired busy bodies. To keep my patsy calm, I offered him a cup of tea. The spices worked wonders on his anxiety and the arsenic promised no pain when he settled to a sleep from which he didn't wake.

Of course I did not attend the funeral, I was a busy woman and my dead adopted father's will to probate. I had no time for little people but when he came to the door, William Purvis insisted that he would not bother me for long.

Patrick is dead?" I gasped. "That's terrible."

"Yes," William agreed. "You seem to have had an unlucky run of late. So much so that I'll post a policeman on your door for your protection."

I flinched but didn't show it. "My protection?" I rolled the word around my mouth as if a foreign dialect I was trying to translate.

"Of course," William insisted. "At first I thought it was a simple robbery and that someone had targeted the old man by chance but the fact your lover was poisoned means someone is out to torture *you.*"

I felt my hands shake and immediately set them on busy work, dusting the hallway table.

"P-poison? I thought his burial was today, how did they-"

"Oh, I stopped that," William interrupted softly like a foot in the door. "It seemed too coincidental so I ordered a second autopsy - you understand. First your father and then your lover? No one is that unlucky - someone is certainly after you."

I shuddered at the word lover, my only love was money. I needed nothing else to make me happy.

"So to keep you safe, I'll leave someone posted here," William said. "Someone to watch over your *every* movement - for your own protection, I'm sure."

"Yes, I'm sure," I lied. "Thank you but now I have nowhere

to be."

"Of course, you've already settled the old man's will. I hope you got what you expected."

"What I was owed," I corrected and saw a shadow hover on the front door glass, the outline of a small policeman "Ah, my guardian angel - and what do I do if someone gets around him?"

"Oh, you can use that phone box at the bottom of your street," he suggested. "Or maybe use that great intellect of yours."

"You think I'm clever?" I asked. Rare praise indeed.

William smiled and seemed to stare through me.

"Oh, yes," he agreed, finally. "Very clever."

*****

Being rich is no fund when you cannot spend it as you wish. I felt hounded as every time I went out drinking I saw a policeman, every time I kissed a young man's ear and asked him back to my house, a policeman told the man someone was out to kill me.

I felt hounded and as much under the spotlight as if the old man had never died.

But I smiled and had to even thank William for such unwavering protection. It was good that I was never alone, that he had had his little busy bodies always watching over me, writing in their little books and looking disapprovingly when again I went into the high street to buy another necklace.

I had lived such a strained existence under the old man's thumb - did I not deserve some happiness? I had earned that money having the life wrung out of me.

His murder was self defence because day by day he was killing the happiness in me.

But a fool that wears his carrot colored hair in wild garish mutton chops could never believe that.

I needed to get away - a holiday at the lakes and although William disagreed, I insisted that I needed some happiness as he set his men about my gardens with metal detectors. William said that they were looking for a gun but I heard one of his grunts mention that they were looking for buried silverware.

I promised to return in the week and no I wouldn't tell anyone where I was going. My holiday would be hush hush - I would be quite safe and for a while I was happy. I spent more money and drank more wine, maybe too much but I needed something to dull the pain when I reloaded the old fellow's murder weapon, put it against my shoulder and blasted a piece of meat from my bone.

If William wanted to concentrate on some shadow pursuing me then I would feed his delusion. I would tell him that some madman had followed me from the capital to my new summer home and tried to kill me.

I was lucky again to have survived. No doubt the gun they found on my bedroom rug would match the old fellow's murder weapon.

It did.

But when I awoke in the hospital, William didn't seem pleased to see him. But he did allow himself one smile when he slapped the handcuffs on me and read my rights.

I was right - I'd had too much wine and had not held the revolver far enough away from me to escape the gunshot residue. My report said the shot came from the doorway several feet away but how had the GSR gotten on my arm?

"I take it you'll be wanting these back?" William said, depositing a dirt covered sack upon my bed that annoyed the nurses but he begged a small reprieve from their fire.

I tried not to give him the satisfaction of turning my head but then the silverware inside the sack caught sunlight reflecting through the window and dazzled my eyes to such an extent that the room rolled over and I almost vomited.

"You — you have terrible hair," I said, having waited many years to admit that.

"That's all you have to say?" William asked and I wished only for my dinner.

I was hungry, wanting to be well fed before they moved me to my cell.

"Tell me, William - do you think you could have made me happy?"

The unusual question took the policeman back but he seemed to give the matter consideration and then said, "I think I would have tried my best."

I thought of money and weighed the two options up.

"Yes," I said as more policemen entered the hospital room to ready my wheelchair to take me to an awaiting car. "I rather think you would."

Woman Lost

Russell Richardson

At 2a.m., Dale shambled out the back door of Dundilee Grocery. This store was the last stop of a twelve-hour day spent hauling vegetables across upstate New York. The workday had exhausted him. Pocketing an invoice, Dale swung up into the box-trailer of his rig and paused to inhale a breeze that drifted across the lunar-like parking lot. He struggled to summon the last reserve of energy needed to strap down the palettes and crates in the truck.

Kamikaze bats zigzagged after mosquitoes in the yellow glare of the light poles. At the lot's dark perimeter, trees and thickets swished upon a grassy knoll. Occasionally, cars screeched and revved down Route 11, but a different noise made Dale stiffen and peek his head out the trailer.

Something had shuffled beyond the light. A nocturnal animal? A bandit? His senses became suddenly attuned. Unlike other drivers, he had not been robbed yet, but remote locations and wee hours made him jumpy. Finally, he slid his palm over his skin-bald head. He must have mistaken the sound. The mind generated phantoms for tired drivers all the time. Retrieving his metal hook—his trusty lifting tool—Dale sighed and trudged into the dim, cavernous trailer.

Intermittently cursing, He began his tasks. He stopped once to stretch and yawn, and, when he swiped the hook at a stray crate, he heard:

"Hey-y-y!"

Dale spun with a "Whoa!" and hoisted the hook above his head in a scorpion pose.

A thin, longhaired woman wearing cut-off denim shorts and a white halter-top peered into the trailer. Her appearance suggested that she had come from a party that she should have left sooner. A red plastic cup in one hand traced figure-eights on the air. She was shit-faced drunk.

From deep in the box, Dale barked, "Do you know what you almost just did?"

The inebriated woman repeated a raspy, "Hey?"

"You nearly got brained," Dale growled. His trembling fist choked the handle of the hook still suspended overhead.

"O-h-h," said the woman, holding the metal bumper for balance. She smacked her lips, had a thought, snapped upright, and, slurred five words together, asking, "Can-I-get-a-r-i-i-i-d-e?"

Dale lowered the tool. "No rides," he said. "Get lost."

Minding her cup, the woman dabbed her wrist to her brow as if checking for fever. Despite smudged mascara and lipstick, and her scrawniness, she was prettier than the lot lizards who serviced long-haul truckers, the disease bags of whom Dale prided himself in not partaking.

He turned and hastily secured the remaining palettes with slams and grunts. Sweat seasoned his forehead.

"Hey-y-y," she said again.

Dale wheeled around. "You're still here?"

"Where you headed?" Her hips gyrated suggestively.

"Don't matter," he said, "because you ain't coming."

She tilted to one side, gaping at the moonless sky, receiving voices through her stupor. From a cautious distance, Dale awaited her next move.

Her eyes fell upon him again. "S-o-o-o?" she asked over the cup from which she sipped.

"Scram," said Dale. "No rides." He motioned the hook to implore her onward. "If my kid can't ride shotgun, nobody can."

She pouted and blew aside her bangs, slurped her beverage, and, with a surprisingly graceful swoop, stepped out of sight.

Dale crept to the tailgate. He squinted, surveying the lot's shadowy surroundings, but saw the woman nowhere. Brandishing the tool more bravely, he reprimanded the night. "That's right! I know you're out there. I've already called the cops, so don't even think about jumping me. You and whoever's with you should just get lost."

He held his breath to listen for sounds—voices, legs tangling bushes. Other than his hammering pulse, no noise came, although that did not disprove she had been robbery bait.

Dale flew into action. He jumped to the pavement, slammed the trailer door, and, hook at the ready, he hustled to the cab. Before yanking the driver-side handle, he peeked through the window in case a bandit waited with a gun aimed at his face.

He climbed in, tossed the tool to the floor, cranked the engine key, and punched on the truck's headlights. He locked the doors and tried to calm himself. Scrutinizing his high beams, he saw no woman. Maybe the angels had traction-beamed her to outer space. As long as she was gone, Dale gave not one shit about the how or where.

But, still.

Dale had never cheated on his wife and therefore considered himself honorable. However, a deserted lot without witnesses and a frisky woman in a blackout made for a unique situation. Temptation tugged at him.

Replaying the scenario, he tried to imagine how he would respond if she had initiated sexual contact. He saw her kneeling while she unbuckled his belt, and he slammed the lid on the fantasy.

That nothing had transpired was for the best. Her drunkenness put the whole thing in the neighborhood of rape, and he was no rapist.

Besides, who knew what STD he would bring home? Try explaining that to Cindy.

But, still. Still.

He drove to the lot's exit and stomped on his brakes. A trio of state trooper cars screamed past, their red and white lights spinning.

A mile down-road, Dale saw what convened them.

The strobing, parked cruisers surrounded a broad oak tree alongside the road. A driverless hatchback was wrapped around the tree's trunk, all twisted metal, splintered glass, and smoke.

Troopers on foot bounced their flashlight beams across the forest, searching for the driver. Dale passed slowly and opened his window to listen. Burning oil scented the breeze. He considered stopping and pointing the boys toward where she had been—but, instead, he put the hammer down.

Normally, he enjoyed long drives. The rhythm of the road corralled his thoughts. Without distractions, he could consider a subject from new directions, rather than his usual straight-on way. After some trips, he had even apologized to his wife for bad behavior, because he'd been afforded time and space for reconsideration.

Tonight, he did not enjoy the drive. The mystery woman kept rising up like a phantom from the pavement before him, only to be driven through again and again. He could not escape the vision of her and could not wait to get home.

*****

The following Sunday, at his son Sean's fifth birthday party, Dale told his anecdote to another father.

Dale had traded shifts so he could attend the celebration, though he did not participate. He and the other father, Jim, secluded themselves in Dale's kitchen during the party. Leaning against the counter, they held green beer bottles over their bellies and bandied off-color jokes.

Jim's daughter attended Pre-K with Sean. She periodically visited the antisocial men, soliciting hugs. After collecting them, she would gallop back to the party, her ponytail bouncing behind her.

She had just left when Dale commenced telling the drunken woman story.

Jim was a good audience, nodding and grunting. An indulgent raconteur, Dale enlivened his story with evocative imagery and bodily expression. Dale captivated Jim. Midway, however, he blundered.

"If I were a different guy, that woman would have been a stain. I could have clubbed her with the hook, dragged her into the trailer, hog-tied her, drove 50 miles to nowhere, did her any way I wanted and dumped her. She has no idea how lucky she was."

A taut smile pinched Jim's face. "Yeah," he said. "Whooph." He dropped his gaze toward his sneakers and shifted his weight. "Awfully... descriptive."

Dale felt shame imposed upon him. He cleared his throat and finished the story. Jim's features remained dour, however, and unnerving. Their bottles empty, the host offered his guest a fresh beer. Broken from his trance, Jim said, "Oh. Alright."

When Dale passed him a full pony, Jim said, "You must have a lot of wild road stories. I mean, that doesn't happen where I work."

Dale tasted his beer and said, "Yeah, some stuff." And to break the silence, he added, "One night, I parked in an alley to nap. I had just drifted off when I heard pops and caught a flash in an apartment window. Not my business. I tucked in and went to sleep. Found out the next day the shots were a murder-suicide. Believe that? Yeah. The road is weird."

Jim's daughter burst in for hugs. Jim snarled at her. "Get out," he hissed. "Can't you see we're having man talk?"

The girl stood and wilted at the center of the kitchen. Her eyes shimmered. "Okay, daddy," she said and ran out.

Jim started to say, "Honey," but it was too late. The men exchanged a glance. "Kids," Jim said, studying the floor-tiles. "No boundaries."

"Uh-huh," said Dale, examining his bottle.

Dale's wife, Cindy, came to get the cake then. "Come sing happy birthday, you two," she chirped, and both men deflated a little, relieved by the distraction.

*****

Thoughts of the woman kept him awake that night. He sprouted an unexpected erection, but with his wife asleep beside him, he could do nothing about it. Eventually, the alarm clock read 6 a.m. He had to leave for a shift.

He sat up in the dark, on the edge of the bed, and slapped his cheek three times. Cindy stirred and checked the clock. "What are you doing?" she asked.

"Going to work," he said. The streetlight through the blinds cast bars across his bare, bent back.

"Can you do it without abusing yourself, please?" she asked. "You scared me."

"Sorry," he said. He turned toward her, yet stayed quiet.

She made an impatient noise. "Everything alright?"

Dale's hand smoothed the bedcovers beside him, his fingers moving in and out of the feeble light. "Yeah," he said. "Thinking."

"About?"

Dale measured his words. "Had a weird talk with Jim yesterday," he said.

"And?" asked his wife. He heard her body move beneath

the sheets. His conscience wanted to say dangerous things. He grunted and asked, "If a person can imagine horrible stuff, do you think they're capable of doing it?"

"Like what?"

"I don't know." Dale's fingers squeezed the bridge of his nose. "Hurting people. Murder. Whatever."

Cindy rolled to contemplate the ceiling. "Seems like everyone's got a devious streak. If a guy can imagine evil shit, he can probably carry it out. Under certain circumstances."

Listening, Dale stepped into his pants and zipped up. He said, "Yeah, what do you know."

His wife lifted her head, an anonymous, faceless shape. "Then why ask me?"

Dale said, "I gotta go to work." He circled the bed to her side.

"Seriously, why?" She propped up on an elbow. "Did Jim say something? That guy's an odd duck. Did he—"

"Never mind," Dale grunted. He wanted to remind Cindy that she was lucky that he was unlike other men. For instance, he was a loyal and never violent toward her. That proved his character. "I gotta go," he said. He kissed the air above her head, leaving her questions unanswered.

*****

In the mudroom, Dale pulled on his boots and checked his watch. He still had time before he was due at work. Maddeningly, that woman haunted him still. In the garage, he patted his pockets, stopped, and bristled. He was so discombobulated that he misplaced his keys. Grumbling, he went back to the row of hooks just inside the door and snatched the spare key. Cindy always scolded him when he took the spare—for emergencies only—but he didn't feel like searching for the master set. Something more urgent pressed at his subconscious.

He reversed the car from the garage and paused at the end of driveway. Behind the wheel, he watched the sun peek into the sky. His thoughts confounded, and his molars hurt from grinding. An illogical compulsion nagged him to drive North, the opposite direction of work... toward the mystery woman.

Also, however... it occurred to him that Daylight Donuts was northward. Suddenly, he wanted coffee and a donut. He could drive that far, at least.

Leaving his block, he checked his mirrors to see if Cindy stood at their window, watching him go the wrong way. But, of course, she was still in bed. Cindy lacked ambition, hobbies, had a lazy streak. If he had known that before they got married, he might have reconsidered.

Coffee aside—what the hell was he doing chasing a fantasy? What outcome did he expect? The odds of finding the woman again were a million to one. Maybe a billion. But, still. To shirk work and chase forbidden fruit gave a tingle. This she-demon had possessed him, for sure. And there remained a very convincing, tiny fraction of a chance that he would return to the lot where they'd met, and she would be sitting on a concrete embankment, awaiting him.

By the time he reached the main road, the mystery woman had returned in Technicolor. She beckoned like a siren. He blared music on the radio. Nothing shook her. He couldn't resist the fantasy—envisioning her hand touching her mouth, sliding over her conical breasts, down her hip.

He sprouted another goddamn erection.

At Daylight, he got a coffee at the drive-up window and circled to the exit... and the lure persisted.

Rather than turning left, toward work, he spat an obscenity and jerked the wheel to the right.

Dale sped along the main route, guided by his absurd urge. He would humor it just long enough to check the gas prices at the Sunoco near the highway. That marked the limit.

Meanwhile, in his head, the woman began stripteasing. To his frustration, his mental camera blurred to hide her private parts. When he reached the Sunoco, he'd forgotten all about gas prices. A fever had consumed him: he had to find this woman again.

Then, from the depths of its banishment, a rational voice pleaded. He was a fool. At almost the top of the hour, he was miles from work. They'd dock his pay for punching in late. How would he explain that to Cindy?

Or, what if he never went home?

With a roar, he swerved the car dangerously across traffic, into the other lane, and raced toward his job.

He ignored the cars that honked at him. In his mind, the woman held out her arms while receding from him, into blackness, as if being blown away by powerful, unjust winds.

*****

For the ten hours spent making deliveries, Dale was divided between two obsessive thoughts: first, that it was shameful for a married man to be susceptible to such carnal cravings and juvenile reveries; and second, that in a few nights he would make another delivery to Dundilee Grocery, where he had met the mystery woman.

Perhaps she would present herself again.

He returned to the yard at almost 5 p.m. Upon arrival, he parked the rig, stretched, gathered his belongings, and ambled toward the main office to clock out.

He got only halfway.

The company's dispatcher rushed out and waved her arms. "Dale," she cawed, her voice piercing the noisy clamor of the lot. A mechanic who banged beneath a truck's hood lowered his wrench and raised his greasy mug to snoop.

"There's a policeman here for you," the woman yelled. "Dale!"

Queasy, Dale froze. A sofa-sized, older man, trailed behind the dispatcher. He wore a blue suit coat and a snout-full of mustache.

The buzzing dispatcher fanned her neck. "He arrived a bit ago... he's been waiting... won't say why—"

The man introduced himself as Detective Hornback to Dale. He flashed a badge. "Got a minute?"

"Sure." Dale's eyes could not stay level on the man.

The smiling detective appeared amused by Dale's uneasiness. It gave him an upper hand. Hornback pocketed the wallet inside his coat.

"Might we have a moment?" he asked the dispatcher. Reluctantly, she retreated to her office confine, glumly peeking over her shoulder.

"I wanted to catch you before you left." The detective possessed an easy, avuncular manner. While talking, he displayed a photo for Dale. "Early Wednesday morning, you encountered this woman, correct?" he asked.

Dale took the wrinkled photo. It showed the woman he had met, but sober. She, a young boy, and a girl kneeled happily on the lawn of a lakeside cottage. A mother and her children. The picture wavered in Dale's grip.

"Yeah." Dale stared at the snapshot. "Looked pretty haggard, though."

"Her name's Linda Strundland." Calmly, Hornback searched Dale's face. "I've been tracking where she might have gone. The Green Mills warehouse has a surveillance camera, so I had them pull the tape. Guess she startled you, huh?"

Dale nodded. He reached to return the picture, but it fell to the pavement.

Fat Hornback collected the photo with a labored exhale. He said, "Relax. Everybody I interview gets jittery. Makes me self-conscious."

He chuckled and produced a pad and a pen. He wedged the pen-cap in the corner of his mouth like a stogie. Poised to write, he said, "What can you tell me about that night?"

Dale chronicled the details of the experience. A slight stutter tangled his tongue now and then. Hornback scribbled, saying *hmms* and *ah-has*. In the end, he studied Dale and asked, "Nothing else? No rendezvousing down the road?"

"No, sir, no way."

The detective brightened and whip-cracked the notepad against his palm. "That's what I surmised from the footage. I apologize for the inconvenience, but we check our leads. Helluva story, though. Surely not a daily occurrence."

Dale shook his head.

"Take my card. You remember anything, call me, okay?"

Dale scanned the details printed on the card, but he could not see straight. He asked, "What do you guess happened to her?"

"That's why she's a missing person," said Hornback with a wink. "If I knew, she'd be a found person."

Spontaneously, Dale covered his heart and testified, "I've got a wife and kid. I would never hurt anybody."

"Of course you wouldn't," said Hornback with a reassuring drawl. "The woman was plastered. This is commonly a death by misadventure case. She'll bob down the Susquehanna soon enough, or a hiker will find her in a gorge. If she hasn't contacted her family after a few days, you can assume why."

Hornback dragged his index finger across his throat and said, "S-k-k-k."

Dale looked mortified.

"Sorry to rope you into this buddy," said Hornback. "Remember—call if you see her."

*****

While the detective left the lot, Dale's own legs wobbled. He advanced toward the office, where the logbook still listed him as on-duty. He sensed the mechanic leering and the dispatcher spying.

The office lacked typing sounds or phone chatter. From behind her desk, the dispatcher greeted Dale with an unctuous smirk. "Everything okay?" she asked. Her hands fidgeted atop her paperwork.

Dale hung the truck's keys on the pegboard. He wrote the time in the "out" column of his row in the ledger on the conuter and set aside the red pen.

"You ever see a photo in the paper," he asked, moving toward the door. He held the knob and spoke without turning to the dispatcher. "And you think, *hubba-hubba*. Right? Good-looking chick—or dude, I guess, in your case. And then, the headline says, 'Young woman raped and murdered,' and makes you feel like a creep?"

He stole a glance at her. The dispatcher's mouth hung to show her bulldog teeth, and she stared as though he was a criminal. With nothing else to say, Dale hurried out.

In his car, he stared out the windshield. His imagination cranked in high gear.

The woman—Linda Strundland—was mincing on moonlit gravel, toppling, going ass over teacup down a rocky slope, cracking her skull, ending up in dark water.

Then her kids squirmed on a couch while a cop squatted on the carpet before them.

And then, he, Dale, lifted Linda up into the truck-bed, and together they pulled her shirt over her head. They kissed while his hands availed themselves of her naked body, and they were definitely going to have consensual sex.

Sudden shame cut the vision to black. How could he think such things? Here the woman was likely deceased, and her pitiful kids might never get a body back to bury. He was a pervert.

But, still. He felt her presence.

Cindy would scent his guilt and ask what was up. He had

done nothing, but dodgy behavior would amplify her suspicion. And what would work be like, once the gossip mill got grinding? To the dispatcher, Dale was now a bad guy. She would tell everyone she knew about him being a creep. Sitting alone, adrift, Dale could not dispute her claim.

Point Taken
Ange Morrissey.

Barry Bigelow's Mother often said, 'Mr. Manilow's eyes meeting mine at that concert released the mother in me, I couldn't believe it, wanting a baby at forty one.' Then she'd sigh.

Making a baby required physical engineering. At work she found a partner who claimed having an affair was top of his bucket list. Canteen gossip said sex without strings was all Magic Moments for men, seemed like a mucky mess to her. She wasn't surprised when he became demanding, he, however, was shocked to find himself dismissed, purpose served.

Twenty three years later Barry's Mother told him she was dying, which turned out to be true, and any Magic Moments he might have, which she doubted, would be a disappointment, as were most things in life. He hoped she was wrong.

*****

His third birthday present was a sewing basket, antique, Mother said. Later he saw it was simply old. Hers when she was a girl, she said, which was possible. 'Sew something pretty for Mother,' she said.

It never occurred to Barry to ask for a ball, or a bike. He

enjoyed needlework, enjoyed pleasing his Mother. When his skills surpassed her own, she never let on.

She left him a house and a bit to live on. He promised himself two Victorian Avery needle cases, the Artist's Easel and the Butterfly, once the funeral was done, and sent her into the furnace to Mr Manilow crooning, 'Come, come, come into my arms…'. A truly satisfactory Magic Moment, he thought.

Marji came, even though he hadn't asked, clearly relieved to find him calm and collected. She winked at him when the soundtrack kicked in.

She poured time and energy into creating her college show, keeping her part time job with a demanding, high end fashion retailer boss, getting her website, Dressi, up and running. Thinner than she should be, she drank black coffee and didn't touch the sausage rolls he warmed in the oven. 'Don't stay home alone every night, Bar,' she said. 'Join a needlework class. Just until I get back and you're working for me. You'll be a sensation.' She raised her coffee, 'Here's to rave reviews, rich clients and a boutique of my own.'

Barry agreed, he trusted Marji. She joked she only wanted his sewing skills, but she never caused him to doubt her, never frightened him with demands for gratitude, or obedience. One day he'd tell her what she meant to him, or embroider it on his arm, like a tattoo, only better.

Mother wasn't there to insist he stay in, safe from the world's wickedness. His promise to Marji got him out of the house and into night school. Thinking about her made it possible to enter the dimly lit hollow halls and join the marvelling ladies.

Sandra Rossiter stole his heart and his sanity the instant she tumbled, laughing, into Advanced Tailoring and Cutting. He followed her home, sent flowers, a book about Coco Chanel, a tortoiseshell kitten from the pet shop nearby. He rang her estate agent boss to praise her sewing skills, shocked the man was more angry than interested. She stopped coming to class.

The others looked at him accusingly. They didn't understand. They said he should go so Sandra could come back.

Sandra stayed away, so did he. He grieved. It was worse than when Marji left for College. She hadn't wasted time insisting he wasn't losing her for ever, the first postcard arrived the day after he waved her coach out of town. Cards came every week, please could he send ideas for hemline embroidery, appliqué patches. Card, after card, request after request.

Barry fulfilled each demand, never wondering if she actually needed what he sent, or how she afforded the postage. He was happy, until Sandra stayed away. He thought he might die.

Barry patrolled the street where Sandra worked, waited outside her flat. The police paid him a visit. After they left, he rang Raylinda, his childhood neighbour, classified locally as even odder than him.

Raylinda's Father wanted a son, Mother a daughter. Raylinda survived in the space between their desires, developing a perversely peculiar personality which eventually found favour. Once denigrated and denied, she became cool and courted, a celebrity he wasn't allowed to visit, not being bizarre enough.

For the sake of old times Raylinda still answered when he rang. Her attention span was short, but she would listen and occasionally comment. 'I explained I wasn't pestering her,' he hiccupped, 'She's my muse.'

It was all quite entertaining. She could use it, tell it, make herself a hero of the performance. With unprecedented sympathy, Raylinda didn't remind Barry Sandra sent the cops, or ask worrying questions about the girl's accusations. 'Prove your intentions are pure,' she yelled. 'Sew something pretty for her.'

Raylinda remembered his Mother, naturally.

Barry put the phone down, tingling all over.

*****

Worried Marji's workload wouldn't leave room for him, desperate to keep her interest, Barry had created a collection of his own, hoping for an emergency when only he could help. Now, anxious to support her while keeping her at arm's length, he sent her his sketches, slashed garments with torn hems, ragged necklines, twisted sleeves, and his logo, two stylised Bs, back to back, looking very much like a butterfly. 'Wrecked,' he wrote, 'Hope you like it. Good luck. Bar.'

He stood outside the post office, longing to see his perfectly packed parcel leave. Anything might happen. The building might burn down.

Exclamation marks ringed Marji's message, 'We have to talk, after the show.'

*****

Barry could summon Sandra's supple silhouette to mind at will. He knew how her body stood, sat, walked, put on a coat, ran upstairs. She shaped his day. He dreamed and planned, waiting for the right time to act.

Marji came with a demand for more double B designs, news of rave reviews and potential investors. Run ragged, tired to the point of tears, she drank black coffee, ate nothing and fell asleep at the table. Barry whispered his plan to her, waking her in time for her coach, hating himself for being glad she wasn't staying longer. He was ready.

*****

Getting into Sandra's flat was easy via an alley, a flat roof and a window left on a latch. He borrowed her white bedding, piece by piece, embroidering his logo in white into tiny corners. He sat on her chairs, pressed his lips to her cups and glasses, wiping them carefully afterwards. He stood in her wardrobe with the doors closed, pushed his face into the delicate, unidentifiable items in her drawers.

A home shopping catalogue provided names, camisole, bra, panties. Lingerie. He borrowed and double B embroidered them, black on black, white on white, hiding the butterfly between hooks, on straps, in bra cups, along panty hems.

His secret signs ceased to satisfy him, they weren't enough.

Sandra was an open, smiley girl who told anyone who'd listen she never wanted children. But all girls want a wedding. He dreamed a wedding might be possible, once he reassured her physical engineering wasn't necessary. He began her trousseau, determined to give her things his Mother never had.

No chaotic crinoline or pretentious party dress for Sandra, a fine white worsted jacket with contrasting fur panels over a white silk sheath embroidered with white symbols of love. They'd choose the pillbox hat and kitten heeled shoes together.

Curing the tortoiseshell cat hide for the jacket was a complex process. He thought it turned out well.

At 3 p.m he displayed the garments across Sandra's bed, then went home to wait. At 3 a.m., full of foreboding, he packed his designs and samples and left a message on Marji's phone, 'Parcel in the shed. Dress + jacket = Pretty Pussy, for Dressi. The lingerie too, once I find the right name, if you want it.' After all, he thought, Sandra doesn't.

When the police knocked he answered the door promptly and, feeling oddly powerful, didn't bother trying to explain.

The case drew publicity even before Raylinda hit the headlines. An officer handing him the newspaper, said, 'The tabloids must've paid her plenty.' There was a photo, Barry, aged ten, wearing an embroidered shirt, plaiting Raylinda's hair.

Marji referred to him as Heartfelt's reclusive and sensitive designer, which was either great publicity, or a dangerous acknowledgment. Certainly a risk.

Barry knew he was being unreasonable, only he wished she'd called him inspired, innovative, impassioned...

He shook off his displeasure, determined to forgive Raylinda and love Marji more than ever. Neither proved difficult. He told Marji not to come, to court or prison.

Raylinda gave evidence in a pin striped charcoal tailored suit. She described here distress on hearing he'd heartlessly killed a cat. She didn't look at Barry, busy twisting her fiercely smoothed hair into knots.

Marji wrote, 'Lease signed, Bar. Raylinda's saving us a fortune in advertising. Orders soaring since Sandra's tearful testimony.' The message was too serious for exclamation marks. He missed them. She asked if he had a name for the lingerie.

He wrote, Good news. Not yet. He gave it to the lawyer to post. His lawyer brought another newspaper back, 'You seem to have a hit on your hands, despite the cat.' One headline shrieked, 'Couture? Not!' over a picture of the fur panelled jacket, which showed to advantage thanks to innovations in colour printing. The modifier beneath read, 'The workings of a tortured mind?'

Barry's lawyer advised against any attempt to explain.

*****

Two hand drawn cards arrived. Each carried a satisfying amount of exclamation marks and, 'By my artist friend,' beneath the illustration.

Watercolour cute bunnies chomping carrots in classic couture told him, 'Fake can't cut it. Thinking well fed, happy rabbits. Lingerie manufacturers lined up. Decide on a name and your hidden butterfly range goes into production.'

The second was a pen and ink sketch, a Wrecked dress in a shop window. Marji's message said, 'Opening tomorrow, Bar. Never forget, we're waiting for you. Dressi needs you. I need you. Trouble soon over, Bar. Soon.'

Barry wondered who the artist friend was and, briefly, who the other parts of 'we' were, then went back to building a wall of design between him and the world where Sandra thought badly of him.

*****

Clocking the Catskin Coat on the national news, a farmer from Suffolk bagged some rabbits and found a dyer. Exclamation marks peppered Marji's description of him, marching into the boutique with a perfect pelt, smelling faintly of farmyard.

She told Barry jersey teamed with false fur was appearing on every High Street, insisting this was flattery, not competition.

The farmer proposed romance on 250 ramshackle acres with the opportunity to spend freely on the rural retreat. Marji refused. She proposed a line of tortoiseshell fur accessories. He accepted, bred more rabbits, made and spent his money alone.

The card illustrating Marji's report of the non-romance showed a capped chap in wellies and waistcoat reaching wide open arms across a broken gate and Marji, one baseball booted foot on an office chair piled high with fur and fabric samples, frowning forbiddingly.

Marji loved baseball boots. Her friend clearly knew her well. Barry decided that was a good thing.

*****

The newspapers published a vegan policeman's pro plant based food rant alongside a photograph of Raylinda leading an anti-fur-in-fashion demo. They spelt the policeman's name correctly, got his age right, he didn't anticipate any harm to his career.

Privately, Raylinda ordered Pretty Pussy. Marji branded Raylinda a hypocrite and refused to accept her order on morning tv, live.

Her next card showed money cascading from an antique till. 'We've given you a raise,' was accompanied by one large exclamation mark.

*****

Barry believed killing and skinning the cat made the judge send him for psychiatric evaluation. His lawyer blamed Raylinda. The woman analysed every word Barry said in a bored tone not unlike his Mother's 'Is That ALL?' voice.

Things got very hazy. He definitely broke some furniture, a gratifying

Magic Moment. They said he hit the psych. He preferred to believe it was the guard.

When he got to the secure unit there were postcards waiting. His roommate, Man Rob, had already read them.

At school Marji and Barry had one rule, if you can't slide round it, over it, under it, the only way is through, and no moaning. Barry smiled and stayed silent.

'Look, here,' Man Rob marvelled, 'Where it says, 'Wait til you see your bank balance.' He shook his head admiringly. 'Wish I had someone like that, on the outside.'

A nurse, which was what guards were called, gave Barry a questioning look. Barry nodded, I'm fine, back. Straight through, no moaning. Following that, the nurse made a point of finding Barry alone and putting his post in his hand. At least

Barry read Marji's cards before Man Rob took them.

'Marji calls you Bar.' Man Rob muttered, poring over her latest.

Without considering the consequences, Barry snapped, 'Only Marji.'

'I'm cool with that,' Man Rob said, after a while.

Man Rob introduced selected inmates with a potted version of Barry's offence, adopting Barry's theory, 'Guy's in here 'cos he killed a cat much as anything.'

He even persuaded Welshy Salvatore, who didn't associate with anybody, to teach Barry prison slang, the subject of Welshy's BA dissertation, of which the whole unit was proud, even though Welshy mostly ignored them.

Having put them together, Man Rob couldn't object whenever Welshy took Barry off to the quiet table, to talk.

Welshy confided, 'Gonna make this dissertation into a book, Prisnish, Imprisoned English. Old lags do great with books, see.'

Barry gave Welshy a drawing of his updated logo, prison bars confining his butterfly. 'I won't let anyone see,' Welshy whispered, 'They'll all be tattooing it on their arses.'

Later he asked if Barry would design his book cover. 'Not if you don't want, mind you, Boyo,' he smiled. 'Be a big boost for me. No probs if it's not your thing, we're proper friends, like.'

*****

The cut out Statue of Liberty card said Marji was in America. Barry wondered if she still had her artist friend. Only that was

Marji's business. All he had to do was like whoever she liked.

Exclamation marks crowned every word. Wrecked and Pretty Pussy had made it to the States and made it in the States. Did he think now might be a good time to do something new? Like lingerie? She was ready to roll, once he gave her the name. She'd be home on the 10th. Which meant she'd been back a day already.

Guilt held Barry back. Though he'd found sweet spots to hide the initials, the garments were copies of the clever underpinnings Sandra chose. No matter how hard he studied them, he never found the confidence to design his own. Everything Marji had to work with was borrowed, copied.

Man Rob grabbed the card. 'You gotta give the girl whatever she wants bro!'

Barry walked out, worrying. Would hidden embroidery alone make the line good enough for Dressi?

Welshy strolled over, then stopped, stepped back.

'No, it's ok,' Barry began.

Welshy shook his head. 'Not this minute it's not, Boyo. Your face looks like mine feels when words won't come.' He raised a hand and turned away.

Barry walked back. Watching him Man Rob's thick cheeks twitched nervously. Barry nodded towards the door. Fail now and Man Rob ruled forever. He didn't breathe until Man Rob sauntered away.

Blank paper waited for an affectionate, enabling letter. Barry wrote, Secret Sensations, go ahead. He added some exclamation marks. He'd tell her what she meant to him out loud, one day.

*****

Marji's press release grabbed the fashion pages, Easier to change than a tattoo, they said, New man, new knickers. Celebrities, apparently spontaneously, begged for lingerie with special initials added.

Barry had a head full of ideas. He had Marji. And Welshy. He pretended Man Ray was a wild animal he'd found and decided to look after. Sometimes he forgot he was detained at her Majesty's pleasure. But never at night. He lay in bed trying to replace Man Rob's nocturnal fantasies with the problems of form, fabric, effect. The gut level activity, the thick yeasty smell, the short, hard words, penetrated Barry's innocent ignorance, tearing it apart.

Man Rob wasn't alone. Listening to the cruel urgency of driving desire and unresolved rage, Barry finally understood his unwanted adoration had frightened Sandra. He had to make amends, but how?

*****

'Bigelow! Gov'ner's office, sharpish!' The order sent him running.

The parcel was open, naturally, the contents arranged on the Governor's desk, 'A cornucopia, a superfluity some might say,' he smiled.

Barry wasn't listening. Embroidery frames, fabrics, dozens of silks; a small shagreen box, its deep, hinged lid open to display several ivory handles protruding from the padded velvet lining, tools the Governor hadn't thought to examine.

Barry recognised the antique set of stilettos, single steel prongs for piercing fabric, or leather. Weapons, in the eyes of some. He guessed he wouldn't have a choice, but he'd happily leave them with the Governor, until he went home.

The Governor steepled his fingers, elbows on desk, wishing his wife hadn't refused to discuss Barry. She had forbidden the mention of Barry's name, which was a shame, her insights concerning previous inmates had proved invaluable. Seemingly killing and skinning a cat was going too far.

Chap's bound to be in a good mood after this, the Governor thought, No better moment. He waved Barry into a chair. 'Still coming up with the goods, Bigelow, you know, new designs for that friend of yours?'

Barry perched warily on the edge of his seat. 'Trying to,' he said.

'More in the pipeline, is there?'

Barry looked puzzled.

The Governor coughed. He had it all off pat earlier, now the words were rearranging themselves, floating away. Chat wasn't his thing, he was better at addressing groups, he should just come out with it. 'Mr. Nichols commends your efforts in the carpentry class, I'm also informed you exercise a calming influence. We see a notable behavioural improvement in your cell mate, Robert Manning. Approachable, less vicious, more welcome in the workshop these days.'

The Governor would know about men like Man Rob, whose threats to punish Sandra frightened Barry. 'You get fuckin' time, she walks away with a halo, the bitch. Needs to be taught a lesson, that one.'

Was the Governor saying Man Rob was improving? Barry leaned forward, hoping to hear more.

Encouraged, the Governor ploughed on, 'However, we recognise carpentry isn't your metier. We think it would be good all round if you had your own space in the workshop,' he waved a hand at Marji's glorious gift, 'A chance to pursue your own objectives, so to speak. Or might you consider taking a class? Unofficially?'

Raylinda swore instant agreement was giving power away cheaply. Barry lowered his head, raising it only when he had a suitably solemn look in place, 'I think, yes, I'd like that.'

The Governor spluttered, his waving hands requesting patience. 'Naturally not expecting... not all one sided... perhaps a little more contact with that post card girl of yours? Pretty good business woman is my guess. Smart. Does she visit? We could arrange....'

Barry swallowed, speechless.

The Governor jumped up. He knew full well Bigelow was 'No Visitors'. What a ridiculous mistake, the man would think he was utterly out of touch.

'Apologies, unforgivable. Bigelow, No Visitors, stipulated. Of course. But phone time, perhaps? Use of an office? Privacy, no interruptions...'

He was relieved to see Barry's face brighten. 'So, definitely, all can be arranged. Timing, must consider the timing, young business woman, many commitments....' he was losing himself, forgetting more important topics. 'However, if there was anything she felt she could...to support your new enterprise...materials...craft magazines...outside today's prison budget, understandably, though remiss in my estimation...begging bowls...grateful...'

Privately the Governor thought Marji, at the helm of an infant, runaway success venture, wouldn't have two seconds to spare in any day to arrange embroidery supplies, or the money to throw at a prison craft community. However, she was clearly willing to do a lot for this man, and the Governor was not above pleading his case in austere times.

Several silent minutes passed before Barry agreed.

Marji sorted everything, including publicity, 'That'll fetch the funding,' she said, and she was right.

Deal done, Barry spent most days in E&T, and had his post delivered there, though it went to Man Rob eventually. He was surprised how often he thought about the man, how responsible he felt for him.

*****

The first, private, phone call found him tongue tied. The second was excellent. It was also too much of a privilege. All inmates could use the phone, but not by the half hour, from a revolving chair in an office with a view across the back end of town to the fields beyond.

He asked to use the phone in the association space. Inmates and nurses made great show of staying out of listening range. Which was just as well on the afternoon Marji told him Sandra was getting married. 'The Papers will be all over it, Bar, best you heard from me first,' she said. 'Don't worry, that girl is fine. She's fine.'

Barry said, 'Of course, of course. Thank you,' and other stuff, nothing he remembered later.

He didn't tell Man Rob, who questioned him after every call. He'd never been jealous. He hadn't recognised it in his

Mother, or his cell mate. He decided to be happy for Sandra, and he was.

*****

His Barefaced Cheek designs sent Marji into raptures. The card showed a fashion show runway at stage height, slender, long footed legs walking beneath swirling silks, linens, furs. A trailing ribbon of tiny script said, 'To a genius with respect and admiration. AJH.'

'Hello, AJH,' he whispered, 'Look after Marji.' He read her message over and over, 'Bar, the tabloids are in turmoil, a tribute to your tremendous talent. Love Marji.' Sober, earnest, no exclamation marks. Love.

After that the papers couldn't trouble him, 'Takes a bum to know a bum,' left him pitying the writer, but Man Rob paced, raging. 'I shoulda known, shoulda got you ready for it. Bastards.'

Marji's favourite article followed, pinned to a note in someone else's handwriting.

The banner headline read, *Now you see it, now you don't*, over front and rear catwalk shots. In the margin Marji wrote, 'Fellice LIVES Barefaced Cheek. She made me promise no-one else will ever walk this. Her understanding, her grace, are vital to your vision. Backstage is hell.'

Fellice looked delicious, the severely cut frock ridiculously modest, until the model moved, when, if Fellice allowed it, perfectly engineered slit seams gave a glimpse of bottom, a split second revelation of breast.

The note was from her, 'Marji tells me I may address you as Bar, this I would like if you, yourself, find it agreeable. I have said to Marji a thing Marji says is important you should know. This thing is, I feel most strong, most sexy, walking your design than in any other ever. I engage the world on my own terms.'

'On her own terms,' Barry murmured, thinking of Sandra.

*****

A bishop wrote to the Governor, the Governor came to Barry, pink faced and jubilant. 'Not that you must, you understand,' he began, looming over Barry's work station. 'I simply put it to you, this would do you, and us, some good. As I see it.'

Barry nudged a chair out. The Governor sat.

Five students bent to their work, smiling.

The Governor didn't relinquish the letter, he read aloud, his finger wondering across the page, 'Hearing many impressive reports, blah, blah, might you,' he raised his even pinker face to Barry, 'He means you, via HMP, but you, Bigelow, in the main,' he blinked and went back to his precious piece of paper, 'Might you accept a commission to design and execute a work for the 300th anniversary of St. Clare's church? St. Clare being, you will appreciate, the patron saint of needleworkers.'

The Governor fell anxiously silent, hands on his knees, letter dangling.

'I didn't know we had a patron saint,' Barry grinned.

*****

A blizzard of postcards followed Welshy's release, castles, cakes, spoons, lakes, leeks, mountains, pit heads, parks. The storm slowed to a shower, but didn't stop.

Wrecked, Pretty Pussy, Secret Sensations and Barefaced Cheek continued to sell. Barry hoped he'd come up with something new when he got home.

On release day Marji was waiting in her bright red mini, though he hadn't asked. A detailed drawing of a Palais Royale sewing box, lid open, contents on display, lay on the passenger seat. AJH's tiny, tidy, 'Welcome Back Mr Designer,' coiled round the keyhole.

Marj's fluttering fingers told him to turn it over. It read, *With love from Marji.* No exclamation marks. Love, again. They parted wordlessly, warmly at his door, the box was waiting on the kitchen table.

He planned to see Welshy, discuss the book jacket.

He had ideas for Dressi.

He would visit Rob.

There was one thing he had to do first.

Hollamby was an unusual name, tracing her was frighteningly easy. He saw her, just once. She shone colourful and clear as a window from St. Clare's. She was pregnant, her remembered silhouette shattered. He adored her, unreservedly.

*****

The Pret Pour l'Amour collection of single fastening garments created a furore. Celebrities continuously lost control of the cunning clothes, though Barry hadn't actually made it all that easy. Only on their own terms, Sandra, he thought.

Marji persuaded Barry into Dressi, where Niamh, Christine and Nicholas christened him Double B and competed for his approval. He wondered when, or if, he'd meet AJH, but didn't ask.

He invited Man Rob to stay on his release and began calling him Rob, a new name for a new start. Meeting Marji was all Rob talked about.

Marji smiled when Barry mentioned it to her, shrugged, went back to work, and began fretting. This man might be a major distraction.

When the day came she hugged Barry like she didn't want to let him go, then she did, with a shove and a melon eating grin. He had no idea how worried she was.

*****

The two men managed well, Rob on his best behaviour, grateful for a warm room, opening windows, a huge tv and pizza deliveries.

At work Marji watched Barry, fighting the urge to ask. He seemed a little uptight. She was permanently dizzy from lack of sleep, she gained five pounds and was cross with everyone except Barry, who didn't notice.

To please Rob, Barry asked, to please Barry, Marji agreed to come for dinner.

Rob prowled around trying to decide where to display the box he'd made to hold the cards she'd sent Barry, then took it back to his room, 'For when she knows me better,' he said.

That night Rob drank, but not much, and was incredibly funny, a trait Barry had neither seen nor suspected. Barry sat back and let Rob entertain.

Marji went home, reassured.

A shining eyed Rob went to bed.

Barry counted his blessings over a last glass of wine; the best job and the best friend in the world; Welshy, soon to be visited; Sandra, distantly adored; even Rob, not such a wild man now.

Then he heard Rob's long silent prison voice grunting his loathing for Sandra and his desire for Marji.

Night after night Barry watched Rob drink, then sat on the stairs, ready to stop the man if he tried to leave, snatching sleep, hoping for silence, hearing horrors.

He said he was working from home. Marji rang twice a day, their calls didn't last long. He wrote two letters and hid them in his bedroom.

*****

One morning Rob disappeared. Barry panicked. He couldn't protect the distant Sandra, or Marji, who maintained mobile phones meant no-one needed to know precisely where she was, 24/7.

Rob returned that night, dejected, without the right present for Marji.

Barry offered him an all-expenses paid cruise, a chance to spread his wings.

Rob asked if he could take a friend, Barry agreed immediately, anything, any cost, to get him away. Rob rang Marji and asked her to go with him.

Barry listened, hoping Rob would accept whatever reason Marji gave for refusing.

Rob threw the phone at the wall, ranting.

Barry opened bottle after bottle, filled glass after glass,

pretending to keep pace, watching Rob's face thicken and dull until he collapsed, curled up under the table, a small, safe space.

Barry grabbed the letters and ran to the post-box.

He'd used as much Prisnish as he could remember writing to Welshy. Some passages were, intentionally, funny, the final sentence stark, 'No point me designing the cover, not after I've done what I have to do.'

Marji's envelope was fatter, new designs, letters for her, his bank and his solicitor. He gave her his house, his money, his final collection and her freedom.

When he tiptoed in Rob rolled over, cursing, fell back snoring.

Barry opened the small shagreen box, made his choice, then knelt. Rob shuddered when the steel entered his ear. He soon stopped.

****

Letters and sketches tumbled into Marji's lap. Mohair coats banded in hole-punch patterned felt; jersey gowns detailed with metal eyelets; linen outfits laced together with lengths of leather.

When she heard the police arrived she hid the letters and spread the drawings across her desk, same old, same old to any outsider. She cried later.

'You aren't safe. Sandra isn't safe. I can't change him or control him. No cards, no visits, no phone calls. Let me be nothing to you. Pierced is yours, if you want to use it. All My Love, Always, Bar.'

A Career Killing
James Roth

"Let's return to the hotel," Yoko said, "and wait out the typhoon there. The bridge could give way."

"I have an important meeting in the morning," Masao said.

"That's hardly surprising," Yoko said.

"Why is it you don't understand? This week was the only time I had."

"All you think about is that promotion."

The windshield wipers flopped back and forth.

For years Yoko had been a dutiful wife, raising their two children and supporting him as he pursued his career, first as salesman in Miyaka Life Insurance, then as section and department chiefs, but she had changed recently. Masao had convinced himself that a young lover had gotten to her and put foolish ideas of traveling and learning to scuba dive in her head. Then when he got his hands on his money he'd dump her.

Between the swiping blades of the wipers, Masao could just make out the abutments of the bridge and, in the muddy river, logs and chunks of Styrofoam flowing past.

Over the past few days he had tried his best to talk Yoko out of divorcing him. She'd always been thrilled to go to an *onsen* to enjoy a relaxing bath and savor the specialties that each onsen's chef offered. But that hadn't been the case this time. They hadn't talked much. She'd spent most of her time watching Korean dramas on her telephone.

A divorce would put an end to his ascent up the corporate ladder. And she knew it, too. For the first time in her life she had the power. If a man couldn't handle his wife, how could he possibly handle a company of men? That's how the president of Miyaka would see it. Yes, a weekend at a hot spring resort, to try and convince her to stick it out with him, had been a waste of his time. Now he had to go through with what he'd been thinking about but had wanted to avoid-- hiring a private investigator to take some photos of her going into a love hotel with this young stud. Then he'd have the power once again.

He began to nudge the Toyota Century across the narrow bridge. Yoko said, "You're driving too fast! You do everything in a hurry!" She laughed. Yes, a young lover had gotten to her. Only a young lover could make her come out with these veiled comparisons. Other women hadn't complained about him. They thanked him, complained to him about their boyfriends or husbands, how they didn't know how to satisfy them.

Then it came to him in a rush, how to put an end to this problem of his. He wouldn't need a private detective. He flipped the electric switch that locked Yoko's door and unfastened his safety belt. As he did, Yoko snapped her head around and glared at him. The right corner of her mouth was twitching. She knew what was coming next. But it was too late for her to do anything about it.

Masao spun the wheel of the Toyota to the left, gunned the

engine, and, just as the Toyota's grill broke through the bridge's guardrail, shoved open his door and rolled out of the car, splashing into the river. The Toyota crashed down beside him. Steam issued from the hood.

Masao swam over to the bank and pulled himself out onto the mud. He looked down the river at the Toyota bobbing along among some logs. Somehow Yoko had managed to unfasten her seat belt and had scrambled over the backseat and was pressing her face against the rear window, where a pocket of air had formed. Then the car sunk. Masao thought, *My career is back on track. Sympathy! That will take me places.*

He clawed his way through some reeds, up to the road, and waited for someone to drive by.

A few minutes later a farmer showed up in his K-truck.

"There's been a terrible accident!" he said. "My wife!"

*****

"Mr. Kikuza, tell me once again what happened? I know it's difficult. But try."

Detective Yamashita, a young man who wore frameless glasses, had a baby's soft complexion, and looked as if he would be more suited to be a florist than a policeman, handed Masao a box of tissues. Masao plucked one out and dobbed his eyes with it. He dropped the tissue into a bin. He sniffled. He shivered. A uniformed policeman had taken his clothes, given him a robe and towel, but hadn't allowed him to clean up. His hair was grimy with sand. There was the matter of questioning him before he possibly forgot the details of the accident.

Masao told Detective Yamashita the story again.

"You knew there was a typhoon approaching?"

"Yes."

"You heard the warnings?"

Masao said, "We decided to take our chances."

Just then a girl who served tea came to Detective Yamashita's desk and set down two cups of green tea. She was perhaps twenty-five and had a pleasantly non-threatening round face. Her lips were a glossy red. Her complexion white. She had formed her hair into one braid, which fell down the center of her back. There was an inviting red ribbon at the end of the braid, which Masao fantasized about untying, so that her thick black hair lay on her shoulders. She said, "Dozo."

Masao was certain that she smiled for him, and so he smiled in return. She was wearing a name tag. Her name was Hanada. Masao wanted to ask her about her first name but resisted.

Ms. Hanada nodded her head and walked off.

Masao drank the tea. It, and the sight of a pretty girl, warmed him inside. He could do with a girl, to make him feel like a man again after what Yoko had said.

"Mr. Kikuza," Detective Yamashita said. "I know you're traumatized, but we need to know the details, if you don't mind."

Masao repeated what he had said one more time, and Detective Yamashita said, "There will be an investigation, you understand, even if it was an accident."

Masao said, "You're just doing your job."

"Thank you for your understanding," Detective Yamashita said.

A uniformed policeman came to the desk. "The taxi has arrived, sir," he said.

"That's all for now," Detective Yamashita told Masao. "You're free to go." He handed Masao his card. "If you recall anything, please call me."

The uniformed policeman handed Masao a plastic bag which held his trousers and shirt and showed him out of the Kagoshima police station. A taxi was waiting at the curb. Masao got into the taxi and thirty minutes later was home. He dumped the trousers and shirt in the trash and stepped into a hot bath, which Yoko used to draw for him, and hadn't been there more than ten minutes, relaxing after a stressful weekend, when his mind began to wander. Soon he found himself fantasizing about Ms. Hanada.

*****

Yoko's funeral was held the following Sunday. The president of Miyaka Life Insurance, and his entourage, attended. They all expressed their sincere condolences, and it occurred to Masao as they were leaving the temple that their sympathy practically guaranteed him a promotion to vice president. His rival, Mr. Sawaguchi, was more qualified—his management skills were impressive, and he was married, had two children, one in Tokyo University, the other working in high tech—but a man who had suffered a great personal loss was the one who would be the popular choice.

"How are you going to take care of yourself?" Kenzo, his son, asked. They were standing at the entrance to the temple. The Buddhist priest who had performed the ceremony was standing there beside Masao.

"I'll manage," Masao said.

"I'm worried about you," Atsuko, his daughter said. Her eyes were red.

Both of his children were out on their own. Kenzo had joined an engineering company two years before, and Atsuko was finishing up her last year at Kyoto University. She hoped to land a job in advertising.

Kenzo and Atsuko walked off.

The priest said, "Cash, please," and bowed.

Yoko's ashes were interred in Masao's family tomb.

*****

On a bright spring Sunday in March, Masao went to a golf practice range to work on his game. Playing golf, too, was necessary to continue on up the Miyaka Life Insurance corporate ladder. Masao had never really held a passion for the game. It required too much patience. He felt he had to play. But over the years he'd gotten his handicap down to a twelve, which, he felt, should be good enough to show the president, and members of the company's board, that he took golf seriously.

As he was stroking 5-iron shots into a net in the distance, a woman set her golf bag down in the slot next to his. He couldn't help but stop to watch her. She was in her mid-thirties, he guessed, well past the marriageable age, an office lady, probably, who did what she wanted and took lovers for her own entertainment. He had been to love hotels with women like her who worked as office ladies at Miyaka Life Insurance. They were there for the taking, and most of them wanted to be taken. They hadn't placed any demands on him.

A woman like her would be a pleasant distraction from his worries about the police investigation into the accident. It was still underway.

He stood there, leaning against his 5-iron, watching the woman. She was tall and athletic. Her shoulders were square, her legs slender, her hips pronounced. She was dressed in a yellow golf skirt and blue golf shirt and matching blue visor. Her hair was gathered together by the band of the visor.

She hit some wedges and was working her way up through her irons, when she suddenly stopped and turned, facing him, and said, "I have trouble with my long irons."

"Doesn't everyone," he said.

*****

Her name was Chie Okada. She was, just as he'd thought, an office lady who worked for an export company.

That night they had dinner together at a tempura restaurant and from there went to a nearby love hotel, the Blue Moon, which Masao was familiar with. In the morning she said to him, "Last night was the best I've ever had." She rolled over and put her head on his shoulder.

"I hope we can do it again," he said.

"Why of course," she said. "What about now?"

"I'm ready when you are," he said.

Masao started to meet Chie in the evenings, after work, when they would have dinner together, and on the weekends, too, when they would play golf or visit a hot spring.

When the cherry blossoms were in full bloom they had a picnic in Shiroyama Park, taking along a bottle of

Takashimizu sake and a lacquered container of sushi--tuna, shrimp, and yellowtail. Chie wore a blue kimono embroidered with a Japanese crane. Her hair was held up by an imitation tortoise shell broach. The nap of her long neck was white and elegant.

Here are there in the park drunks were bellowing to the electric amplification of a karaoke box. Now and then a man stumbled past them, stopped, and puked at the base of a pine.

"Drunken fools," Chie said. "I'm so lucky to be with you, a gentleman."

Masao raised his sake glass. "To me," he said, and they clinked glasses together and drank.

It must have been the sake that emboldened him, because after a few more cups of it he said what he had wanted to say to her since they'd met. He felt a need to share his cleverness with her. He said, "The police had some suspicions about the accident, but it's all cleared up now. The stupid detective called me yesterday. The case is closed. My insurance even paid the fine."

"What kind of suspicions?" Chie said.

"About me," Masao said.

"How could they?"

"Maybe he heard something from one of her friends."

"What do you mean?"

"She wanted a divorce. Do you know how that would have damaged my career?"

"I certainly do. There's a man at my company whose wife divorced him. He'll be sitting at the same desk until he retires."

"You understand."

Chie said. "Isn't a woman supposed to be there for a man, to support him?"

"Exactly," Masao said. He drank some more sake.

"Tell me about your wife," Chie said.

He said, "I think she had a young lover who planted ideas in her head. She wanted to learn to scuba dive. She couldn't have gotten such a crazy idea on her own. No. She had a young lover."

Chie poured some sake into Masao's cup. "Drink," she said.

As Masao drank he felt the need to tell her more. After a while he said, "It wasn't an accident." And with that admission he felt like the petal of a cherry blossom floating by. Carrying around a secret, he realized now, had been such a burden.

"You had to do it," Chie said, "for your career." They clinked sake cups together again and drank. Masao then lay on his back on the straw mat, looking up through the canopy of cherry blossoms at a blue sky and passing clouds.

He drifted off to sleep and was woken by someone nudging the bottom of a foot with the toe of a shoe. Masao opened his eyes.

Detective Yamashita was staring down at him. "I can see you're still in mourning," he said. He looked at Chie, then back at Masao, who said,

"What do you want?"

"Chie sent me an interesting text."

Chie took her phone from her handbag and played the

conversation they had just had. Masao felt as if he might need to puke.

"Your secret is safe with us," Detective Yamashita said.

"Congratulations on your promotion," Chie said.

Detective Yamashita took off his shoes, sat on the mat, and ate some tuna. Chie poured him a cup of sake. "The cherry blossoms are exceptionally beautiful this year," he said.

Masao stood and went over to a stately pine.

Night After Night

Brandon Barrows

There was a knock on the door of my studio. I looked up from the drawing-board, covered in rough layouts for the issue of *Green Archer* I was working on. The room was bright with the reddish-gold light of the still-rising sun. The only window faced east, looking out over the big side-yard that stretched between the house and our next-door neighbor's; it was only a little after seven in the morning.

"Nick?" The door crept open.

I put down my pencil and turned. Through a yawn, I asked, "Yeah, hon?"

Amy stood in the doorway, one hand on the frame and the other on her hip. She wore a look of mild exasperation. "You didn't even get any sleep in *here*, did you?"

My studio was small and cluttered. Stacks of books, both reference material and things I worked on as well as boxes of complimentary copies of comic books I drew, were piled everywhere. There was barely enough room for the drawing-board, computer, a chair, and me. I don't know where I'd sleep even if I wanted to.

I yawned again and knuckled an eye. "No, I guess not. I've

only got a few days to finish these pencils, though."

"You have to sleep sometime."

"I know, but they've got me inking my own work again. It's more money, but it means twice as much work in half the time."

Amy came into the room, put a hand on the back of my chair, and another on top of my head. "You really love your job, don't you?" I looked up, over my shoulder. She was smiling down at me, the same sunshine smile and bright, blue eyes I fell in love with. As far as I was concerned, she was brighter than the sunrise. I loved her more than anything.

She was right, though; I loved my work, too. A wife I adored, a job I enjoyed and made decent money at, a home of our own… it was more than I ever dreamed of and more than I deserved.

Until my late teens, I was a piece of shit. I'm not going to sugarcoat it. Except for a minor miracle, I would have ended up rotting in a cell or O.D-ing on meth in some rat-hole.

My one saving grace, the one good thing about me, was I had a skill. I always liked fooling around with art, drawing mostly, because paper and pens were easy to come by even when nothing else was. I never thought I was that good, until someone noticed it—doesn't matter who—and pointed my life in another direction. By the time I was twenty-one, I was one of the best forgers in the state.

My mentor helped me get clean, helped me get my G.E.D., all while I made a fortune for him. It's funny to think of a career criminal being a good guy, but he was – he didn't even implicated me when he took his final fall. He took all the blame and he's probably still in a federal pen somewhere, while I'm free as a bird, without a record, despite being as guilty as he was.

Being that close to the inside scared hell out of me and it was the best thing that could have happened. One of the federal cops, convinced I was just a dumb kid, even took pity on me. She saw I had talent and introduced me to an art agency that got me my first legitimate work. I never before thought about drawing comic books, but within a year, I was making a decent living. It's hard work, and I put in a lot of all-nighters, but I'm happy. I still send Agent Mendez Christmas and birthday cards. Amy thinks she's a favorite teacher of mine, which she was in a way. Amy doesn't need to know the truth. We have a good marriage, but as great as my wife is, she's not the type of person who would understand that part of my life. To say she grew up privileged would be putting it lightly.

"Yeah. Sorry I never came to bed."

She tussled my hair. "You want breakfast?"

Shaking my head, I pushed back the chair and stood. "Not now." I stretched, trying to get the kinks out of my shoulders. "I think I'll grab a shower and head into town. I'm running low on Bristol board and the Amazon shipment isn't due 'til Thursday."

"Sounds like a plan." Amy leaned up to be kissed and I obliged.

Half an hour later, I was in the car, heading towards Granton. It's a small town, in the boonies, but it's perfect for us. Amy loves the outdoors, which there's plenty of, and the cost of living is low enough that I can support us on my own. Whatever inconveniences there are, we deal with.

It was still early, so I had some breakfast in a café, then headed to the art-supply store. When I got back to the car, there was a brunette head leaning against the back of the passenger seat and a slim arm hanging out of the window. *What's Amy doing here?* I wondered.

I opened the driver's door and slid under the seat, reaching a hand towards my wife for a friendly squeeze – only it wasn't my wife. It was someone I never wanted or expected to see again: Crystal Hoggerty, a name and face from a past I spent a decade trying to forget. It was like being shot in the heart.

"What the hell are you doing in my car?"

"Hi, there, Nicky," she drawled, slow and lazy, a smile on her face. Crystal was part of the fast crowd that at one time I wanted to be in with so bad I forgot about everything else. The group that would have killed me if I hadn't been lucky. Seeing her here, after all those years, was like seeing a ghost. But ghosts don't age and Crystal had. Fast living was catching up with her. She couldn't have been more than thirty, but you'd have guessed five or even ten years older. She still looked okay, in sort of a trashy-sexy way, but a lot of that was knowing how to dress and wear her make-up. Before long, that wouldn't be enough to hide the damage she'd done to herself.

"You're staring, Nicky," she said. "You like what you see?"

"Not at all. What are you doing here? No, you know what?" I climbed out of the car and hustled around to the passenger side, pulling the door open and latching onto Crystal's arm. "I don't want to know. Just get out and go away." I tried to tug her out of the car, but she went limp, becoming dead weight. And all the time, she grinned at me.

"Don't be like that, Nicky. Aren't you glad to see me?'

A middle-aged couple walked by, hand in hand and eyes glued to the scene we were making. I felt heat rise to my cheeks, so I closed the passenger door and got back in the driver's seat.

Without looking at the intruder, I said, "Please, Crystal… I have a life here. I've worked my ass off to make something of myself. I don't know what you want, but—"

"That's no way to talk to your long-lost cousin, is it?"

"What the hell?" I wondered what the joke was. I had family somewhere, but nobody I talked to since I dropped out of high-school and even then, Crystal wasn't any part of it.

She leaned across the seat, her breast brushing against my shoulder. "I'm your cousin. I'm going through a bad divorce and I've lost everything and I need a place to crash for a few weeks. That's the story we're going with. You wouldn't put family out on the street, would you, Nicky?"

I pushed her back into her own seat. "The hell are you talking about?" I felt like a broken record.

She leaned back against the seat and stretched slowly, like a cat in the sun. "I just told you. I need a place to stay, so I'm your cousin."

"I'm married, Crystal."

She turned to me. "I know. Who do you think the story's for? When I saw your name on one of those comics, I couldn't stop laughing. It was the craziest thing, totally random. But then I Googled you and what do you know? You're doing pretty good for yourself. You shouldn't tell those websites as much as you do, Nicky."

"Get out of the car or I'm driving right to the police station."

Crystal laughed, loud and raucous, like a sitcom laugh-track. "Oh, that's good, Nicky. You're gonna go to the cops? Do they know about you? How about your little wifey? I saw her on FaceSpace and I bet you never told her about yourself, did you? Not *really*. She ain't the type. You go to the cops and maybe you'll get rid of me, but you'll have to explain how come you know me, won't you? And don't think I won't be talking, too. I bet you there's still some stuff the cops back home wanna hear about." She grinned and this time it was feral.

"God damn you, what do you want from me?"

Crystal looked out of the windshield, forcing a yawn. "I told you. A place to stay. I've come a long ways, Nicky, running all the way, and I'm tired. I've been running for so long and now I need some rest and relaxation."

She opened the passenger door and slipped out, then leaned back inside, saying, "I got your number online, so I'll give you a call in a couple hours and you can give me directions to your place. I've got my car down the block."

"Crystal, you can't do this." Even to my own ears, it sounded pleading and whiney.

She gave me that nasty, predatory smile. "I'm doing it, baby. Ciao." Then she turned and hip-swung down the sidewalk.

I pounded my fist against the steering wheel, swearing and

feeling like I might cry. I was trapped and I wasn't even sure how it happened. I spent so long working so hard, and along comes the last problem I ever imagined. And it was a problem, because Crystal was right; after eight years of marriage, telling Amy now would mean admitting I'd been hiding a huge part of my life. Amy wouldn't understand that. She would see it as just a colossal lie that stretched over our entire life together. And if there was one thing Amy hated more than anything else, it was liars. I'd seen her cut friends out of her life over little things, and this wasn't little. I didn't know what she'd do if she found out and I didn't want to risk finding out.

I punched the steering wheel again then drove home, feeling sicker than I ever had in my life.

*****

I was on the couch in the living room, pretending to catch a nap, when the phone rang. I should have been working, but Amy insisted I needed some rest, and I wouldn't have been able to concentrate, anyway. I couldn't sleep, either, though. My head was a mess and my heart kept skipping beats.

The noise cut out mid-ring as Amy answered it. Then: "Nick, call for you."

I went into the kitchen. Amy stood by the phone-nook, her hand over the mouthpiece of the cordless. She was wearing tiny cut-off shorts and a ratty old t-shirt, smudged all over with dirt from her garden. She was lightly tanned and fairly glowing from the late-spring sunshine. She was gorgeous. Something struck me in the guts.

"It's a woman," Amy mouthed, handing me the phone.

"Hello." My voice sounded hollow.

"Make it sound good, Nicky," Crystal purred in my ear. "Your pretty cousin you haven't seen since you were a kid coming around is exciting, isn't it?"

"Yeah, sure," I said, not bothering to fake the enthusiasm she wanted to hear. She was chattering some more, but I didn't hear it, all I was thinking of was that I was trapped. I broke into the one-sided conversation, giving her directions from route 114, then hung up.

"Nick… who was that?" There was concern on Amy's face. I told her the story Crystal came up with. "Your cousin Crystal?" Her brows wrinkled.

I didn't blame her; she never met any of my family. There was a good reason for that and the half-truth I told her when we met, that I never got along with them and that I left home early, seemed to satisfy her to a degree. To accept a supposed member of that family into our home now must have seemed strange.

Shaking my head, I told her, "I had no idea, but she's already in town… what can I do?"

"Well…" Amy shrugged. "I guess you're right. It'll be fine." She put on a smile. "It'll actually be nice meeting someone from your family and it'll give me someone to talk to. You're always cooped up in your studio, anyway."

"Yeah… Speaking of, I better get a little work done before Crystal gets here."

The look of concern was back, but all Amy said was, "Okay. I'll hop in the shower."

I went into the studio, closed the door, and sat down. My chest hurt so badly I could barely breathe and this time, I let myself cry a little. Hot, bitter tears of frustration. I couldn't think of anything else to do.

*****

"Nice place you got here, cousin Nicky." There was only a hint of sarcasm in Crystal's voice as she climbed out of a beat-up Chevy sedan with more rust than paint. She was wearing a halter-dress that was much too young for her and when she stretched as if she was reaching for the sky, the hem came nearly to the tops of her thighs.

She put her hands on her hips and added, "I prefer bright lights and sidewalks and all that, but this'll do for a vacation."

"A very short vacation," I told her.

She smirked. "Help your cousin with her bags, will you?"

I opened the rear of the car and took out two suitcases, both nearly-new, and lugged them up onto the porch.

Amy met us at the door, sunny smile plastered in place. The women exchanged greetings and little half-hugs and began chattering away in the get-to-know-you sort of shallow friendliness you reserve for relatives you've never met and expect never to see again before too long. I stood there, dumbfounded, thinking maybe this would be okay after all. If the two of them got along, Crystal could stay for a few days and then be on her way and things would go back to normal.

"Hey there!" a new voice called from down by the road. As one, all three of us turned and saw my next-door neighbor, Todd. He was wearing skin-tight spandex in green and black and straddled a professional-looking bicycle. He was one of those guys who went nuts for his hobbies. For the past couple years, it was cycling. He biked rain or shine, even through the winter. He was dedicated and I had to admit, it did him good. He must have dropped thirty pounds since he started and it made him look a lot younger his fifty or so years. But along with renewed health came the arrogance that a lot of hardcore cyclists have. I never really cared for him much before and that didn't help at all.

"Oh, hi, Todd!" Amy gave him a little wave.

Todd took it as an invitation and walked his bike up the flagstone path from the mailbox to the house. "Who's this lovely lady?"

Amy looked to me to make introductions. With as much grace as I could muster, I said, "Todd, this is my cousin, Crystal Hoggerty. Crystal, this is our neighbor, Todd Cartwright."

Todd thrust his hand out and Crystal took it gingerly, playing the coy maiden. It was hard to keep from rolling my eyes. "Glad to meet you, Mrs. Hoggerty. Up here for a visit? Your husband here you?" He tried to look past us into the house.

"I'm in the middle of a divorce, actually," Crystal said, faux sadness replacing the faked shyness.

"Is that so?" Todd practically beamed. "Well, if you're in town for a while, maybe I can show you around."

Amy made a disapproving face. I turned from the group. I couldn't watch anymore. I hefted Crystal's bags. "I'll take these to the guestroom."

Nobody seemed to notice as I left.

*****

"Crystal seems nice enough."

Amy and I were in bed. Through the door of the bathroom shared between the master and guestroom, I heard the sounds of Crystal showering. It was after eleven o'clock and I wanted nothing more than to sleep, to catch a few hours of blissful ignorance.

Amy, Crystal, and Todd chatted on our porch for a while and the end result was Todd being invited for dinner. I didn't ask how that happened. He was a widower and it seemed clear he had some interest in Crystal, so maybe Amy was playing matchmaker. At dinner, though, I ended up sitting next to Crystal and Amy next to Todd. The three of them shared a lively conversation that I barely participated in and only when I was asked a direct question. Crystal was always a gifted liar and it seemed she perfected the craft in the years since I knew her. Both Amy and Todd were charmed by her so it went on for hours.

Now, finally, the day was over and all I wanted was some rest and peace.

"I'm glad you're getting along," I told Amy.

"She's had such an interesting life. I can't believe all the places she's been."

I almost told her not to.

I felt Amy roll over. From the nearness of her breathing, I guessed she was propped up on her elbow. "And can you believe her husband? Putting everything in his name so she'd have nothing if she left him? I mean, my god. It should be illegal."

"She'll be fine, I'm sure."

"Maybe…" I felt her lower herself onto the mattress. When

she spoke again, she sounded irritated. "Todd seemed to like her, didn't he?"

I didn't answer. I pretended to be asleep.

*****

Ten days passed. Crystal spent them lounging – on the couch, on the patio when it was warm enough, in bed. She never got up before noon. For the first few days, she and Amy got along well enough. Amy tried to find things for the two of them to do, but Crystal just wasn't interested and the friction between them became apparent pretty soon. They had arguments that seemed to threaten to explode, but never quite did.

Todd Cartwright was a frequent visitor and once or twice, Crystal went out with him. Several times, in the middle of the night, I looked out of the window of my studio and saw a tall shadow that had to be Cartwright coming across the stretch of grass between our houses and meeting one coming from my house. I didn't know what the big secret was, why he and Crystal were being so cagey about meeting, but I was glad they were getting on well. Maybe he'd take her off my hands.

Amy wasn't so happy. She didn't like Crystal lying around the house, but she didn't seem to like her going out with Todd, either. They argued about it. But for the first time since we'd been neighbors, I was happy to have Todd around. Even a few hours of Crystal out of the house was a blessing. I didn't understand why it upset Amy.

The tension in the house was nearly off the scale before long. My work suffered. I got nothing done the first few days and after that, I was playing catch-up, working practically around the clock. By the fifth or sixth day, I barely left my studio. When I worked like this before, it was because I enjoyed what I was doing. Now it was because everything seemed to come out wrong. Perspectives were skewed or inks came out smudgy. I had to re-do two or three times what I could normally finish in one go. My editor wasn't happy with me and I couldn't tell him the real reason I was behind schedule, so I pretended illness. It was only a half-lie. I'd been sick in my soul ever since I first saw Crystal sitting in my car.

On the eleventh morning, I was inking a climactic, double-page fight-scene when I heard a crash from downstairs and raised voices. I raced down and found the two women in the kitchen, standing amidst broken glass, water, and crushed flowers. Both of their faces were red and Amy's hand was lifted as if she was about to slap Crystal.

"Hey! Cut it out!" I inserted myself between them, gently grasping Amy's raised arm.

Both women looked at me as if I was something to be stepped on, but then something flickered in Amy's eyes and she turned away. Without a word, she walked to the sliding glass door, out into the backyard.

I turned to Crystal. Her face was red from anger, but I could also see one darker spot in the shape of a hand-mark. Amy must have already hit her once. I'd seen Amy angry, but never once imagined she could be violent. I couldn't guess what would push her that far.

"Crystal, what happened?"

She put a hand to her cheek, looking in the direction Amy left. "That bitch."

I grabbed her shoulders and turned her towards me.

"Crystal. What the hell was that all about?"

She looked at me finally. "You know what, Nicky?" Her voice was soft, and gentler than I ever heard her speak, even when we were kids. "I almost feel sorry for you." Then she twisted free of my grasp and moved towards the front of the house. After a moment, I heard her on the stairs and then the door of the guest bedroom slammed.

I went to the backdoor. Amy hadn't even bothered to close it behind her. I looked into the yard, but didn't see her. There was a flash of movement in the woods, off in the area abutting the stretch between my yard and Todd's, but it was gone too quickly for me to make out what it was.

I went back inside, closed the door, and headed upstairs. Enough was enough. Whatever Crystal was hiding from, it wasn't my problem. I didn't owe her anything and the anger and sickness inside me was burning out the fear of whatever she might tell Amy or anyone else.

I knocked on the door of the guestroom. "Crystal?" I tried the knob. It was locked. "Open up. I need to talk to you."

There was movement inside the room, but no answer.

"Open this god-damned door!" I shouted, punching the doorframe. "You have to go. Today. *Now*. You hear me, Crystal? Pack your shit and get out!"

The door swung open. Crystal's face appeared. Her eyes were red and puffy as if she'd been crying. "I'm not going anywhere, Nicky, and you should thank your lucking fucking stars that I'm not. You don't have any idea what's going on. You don't know a damned thing." She slammed the door closed and left me standing there, angry and confused.

She was right. I had no idea what was happening. A life that seemed so perfect just a couple of weeks ago was coming apart at the seams. I was a mess, Amy was turning into a stranger, and this intruder who I barely knew was the cause of it all. I worked my ass off building this life and now Crystal was tearing it down.

For days, something inside me was on the point of breaking and just then, it snapped. A wave of ice washed over me, cooling the anger, calming me. I could think clearly and a part me that I hadn't realized was still with me took over. I went into the master bedroom, rummaged in the closet for a box I hadn't looked at or even thought of in years. I pulled it out, opened it and found what I was looking for. The battery in the old phone was dead, but I had the charger. I just hoped the number was still good.

*****

Amy came back around dinner time and we ate frozen lasagna in silence, just the two of us. Crystal didn't come out of her room and neither of us bothered to go get her. As I washed the dishes, Amy came up behind me and very quietly said, "We have to do something about her, Nick."

"I know." Maybe there was something in the way I said it because Amy didn't press me for any further answer.

*****

That night, I was in my studio, but I wasn't working. I sat waiting, watching through the window. Just before two o'clock, the shadows I expected appeared, came together in the open space, faintly lit by the three-quarter moon in the sky, and then headed towards Cartwright's house. I took note of the time and compared it to what I remembered from other nights. Then I went into my bedroom, careful to not disturb Amy, crawled into my half of the bed, and slept soundly for the first time in weeks.

The next morning, I told Amy I had to go up to Montreal to meet with a publisher. She didn't understand; I'd traveled for work before, to attend conventions a few times a year and "all hands" creative meetings once or twice, but never so suddenly. Besides, I was under long-term contract for *Green Archer* and contractually couldn't take on any other work. I told her it was important and she just sort of shrugged. I knew she didn't want to be left alone with Crystal, and I didn't blame her, but she was right: something had to be done.

*****

It was a while since I'd been in a major city but the streets of Montreal weren't that different from the places of my youth and I remembered how to walk, how to talk, how to project the necessary image. It was disturbingly easy to fall back into that character, one that was just as artificial as any I ever drew.

I found the bar I was told to look for. I went inside, sat on a stool. It was awkward with my overstuffed wallet in my back pocket.

I waited until a thin, wispy-mustached guy in an apron came to take my order. "What you 'ave?" His accent was heavily French.

I gave him the name of a whiskey brand that didn't exist and pushed two American hundred dollar bills across the counter. The guy didn't bat an eye as he scooped them into a pocket of his apron, then turned and beckoned with a finger.

I followed him to a door in the back. He opened it and gestured for me to step inside. I entered. The door closed behind me. A light went on and for a moment I was blinded. A voice told me to sit down.

Fifteen minutes later, I was back in my car, headed south, my wallet considerably slimmer. Forty minutes later, I was across the border. Amy never bothered to ask about the meeting or if anything came of it. I guess she had other things on her mind.

*****

Two days later, I sat in my studio, staring out of the window, finally done with work I should have turned in days ago. The afternoon sunshine slanted through the trees, giving the scene a warm look at odds with the chilly wind that had been blowing all day. It was the last gasp of another New England winter that didn't want to let go, like Crystal was the last gasp of my old life. But soon, both would be gone.

There was a knock on the door, then the sound of it opening, and bare feet padding across the wooden floor. I didn't turn around. Arms draped themselves across my shoulders then wrapped lightly around my neck. A warm softness pressed itself against the back of my head, then my cheek.

"Nicky, are you really happy here?" Crystal asked. There was no mirth, no sarcasm, no anger in her voice, just a quiet sadness.

"I was," I told her.

"Do you ever miss the old days?"

I shook my head. "Not for a single second."

"We all had fun together, didn't we?" She sounded like she might cry.

I twisted around to look at her. "How many of them are still alive, Crystal? Alive and walking around free? You and me, and who else? And maybe not you for long. Someone's after you or you wouldn't be here. I don't want to live like that ever again."

For a long moment, neither of us said anything. Then Crystal moved to the door, but before she went out, she turned and said, "Nicky, I hope everything works out okay for you."

I didn't know what she meant. Could she know what I had planned? I didn't see how and I didn't want to think about it. I turned back to the window and waited until I heard her retreating footsteps.

Only a few more hours, I told myself. Then it would all be over. Day after day, night after night, I spent almost every waking hour in this one, small room that used to be my sanctuary and had become a sort of prison.

*****

Dinner was a miserable, quiet affair. Nobody said a word and I hardly tasted the food. Afterwards, as I washed up, Amy came into the bathroom and leaned against the closed door. I looked at her reflection in the mirror. "She'll be gone by tomorrow morning."

Amy's expression cracked and it was like I could actually see some of the stress and tension falling away. "You told her?"

"I've been telling her." I dried my hands on a towel and turned to face my wife. "But this time, I promise, she'll be out of our hair."

"Oh my god." Amy threw her arms around my neck and kissed me like she hadn't in ages. "Oh my god. I can't wait. I'm sorry, Nick. I know she's your cousin, but—"

"I know. Sorry it's taken so long."

"But she'll be gone tomorrow?"

I nodded. "It's almost over."

Amy kissed me again and went out, practically skipping. I followed her into the bedroom, told her I had some work I needed to jump on and probably wouldn't be in bed 'til late. That was nothing new at this point and she was too happy with the thought of Crystal leaving to complain.

So I shut myself in the studio and waited.

I'd done this so many times. Night after night, sitting in darkness, waiting, but now the anticipation made it feel very different.

The hours passed and right on schedule, just before two o'clock, a shadow detached itself from the side of the house. It moved faster than usual, though, the slim figure nearly running in its haste to meet the bulkier one coming from Todd's side of the shared yard.

My heart skipped a beat and then began to hammer in my chest. I pushed back from the chair and stood leaning over the desk, trying to get a better view of what I knew was coming. Sweat formed on the palms of my hands and my forehead and I felt a chill that had nothing to do with the weather.

The two shadows came together in the yard, a stone's throw from the cluster of woods behind the houses. And then a third shadow appeared, stepping out of the deeper darkness beneath the trees. There was a roar and a flash and I knew the anonymous killer I hired used a shotgun. I didn't want Todd killed, only Crystal, but it was an acceptable casualty. I never liked him and I wouldn't feel too bad. It might even muddy the waters more when the police investigated. I would tell them that Crystal seemed nervous, like she was hiding from something, and let them make their own conclusions about how Todd fit into the picture.

The figure from the woods disappeared before the flash of the gun did and I thought for a moment that I heard an engine starting somewhere off in the distance. I turned and raced out of the studio and down the stairs as anyone who heard a gunshot in their yard would. I knew there was no more danger, the killer was gone. All I could think of was that Amy and I were free! Free from Crystal, free from the past, free to live our lives again!

I made it to the bottom of the stairs before a voice called my name. I looked up and Crystal stood at the top, her face puffy from sleep, wearing only a white tank-top and blue panties. "What's going on? What was that noise?"

Something punched me in the chest and my face and hands startled to tingle. When I didn't answer, Crystal started down the stairs. "That sounded like a gunshot, Nick!"

"It was." My voice was so small, I wasn't sure I said it out loud.

I walked through the house, out of the backdoor and across the yard, Crystal at my heels, saying my name over and over, asking me what was happening. At the edge of the woods, she stopped talking. Amy and Todd were huddled together in a pile, their broken forms limned in light from the nearly-full moon.

"Nicky… what did you do?" She turned to me. "You knew all along?"

I collapsed to the grass and started sobbing. It made sense now, why Amy didn't like Crystal seeing Todd, what they were always fighting about, what Crystal meant when she said she felt sorry for me. She found out about the affair, saw what I couldn't because she was an outsider. I spent so much time working, left Amy alone for so long, even before Crystal showed up. After getting in shape, Todd was a decent looking guy and Amy must have been lonely. That was my fault and so was this.

Amy, I thought uselessly. *Amy, I'm sorry. I loved you so much. I just wanted to give you a good life.*

Crystal's hand struck my cheek, bringing me around. "Don't just sit there bawling, Nicky!"

I looked up at her, my mouth hanging open, tasting the salt of the tears.

"Nicky, we gotta go! We gotta get out of here!" She had hold of my arm and she was trying to drag me to my feet, but it was no use. She wasn't strong enough to lift me by herself and I had no intention of going anywhere. What was the point? Everything I did for the last eight years was all for Amy's sake, for the sake of the life we shared. Now, no matter what happened, that was gone forever. It was gone, so I just didn't care anymore.

I lay back in the wet grass, sprawled beneath the moonlight. Crystal kept shouting at me for a while, but eventually she stopped, and soon, I heard the sound of a car pulling out of the driveway.

I just lay there, looking up at the night sky, surrounded by the scents of spring and the stench of death, waiting for the sound of sirens, waiting for what came next. Waiting for another night to end.

Just a Shadow
Bern Sy Moss

The wind came across the lake like an out of control freight train roaring down the track, agitating the water, forming it into great, white crowned waves, pushing them toward the shore where they finally crashed and broke in rapid succession leaving white foamy remains.

It reminded me of Van Gogh's *View of the Sea at Scheveninge,* painted on a day when the wind, like today, controlled the vista. He made a quick interpretation of the scene, as the wind lifted the sand around him and imbedded it in the thick, wet oils layered from paint tubes onto his canvas.

I glanced over my canvas looking for the right perspective to capture the summer cottages, a sufficient stretch of the beach and the ferocity of what was before me.

Like an unpredictable woman, these waters could go from calm to rage with the slightest provocation and were not to be trusted. Not unlike the woman who was approaching me. My perspective no longer my concern, I studied her as she got closer hoping that maybe I was wrong. I did not want to see *that* woman again.

The breeze off the lake was strong and persistent. It carried the woman's hair up off her shoulders and covered her face. The dark hair I remembered. She walked barefoot on the sand with the attitude and determination I remembered. She carried her shoes by their straps with a paper shopping bag in the same hand. With her other hand, she brushed away the hair off her face. When she was close enough she said, "I found you, Turner."

"Want to do that, Sara?" I asked.

"Let's find a quiet place to talk," she shouted over the roar of the wind. "I have a proposition for you."

*****

Harry's bar—my sanctuary—had that old tavern smell and the mustiness that you just can't get out of an old building and maybe that's what made it special. The floor was gritty with sand from the beach and the old wooden tables carved with the initials and sometimes the names of those tourists, day-trippers, and passersby that seemed to find it necessary to immortalize themselves in this manner.

It wasn't the kind of place where you made friends, the cliental mostly just those transits. I talked to no one and no one talked to me and I was good with that. Not even a cell phone. To say I was a loner was underestimating me. I was *the hermit* in a world cluttered with too many people and Sara was one of the too many.

So, when Sara and I slid into my favorite booth, the one closest to the bar, I could understand the surprised look on Harry's face. I held up two fingers. Harry nodded and proceeded to bring two drafts to the booth.

"Drinking beers, now?" she said.

"My tastes have changed."

"What I have in mind will bring you back to where you

were."

"I like beer."

"You'll like what I have to offer."

"What's in the bag," I asked.

She smiled and reached into the paper shopping bag she had carried on the beach. "It's a gift," she said and pulled out a porcelain jar with a Chinese motif.

"A ginger jar," I said. "I don't get it."

"Not a ginger jar," she said as her smile widened deepening wrinkles that weren't there when I knew her last.

"It's an urn. It's him, isn't it? He's dead."

"Yes, he is and since I have no use for him anymore, you can have it. Keep it if you like or drop the damn thing in the lake. I don't really care what you do with it."

I was stunned. "So, this is your proposition," I said.

"No, this is what makes my proposition viable for you," she said. "Yes, Jerzy is gone, but the demand for his paintings is huge right now and there is a way to make his works available for all those clamoring for a Jerzy Hart original, at least on a temporary basis."

"And how will you do that?" I asked.

"Well, Turner, that's the part where *you* come in and make it happen."

*****

I didn't sleep well that night. Memories flooded my brain. Memories of Sara, Jerzy and me. They were not happy memories. The memories followed me into my sleep forming nightmares, reliving that time when we all lived together in that old garage.

I woke in the middle of the night soaked with sweat and wondering if I could do what Sara proposed. Could I create Jerzy Hart paintings again? Jerzy Hart, a common street and alley artist who somehow made a phenomenal entry into the professional art scene, his paintings now desired by the rich, coveted by celebrities. Could I pull this off again? Did I really want to?

It was a simple plan, complete the paintings he had left unfinished and Sara, as Hart's widow, would certify that the paintings were authentic Jerzy Hart originals. Even the big galleries would buy into it with her certification. She promised a fifty-fifty split when all of the paintings were sold and the amount of money, she was suggesting, was very significant making it difficult for me to say no. But could I trust her? It wouldn't be the first time she deceived me.

*****

The next day I loaded my car with what little I owned. My painting supplies weren't much to talk about, some old brushes, paint tubes, a few canvases. I left it all in a pile next to the garbage bin.

As a painter, the soul of originality was not with me, but with the masters that came before me, but I didn't make reproductions. No, my paintings were very good imitations of styles and techniques, not copies of actual paintings and no matter how difficult it would be to differ mine from the so-called masters as far as style and technique went, without certification or provenance, they were my paintings and couldn't be passed as anything else. No point signing with any name, but mine.

Not that there was a great demand for a painting by Turner, but my canvases did sell. I can thank those tourists, day-trippers, and passersby for that because the money made from them were all I had to support my mediocre life style.

I headed over to the art gallery on the main street in the town where I spent the last years of my life, one of those tourist traps that specialized in taffy and fudge, gourmet ice creams, souvenir shops, and lots of craft shops.

I collected the money from the sale of one of my oils, which only gave me enough for gas for my trip. I told the owner to hold whatever was made from my other paintings until I came back.

"Where you going, Mr. Turner?" the owner asked with an accent I could never put my finger on.

"I'm going to," I hesitated and for no particular reason said, "going to Mexico for a vacation."

By noon, I was on my way to Chicago to meet Sara, the paper shopping bag with Jerzy's urn on the back seat of my car.

*****

I found Sara's condo located on Lake Shore Drive. Nothing like the squalor the three of us lived in when we were together. Far from it—lavish with a different view of Lake Michigan than I was accustomed to. Hers was the very pricey view.

"Here," she said as she handed a glass to me. "Better stuff than you've been drinking."

"Have you got a beer?" I smiled, looked around and said, "Pretty expensive place, Sara. Jerzy must have been doing really good."

She smiled back at me. "Maybe, I do have a beer and this place, not mine. I'm apartment sitting for a friend."

"You always had a friend, didn't you?"

"Look," she said as she poured the beer into a glass, "one of us has to be the one to call the shots and I think it should be me."

"Of course, you would."

"I have the buyers and the paintings need buyers or else why do this?"

"You can't do this without me."

"The paintings are worthless without my certification as Jerzy Hart's widow."

"They still may be worthless. What if someone recognizes the difference now?" I asked.

"Did they recognize the difference the last time we did this?" she countered.

"I was just finishing off the paintings. His soul was already in them," I said. "How much is in these?"

"There are about twenty-five paintings, maybe more. I have a show contracted exactly five days from today for, let's say, about ten of them. Ten paintings just need some finishing off like before. They should sell quickly. Do those first.

"I haven't made up my mind yet on the rest of the paintings. I'm working with a gallery in France. They may buy the whole lot. I'd like to dump them all at once, but only if they're willing to pay my asking price. If that doesn't work out, I have a few private collectors with deep pockets that might be interested.

"Then there's the large one near the door. It's going to a private collector upon his approval. The collector is willing to pay a substantial sum and good for the money, but sometimes I have to wait until one of his deals comes through before he can come up with the payment. There's a lot of money to be made here, Turner, if you just do your part."

I could tell she was picking her words carefully, focusing on the money, dangling it in front of me like a carrot. And it was obvious to me why she searched *me* out. She had no one else to go to, no one else she could trust to finish the paintings, as they should be finished. I had fooled everyone who needed to be fooled the last time we did this and she believed I could do it once more.

Again, I asked, "How much of Jerzy is in these?"

She sighed, "Unfortunately, Jerzy's soul, as you say, may not be in that large one near the door and quite a few will require more work than those first ten that just need some finishing touches. You'll have to do what you do. You know his style. You're familiar with his technique and if there are questions, I'll just say he was experimenting. I want everything completed in three weeks. Can you get all of them done in time?"

"A bit of a brake-ass schedule don't you think, Sara?"

"You can do it, Turner. I know you can," she said as she moved closer to me, rubbing against me, her arms embracing me. "I wish things had ended differently between us. Maybe, we can pick up where we left off."

"Is this what it's about, us?" I asked, knowing she was playing me. "It's over, Sara. Get someone else to do this if that's what it's about."

"No, it's about the money and only the money," she said pulling away from me.

"It always was, wasn't it?"

"Don't feel bad. We can still at least be friends. There was a time when we were even more than friends," she said.

"Try co-conspirators, which is what we will be."

"What we always were," Sara said.

"No, not until we were no longer friends."

She smiled. "You mean no longer friends with benefits."

*****

I followed Sara to a parking garage where we stored my car. Then she drove me to a neighborhood of dilapidated warehouses, finally parking in front of a familiar spot. The old mechanic's garage Jerzy's uncle owned and let Jerzy use as his studio.

"Jerzy was still working out of this place?" I asked.

"Seemed to be his comfort zone," she said. "You can see why it was best to store your car. Probably won't last two seconds on the street in this neighborhood now. It's gotten a lot tougher."

It was the same place where we all lived together, the same one I had brought Sara to when I found her living on the street, the same street where Jerzy had found me the year before.

Jerzy was the one with the education. He had attended the Art Institute in Chicago on a scholarship—one of many who did—but his trip to fame started with what some called graffiti and others looked at as innovative.

In the interim, he, actually all of us, lived off the money he occasionally made from the commissioned murals he painted on buildings.

I, in those days, made my contribution working as a waiter and painting when the mood was with me, searching for my own particular style, that something that could make my paintings distinctive and highly marketable, but it always seemed to elude me. My only talent seemed to be in replicating the methods and styles of others.

And Sara, Sara was just there. There for me I thought, but Sara was there for herself and only herself.

Jerzy, so committed to his work, painted day and night and sometimes I think he painted when he was sleepwalking. Out of those subjects in his graffiti art, he created a style of his own invention.

By the time Jerzy's name was being throw around the art scene in a serious manner, I decided to leave. What else could I do? It was getting too crowded with the three of us, crowded not physically, but emotionally.

Distracting me from my memories, Sara grabbed my arm and started pulling me around the garage showing me the unfinished paintings Jerzy left propped up against the walls.

"Didn't he finish anything since I've been gone?" I asked.

"Yes, enough for three shows" she said. "Each time he showed, the prices kept going up. After you finish the other paintings, you'll being doing this one. I know he barely started it, but you were always a master of his style, a perfect imposter, if not *the* master imposter of Jerzy Hart."

We stopped in front of a very large canvas, at least ten feet tall. "This is the one commissioned by the private collector," Sara said.

"How much?" I asked.

She didn't answer. Instead she pulled me back to the smaller paintings "Can you get all of this done in three weeks?" she asked. "I want to be done with this as soon as possible."

"I think I can," I said.

"What do you think was going on with him, always jumping from one piece to another, never really wanting to see the finished product, never feeling the need to complete anything? How hard do you think it was for me to get him to finish his paintings after I made commitments at the galleries?" She stopped her rant, turned to me, and smiled, "But, I don't have to worry about that anymore, now that I have you. Do I?"

I couldn't help, but ask, "The money, how much more are they paying, since the first time he died?"

"The accident was a big help in putting Jerzy on the map, wasn't it?' she said.

Her comment stirred up more memories. After Jerzy was left on the street by a hit and run driver, Sara saw an opportunity to capitalize. Money was never Jerzy's motivation and a meager day-to-day existence seemed to satisfy him. Most of the payments for the murals and whatever paintings he sold at that time, collected in a drawer in an old desk in the garage. With Jerzy hospitalized, Sara was in control. She forged his name and cashed the checks.

She then spirited him out of the hospital and put him in a private physical rehabilitation facility under a fake name. No one knew what happened to him and many assumed he had died. Sara wouldn't confirm this and she certainly didn't deny it.

It was a time when he began to pull his style from his murals and graffiti, experimenting and fashioning paintings from them, showing them at the smaller insignificant galleries.

I finished those Jerzy Hart "originals" — the unfinished paintings he started before the accident. Sara swore to anyone who would listen that the paintings I completed were authentic Jerzy Hart's and the more prominent galleries began to display them. The belief that Jerzy died created a unique demand for his paintings. Sara and I enjoyed the spoils of Jerzy's success while Jerzy endured the pain of his rehabilitation.

When Jerzy finally did come back on the scene, we worried there might be a price to pay, but the art world somehow forgave Sara.

"I never said he was dead," she responded to anyone who questioned her.

But Jerzy couldn't forgive even though Sara's hoax had elevated him to a celebrity status.

Jerzy was livid and most infuriated with me. "There're not my paintings," he screamed at me. "It's not how I wanted them finished and you signed my name."

He was wrong about one thing. I never signed his name, I couldn't bring myself to do it, but Sara could. Sara, somehow convinced him that it was all my doing, my idea. It wasn't and it was when we parted ways, Jerzy and I.

Now, he really was dead and she wanted me to do it again.

"I didn't know he died," I said. "I wish I knew. I would have come to the funeral."

"It was his wish just to be cremated. No funeral. No memorial. Nothing, that's what he wanted," she said.

"How did he die?" I asked.

Sara left without answering my question. I wandered around the garage taking in the fact that nothing changed since I left. The back of the garage still had a kitchen of sorts, an old four burner gas cooking range, a microwave, a sink, table, chairs and a small refrigerator which was now stocked with some cold cuts and bottles of water. A loaf of bread sat on the range.

Junk left from when it was a vehicle repair shop was stowed against one of the walls. Sleeping bags were still bunched up on another wall as if the three of us would again be using them tonight. The only difference was the addition of a cot with a baseball bat under it. Must have been Jerzy's weapon of choice in case of intruders, I decided.

The bathroom still looked like no one had cleaned it since the garage was built some hundred or more years ago and the skylight seemed even more opaque from the years of accumulated grime.

A pile of Jerzy's painting supplies sat next to the door of the storage room where they were usually stored. The storage room door resisted when I tried to open it and left me wondering why it was locked now. It never was before.

The cement floor and the brick walls of the garage would cool the air in the hot summer days ahead unless the humidity took over. Then the oppressive heat and humidity would do what it does, exasperating men and animals alike. Typical for Chicago in July.

The garage smelled of paint, mold, and something dead.

How did we live like this? Why did I? And I was going to do it again. Money is such a powerful incentive and Sara promised lots.

About ten paintings, as Sara said, just needed some finishing touches and to be signed. The others required more work. Then there was the last painting, the large one going to the private collector, which was little more than some rough sketching on the canvas. It would be more difficult. From what I saw, I couldn't determine where Jerzy was going with the painting. He hadn't left any of himself on this canvas only some very vague suggestions of what he was planning.

I remembered him telling me, a little bit of his life ended with each painting he finished. Maybe, that's why he couldn't finish them. It was his weird way of holding on to life.

*****

By the next afternoon, after I finished several of the paintings for the first show, I heard a key turning the lock at the front of the garage. Sara came in carrying two gallons of house paint.

"Got everything you said you needed," she said as she put the paint in a corner near the door.

I noticed someone outside was handing the supplies to her, but staying out of my line of vision. I started to move towards the door. She caught me by my arm and pulled me to the back end of the garage where my view of the front door was blocked by the large painting by the door.

"Are these the ones you've finished?" she asked as we stood

in my work area, where a large fan circulated the air to speed up the drying process on a group of paintings leaning again one of the walls.

"Yes," I said.

She moved around looking at them from different angles. "Very good. I can't tell them from Jerzy's," she said. "But it's not done until you sign them." She read the look on my face. "Don't feel guilty about signing his name. He's not going to need it anymore."

"I don't think I could do it as well as you could," I said.

"Well, then you better start practicing," she said as she walked over to the corner where the things I needed to pull off our fraud were now piled.

A painting sat on top of the pile. She walked over to it and lifted it up for me to see. "Here, his signature in case you forgot how it looked. I'll be back in a day or two," she said as she handed the painting to me and then went out the door.

"Sara, how did he die?" I shouted after her and ran to the door, but her car was already gone.

I sorted through the cans of spray paint and gallons of house paint. Jerzy's choice of materials for his graffiti and murals continued to be his favorite mediums when he moved on to painting on canvases. One of the boxes held paint rollers, paintbrushes sized from one inch to four inches and one, so very slim, purchased, without a doubt, for the sole purpose of signing the finished paintings.

*****

By the third day in the garage, I was nearly out of bottled water and the meager rations of ham and bologna were almost gone.

I had no money to buy anything. All I had went in the gas tank to get myself here.

The ten *nearly finished* paintings were now complete and waiting for me to sign them. I moved on to the paintings that required more work, but this was Chicago and it was July and each day seemed hotter than the day before. I was finding it difficult to concentrate and missed the breezy beach on the other side of the lake where Sara found me.

I kept the windows closed during the day to keep the heat out, hoping, the cement floor and brick walls of the garage still held some of the coolness from the previous night and would make my surroundings a bit more bearable, but by late afternoon, the heat and humidity of the day had settled in. The fan that Jerzy used to dry his paintings was pointed at the recently finished ten paintings. I turned it and pointed it at myself as I ate the last of the food Sara left for me.

I was thinking this was a hell of my own making when I heard the door in the small vestibule by the back of the garage open then close. I picked up the bat from under the cot, raised it above my head and waited to see who would be coming around the corner.

"Who the hell are you?" he said when he saw me.

"No, you first. Who the hell are you?"

He ignored my question and instead asked, "Where's Jerzy?"

"Look, you better tell me what you're doing here or this bat is coming down on your head."

"Jerzy can vouch for me. I come to keep him company every once in a while," he said. "Where is he?"

125

"Jerzy's dead."

"Happens to all of us sooner or later. What did him in?" he asked as he opened the refrigerator and took my last bottle of water. He pulled one of the chairs away from the table, dropped his backpack to the floor and sat down. He began coughing. After a drink of the water, he got the coughing under control and asked again, "What finally did him in?"

I put the bat down and sat on the remaining chair. The guy was probably one of the characters drawn into the area by the homeless shelter a few blocks away. There were times in those years when I lived in this garage that I spent some nights there. He seemed harmless, maybe in his seventies, bald except for a fringe of hair around the sides and back of his head. He wore it long and pulled into a ponytail.

He rubbed the stubble on his chin and said, "Well, are you going to tell me what happened?"

"I don't know how he died. I'd like to know myself?"

"What are you doing here? Squatting? Jerzy won't put up with any squatters only his friends and I know all of them. Come to think of it, I guess, I'm his only friend. Don't consider that wife of his, is any friend of his," he said.

"*Was,*" I said. "Not *is.* Who are you?"

He started coughing again and took another drink of the water. "Been to Nam. Gave my arm for my country." He swung the empty left sleeve on his shirt toward me. "And my mind, PTSD, you know. Now, the docs are telling me lung cancer and some other things. All over but the dying."

We sat quiet for a while. It was he who finally broke the silence. "They tell me what's ahead ain't going to be like going to a picnic. Be a favor to me if someone would just put a bullet in my head. Think you could do that for me, kid?"

I shook my head, "No, I couldn't do that."

He smiled, "Maybe later, when we get to be better friends."

We stared at each other for a while, then he said, "There was one guy, Jerzy said was his friend, but he hadn't seen him in years. A falling out they had, I guess it was over that Sara. Women they can do that, really wreck a guy's life if you get involved with the wrong one. You won't be Turner, would you?"

I nodded, "Yes, I'm Turner."

"Well Turner, let's see, you don't know how he died, but you're here doing something. What are you doing here, anyway?" he asked.

I hesitated and he picked up on it.

"Up to no good for Sara, probably. That woman could twist you and him up until the two of you didn't know any better. Like pretzels. Oh, I know all about the stuff you did before for her and Jerzy figured out whose idea it was by himself. Took him a while he said, but he didn't blame you anymore."

"No, I'm just here to clean up," I said.

"Yeah, clean up with these paintings. I hope she's paying you enough." He stared at the floor for a while. "Hell, Jerzy probably won't care anyway now."

We both heard it, the sound of the lock turning on the door in the front end of the garage. The guy jumped up and ran to the back door leaving his backpack behind. I picked it up and threw it in the small vestibule by the back door before Sara could see it.

Sara came in and strolled down the length of the garage looking for works that were completed. "You've got quite a few done. Think you'll be done with all of them in time?' she asked.

"Where have you been?" I shouted at her. "I'm out of food. Out of water. And I'm sweating my brains out. I need to get out of here for a while."

"Already? You don't need to go anywhere. I don't want you seen by anybody. What if someone recognizes you? There's still some of those we knew before around here. So, get used to it. This is where you stay until the job is done," she shouted back at me.

She placed a case of water bottles on the floor. "I brought you more food and water," she said as she emptied cold cuts from a plastic grocery bag into the refrigerator and dropped a loaf of bread on the cook top next to a box of doughnuts.

"Get those paintings signed," she yelled back to me as she went out the door.

*****

The next morning, I noticed the knapsack was gone and realized that anyone could come in that lockless, back door when I was sleeping and I wouldn't know.

As I breakfasted on a stale doughnut and a bottle of water, I studied the signature on the painting Sara left for me. She was so good at forging Jerzy's signature that I wondered if the signature was actually his.

I always felt, even though I finished Jerzy's paintings, that if I didn't sign his name to them, it wasn't really an act of forgery on my part. Now, I was contemplating doing something I would have never done in the past. The thought crossed my mind, why didn't Sara just do it. She never had a problem before. The answer was easy. She wanted me in as deep as she could get me in case I decided to turn on her and forging Jerzy's signature would put me in damn deep.

Then there was that fifty-fifty split of the money, which was certainly more generous than I'd ever known Sara to be, but it was an opportunity that wouldn't come along again. How many times could Jerzy Hart die and I be called in to finish his paintings.

I found a blank canvas and proceeded to master Jerzy's signature. I spent the morning practicing and in the afternoon, I signed the ten paintings for the first showing.

As I worked the next group of paintings, it was becoming obvious to me something was changing in Jerzy's technique. It seemed the ten *nearly finished* paintings that I completed were the Jerzy Hart style I'd been familiar with, but the ones that required more work, were in a different style. I just couldn't find him in them. What would have made them a Jerzy Hart—it just wasn't there. As I worked, I tried to put him in them and wondered if Sara would have a harder time passing these off as his paintings.

When the light coming through the skylight had just about diminished, I shut off the spotlights that illuminated my work, cutting down the heat in the garage to almost bearable, and sat at the table thinking, bologna or ham tonight. The thought of going to prison—for forgery—floated through my mind, but then prison couldn't be any worse than living in this garage. Nothing could be I decided.

I heard the back door open and close and the old guy came

in. He placed a paper bag on the table and dropped his knapsack to the floor.

"How you doing today?" he asked as he pulled cans of beer out of the knapsack and set one of them in front of me. "Thought you wouldn't mind if I brought dinner tonight," he said as he pulled a Styrofoam container of fried chicken and French fries out of the bag and put it next to the beer.

"You know what, kid, you need a shower. Guys on the street smell better than you," he said.

"Not a kid," I said.

"Compared to me, you are. You want the shower or not? I can vouch for you with Brother Simon at the shelter," he said. "They're getting particular about who they let in nowadays."

Between stuffing my mouth with the food and swigging down the beer, I managed to say, "Sure, I do. What's your name? I don't know your name," I asked.

"Sgt. Arnold Smith," he said saluting me. "You can call me Sarge." He started coughing and squelched the cough with a mouthful of the beer. "You know, you ought to look around some of the junk against the walls, must be a dead mouse or rat around. Place smells like death. Meant to tell you that last time I was here."

*****

I awoke on day five thinking that a shower could do wonders for a man, especially one who lives in Sara's prison. It did wonders for me. I could think clearer now. In my clearer thinking, paranoia was settling in. Did anybody at the homeless shelter recognize me? Would they remember me? Did they even care? Sara had really gotten in my head.

Too much control, just like before, I thought. I knew I needed to get out of this place as soon as possible. I couldn't live like this much longer. But the money—isn't it always about the money.

Also, I decided I needed a new deal with Sara. The original agreement, the fifty-fifty split of the money on all of the paintings when they were all sold, wasn't working for me. That could take months and I wanted to gone as soon as possible. Instead, I would tell Sara, just the money from the first ten—the ones at the show tonight, the ones she should have no problem passing off as Jerzy's work—is all I wanted, but all of the money. The rest of the money would be hers no matter how much she made on the remaining paintings. It had happened in the past with Jerzy's paintings, for all of them to be sold in one showing, and I was hoping it would happen tonight.

Most of the payments would be in credit card payments, money transfers, no waiting for checks to clear, paid to the gallery and then forwarded to Sara's account I guessed.

Sara would be ahead with my new deal. She still would have eighteen more to sell and the large one she was planning to sell to the private collector though these paintings might be less convincing Jerzy Hart art.

I could see it in the progression of his work; Jerzy's soul wasn't there anymore. He didn't seem to care and now I didn't. I didn't intend to spend three weeks in the garage. I would finish the paintings and get as far away from Sara as fast as I could, but in the meantime, I would have to trust her. How else would I know how much money was paid for the ten paintings?

I had it all figured out by the time I heard the old lock turning and announcing Sara had arrived. Without saying a word to me, she pressed the button on the wall. The old garage door squeaked and groaned every inch as it moved on it's track, finally finding its way up to the ceiling.

She walked through the opening it left, got in a white van and proceeded to back it into the garage. When she got out and pressed the button again, the door repeated the noisy return to its former position.

Walking over to me she said, "Help me load the paintings for the show tonight."

"No, I want to talk to you first," I said thinking my new deal needed to be worked out before she could go rushing out the door again.

"Sure, let's talk," she said.

"I want to change our deal," I said.

"How do you want to change it?" she asked crossing her arms across her chest. I could detect the calmness leaving her voice and anger intervening.

"I'll take whatever money is made on these paintings for the show tonight. Just these ten. I'll finish the rest for you, but I don't want to wait until you sell all of them to get my money. I want to get out of here as soon as possible and be on my way. I just want whatever you make tonight."

"If that's what you want," she smiled and said as if this change in the deal didn't really make any difference to her one way or another. "Let's get the paintings loaded now."

I should have realized right then she couldn't be trusted. It just seemed too easy. I'd never known her not have the last word, never known her to let anyone else make the end deal.

*****

The total quiet with only the white noise of the fan to keep me company was unnerving me. I was a loner when I had a choice, but now the lack of human contact was beyond my control and I began to understand what solitary confinement must be like. I hoped Sarge would come and bring some sanity into my situation. He didn't disappoint me.

"Did you miss me?" he asked as he came in.

"Yeah, I did. Talk to me. I need to talk to someone besides myself."

"What do you want to talk about," he asked handing me a beer from his knapsack.

"What was Jerzy like before he died? His paintings…"

"Weird stuff as far as I was concerned," Sarge said. "I don't get this pop art, street art stuff."

"Yeah, but I can tell something was going on with him by the way he was painting," I said.

"You can tell that? I could see that. Not in the pictures, I don't understand them, but in him," he said.

"What do you mean?"

"I guess it started when he fell off the ladder. He was working on that one." He pointed to large canvas that Sara planned to sell to the private collector.

I could understand the need for a ladder. The canvas was about four feet wide by ten feet high and I knew I'd need a ladder to finish it.

"He started that one. Fell off the ladder and never went

133

back to it. Started working on some others, smaller ones. He'd start them but seemed to put even less on the canvases than he usually did. He never seemed to want to finish any of his paintings. Told me one time, only way they would be finished was when he was dead."

That sent a chill down my back and for a weird second or two I felt like Jerzy was near.

I shook off the shiver as Sarge continued, "every time I came, he'd walk me around showing me what he had painted each day and explain some kind of hogwash crap about what inspired him to do this or that, but the big one, he wouldn't work on it. Never did get it, all that stuff he was telling about inspiration and whatever, but we were still friends. Don't have to always agree or understand your friends, just need to find a common ground," he said.

"What was your common ground, Sarge?" I asked.

"We both needed someone to talk to and we both liked beer," he laughed and started coughing, finally stopping it with a mouthful of beer.

"Where was Sara in all this," I asked.

He shook his head. "He was a prisoner in this dirty, damn garage. It was like, what do you call it? Some kind of syndrome. Can't remember the name. The one where your captor makes you think they're protecting you."

"Stockholm Syndrome," I said.

"Yeah, that's the one. Let me tell you how it went down," he said.

I sat there listening. Apparently, Sara and Jerzy married not long after I left. She convinced him he needed someone with the authority to speak for him because of the multiple medical problems he still suffered from the hit and run accident. Someone to talk to the doctors for him, but she wouldn't let him see any doctors. Instead, she kept him contained in the garage with painkillers. Gradually, she became more controlling, not even letting him go to his own painting exhibits at the galleries where she contracted to show his paintings. I guessed it wasn't hard to control him since she controlled the drugs.

"Of course he didn't see it the same way I did," Sarge said. "He always defended her that is until he fell off the ladder. With his bad leg from the accident, he shouldn't have been on a ladder, but Sara had a guy that wanted a big Jerzy Hart painting. When he fell, well then things changed.

"I found him that night," Sarge said. "He didn't even have a phone to call 911. I wanted to get him help, but he said Sara would come in the morning and take him to the ER. Didn't happen. He hurt his arm bad in the fall. His painting arm. She told him all he needed was some more pills. She had him addicted. After that fall, he wouldn't get back on the ladder to finish the big one.

"Sara kept pushing him to paint. Kept telling him he had commitments, shows of his paintings that she wouldn't even let him go to. He pretty much lost interest in everything after that fall and I think it was ticking her off. Looked to me that he was becoming no use to her anymore."

"I could see the change in the paintings," I said.

"Kid, he gave me something for you if you ever turned up," Sarge said as he dug into his knapsack. He pulled out an old leather wallet and handed it to me. The initials J and H were tooled into the leather.

I opened it and found a credit card, and a driver's license with the same signature I'd been practicing to forge on the paintings. There was a clipping from a newspaper, an article with a picture of Jerzy, Sara and me at his first show at a small gallery that gave some of the street artists an opportunity to show their works at a time when no one else would. Ten dollars and a folded piece of paper were also in the wallet.

I unfolded the paper. It was a bank statement for an account held by Jerzy and Sara Hart. I could see the deposits, numerous ones from different galleries and other deposits I assumed were monies, collected from the sale of paintings to private collectors.

I looked at Sarge. "Why give this to me?"

"I don't know. He said you'd know what to do with it."

"I'm surprised Sara let him have this," I said pointing to the bank statement.

"He told me they had a big fight. He told her he won't paint another painting until he knew what she was doing with the money," Sarge said. "I don't think he really cared about the money. I think he knew he was being used and just wanted to put the screws to her in the only way he could."

"As if having all this money was doing him any good."

"Something else for you. Went to the library and got an obit off the Internet." He handed me a sheet of paper and I read Jerzy's obituary.

"It says there was a private memorial attended by his wife and close friends. Doesn't say how he died," I said.

"Doesn't even say who the close friends were or where he's

buried," Sarge said.

"He's not. She brought me his urn and told me there was no memorial."

"Now, that's interesting. You're not a close enough friend to attend the memorial or even know how he died, but she gives you his urn."

"This obituary seems to be the only evidence that he is dead. Could be she concocted the whole thing. Dead artists' paintings are worth more than live artists' paintings. She proved that once already. Maybe, she's faking his death again," I said.

"Or maybe, worse," he said picking up his knapsack. "See you tomorrow, in the meantime, stay cool."

"Very funny," I said wiping the sweat off my forehead.

*****

Sara came every few days to bring me food and water and to check on my progress. I hadn't seen Sarge in the last few days and missed his company. By the count of the lines painted on the wall, my stick calendar told me it was day sixteen in this hellhole.

Somehow, I had completed and signed all of the paintings, including the large one, in less than the three weeks, driven, I guessed, by the need to be out of the garage and the solitary life Sara's proposition had forced on me. Human contact was becoming something I now craved.

It was not my best work—though I would never admit that to Sara—and it was speculative, just my best guess as to what Jerzy probably envisioned, but that wouldn't be my problem. Sara would just have to sell the idea that Jerzy was experimenting with different concepts.

I sat at the table pouring a bottle of cold water on my head when I heard the lock doing what it does when Sara arrives.

"You got them all done faster than I thought," she said as she browsed slowly, through the paintings taking time to study each one. "Some don't look like his work. I don't think I like that."

"Look, the ten that needed only the finishing touches are definitely him. Right?"

She nodded in agreement.

"These eighteen were the ones that needed more work. Some of the techniques I knew that were him, were there, but not enough. It looked like he was purposely changing his style. I can only imitate his style when I can see it and this was something I had never seen before."

I pointed to the four-foot by ten-foot painting and said, "That one only had a rough sketch, no Jerzy Hart soul. I did my best to put him in it, but had no idea where he was going with it. The thing that made the paintings a Jerzy Hart wasn't there anymore. Did my best, Sara. You can't capture a man's soul if it isn't there in the first place. It's like something bad had happened to him and he didn't care anymore. Sara, how did he die?"

She ignored my question. Instead, she smiled and said, "I brought the van today." She walked over to the wall and pressed the button to open the old overhead garage door.

Funny, I thought, I didn't recall Sara smiling much in the past. It was starting to make me uneasy and gave me a feeling she was enjoying a joke she wasn't sharing with me.

We stood and waited as the door creaked and rattled its way to the ceiling of the garage. Sara went to the van and proceeded to back it in. After she closed the overhead door, she walked with me to the back of the garage. She was carrying a grocery bag.

"I brought a few beers for you." She took bottles out of the bag and put them in the refrigerator. One she poured into a glass that she found in the cabinet above the sink.

"You know, Turner, you're starting to look like him with that shaggy hair and the beard," she said as she handed me the glass.

"Didn't need a glass, Sara, the bottle was just fine." I took a long swallow. "I could have used some of this instead of all that water."

"Didn't want you to get dehydrated."

"Not having one too?" I asked.

"No," she said and smiled again. "I'm driving."

"Have you got my money?" I asked.

"I'll take all of the paintings with me today. Tomorrow I'll pick you up, take you over to the condo and you can clean yourself up. Then we'll have dinner someplace nice and I'll have your money for you," she said with that smile that worried me.

I finished my beer and then helped her load the remaining paintings in the van. It was only afternoon when she left, but I was already sleepy. The oppressive heat and the living conditions I allowed myself to be subjected to had finally taken their toll, I thought, as I laid down on the cot for a nap.

*****

"Kid, wake up! Damn, wake up!"

I was in some kind of murky dream. Someone was pulling my arm, coughing and yelling, "You got to wake up! Kid, I only got one arm, I can't carry you. Damn, wake up!"

I was really trying to wake up, but I was so tired and the dream wasn't really a dream and Sarge was now pouring cold water on my face. And the smell, what was it? Gas, damn it was gas. I jumped up and leaned on Sarge as we made our way out the back door. He dumped me on the cement alleyway behind the garage.

"What the hell! Were you trying to commit suicide or what?" he said. "The gas on the range was on, all four burners."

The warm, damp, fresh air of the Chicago summer night cleared my head. "She tried to kill me!" I screamed at him.

When I finally got myself together, Sarge took me over to the homeless shelter. A shower and a decent meal can do wonders for a man. Especially, one who'd just escaped death.

*****

The homeless shelter was close enough for the explosion to shake just about everyone there awake. By the time Sarge and I got to the garage, the fire had consumed it. Fire engines and an ambulance, that passed us on our way there, were already working the scene. I could hear the sirens of more emergency equipment still coming. We watched as the roof fell in and the brick walls collapsed in on it.

"All evidence destroyed and you would have been just some guy squatting there," he said. "Burnt to a crisp."

"I know," I said. "Trust and Sara have always been on opposite ends of the spectrum and I let her sucker me in again."

"Bet it was about the money, wasn't it? Money can kind of blind a guy to what's really going on," Sarge said as he started coughing again. He wanted to say something, but the coughing couldn't be stopped with his head jerking forward with each spasm. It must have thrown the shooter's aim off as his head covered mine for a spit second and stopped the bullet meant for me.

He started to fall, his body hitting the pavement faster than I could stop it. I started screaming trying to be heard over the roar of the fire equipment, "Help! We need help over here!"

I caught the attention of one of the paramedics from the ambulance. He came running over.

I held Sarge in my arms. He was smiling and his last words to me were, "You know she did me a favor. You better run, kid."

I scanned the crowd that had gathered for any sight of Sara at the same time realizing that maybe she wasn't the shooter, remembering the "friend," that helped deliver the painting supplies.

Taking Sarge's advice I did run, as fast as I could, to the homeless shelter. With about fifty guys around me, I decided, it was a place where Sara wouldn't attempt to come after me.

*****

The Chi-Town Bank was walking distance from the shelter. The next morning, I fast-walked it, looking over my shoulder as I went, waiting for a bullet to find me.

I now knew what I needed to do with Jerzy's wallet. Sara's words, "You're starting to look like him with that shaggy hair and the beard," were now resonating in my head.

When I got to the bank, I presented the driver's license and signed Jerzy's name. Jerzy's paintings had been selling very well, even better than Sara had lead me to believe. I'm sure I cleaned more money out of the account than Sara would have paid me if she had kept her part of the bargain.

The local news station covered the fire and the conversation at the shelter centered on the identity of a body found in the rubble, burned beyond recognition. The authorities had already decided it was one of the neighborhood squatters there for the night.

My first reaction to that was he picked the wrong night. Still, it left me wondering about that locked storage room and the smell of death that continuously, permeated the garage. How long had he actually been in the garage?

*****

After Sarge's funeral, I drove down to Mexico for that vacation. I had no idea what to do with Jerzy's urn, so it came with me.

I still paint, sometimes in the style, never copies, of the old masters. I still do Jerzy Hart paintings, but lately, I've been doing Picasso. I am just a shadow behind the masters I immortalize and celebrate.

I have a nice rental on a hillside with a great ocean view that I decorate with my paintings. My lease is for a year and I wonder if staying in one place that long is the smart thing to do. Sara found me once already when I least expected it.

My rental came with a housekeeper who is also a great cook, but her talents are limited to the local cuisine. Lucky for me, I have a fondness for Mexican cooking and lucky for me, Maria speaks better English than I speak Spanish.

Yesterday, I found flowers in Jerzy's urn.

"Maria, why did you put flowers in this urn? Where are the ashes?" I asked.

"Urn?" she said. "Not an urn. No ashes. Just an empty jar."

Secrets of the Inner Ring

Gustavo Bondoni

Inspector Claude Huffmann twirled his moustache, knowing what an impressive figure his Parisian suit and proud bearing must cut among the uncouth locals. He would never have chosen to come to this spectacle, of course, but the young lady had insisted. She was a friend of some distant cousins living in the mid-West, and she'd immediately taken a shine to him. The young police officer, having heard rumors about these American farm girls had done little to discourage her.

A rotund man in a very tall hat directed the proceedings, and as a drum beat to a crescendo and other noise swelled within the small tent – dingy when compared to some of the British circuses he'd seen, that had permanent buildings, true theaters of the circus arts – a group of clowns rolled out a preposterous red cannon.

The ringmaster introduced someone called The Great Morindo, and explained that he was a master of the art of the human cannonball.

Abigail tensed. She clutched his arm and watched intently as a small, dark man climbed into the mouth of the gun.

Claude felt the excitement rising in the rest of the crowd as well. He knew it was all staged, and that it wasn't a real cannon, but he didn't see how anyone fired out of even a spring-loaded device could fail to exit through the canvas wall at the far end of the enclosure, probably taking with him many of the inhabitants of the rickety wooden bleachers which had been set up there.

The drumbeat reached a frenetic cadence and a fat clown ceremoniously touched a burning torch to the rear of the cannon, which immediately responded with a loud bang.

Something flew out of the cannon, followed by a cloud of crimson smoke.

Abigail jumped out of her seat in excitement and clapped her hands, but then turned to him in confusion. "What happened? Where did he go?"

The obvious answer seemed to be that he'd exited through a brand new hole in the canvas, just about where a cannonball would have gone at the angle the gun was set.

But Claude's well-trained senses had immediately fathomed what had occurred. Small parts of something had flown out of the mouth of the cannon, not going particularly far. Plus, he could see the rope that opened the window in the tent fabric, which meant that the hole was decidedly artificial.

So as the ringmaster shouted: "The Great Morindo, ladies and gentlemen!" and asked the crowd to file out in an orderly way, the inspector made a quick inventory of the stuff that had come out of the cannon. He expected to see some kind of ballast material, possibly hay or paper, but was instead appalled to see what looked like a severed arm lying beside an elephant's watering trough.

Worse, one of the clowns was discreetly kicking something

that looked like a human head towards the backstage exit. After seeing that, Claude preferred not to dwell on the red mist which had dispersed through the tent.

No one in the crowd mere feet away seemed to have noticed anything amiss. Most of them were milling towards the exits.

But Claude Huffmann was not one to let something like that pass. He considered himself an example of the Paris constabulary which meant that he had certain responsibilities.

Especially if there was a pretty girl watching.

Taking Abby by the hand, he headed towards the offending clown. "You, over there, halt! Halt I say!"

The clown looked over at him, grimaced grotesquely through his sad-face makeup, and redoubled his pace towards the exit, kicking the leaking head along in front of him as best he could with his huge blue shoes. His course was marked by copious red drops.

"Claude, what *are* you doing?" Abby asked him breathlessly. "We need to go that..." Then she suddenly looked down, stopped speaking and turned a pale shade visible even through her farm-bred sunburn. "Oh, my lord."

Claude felt her sway, and caught her arm before she could collapse. When he looked back towards the exit, the clown and his improvised football had disappeared.

Torn between his duty as a gentlemen and that of an officer of the law – even if he had no jurisdiction on this side of the Atlantic – Claude fumed as he waited for Abigail to recover, but he held his tongue. Even if the clown conspiracy made the head disappear, he had plenty of evidence to confront them with: the arm he'd seen earlier was still beside the trough.

"Abby," he said, "I'm very sorry about this, but I need to speak to the circus owners. That means I need to go through that curtain right now, and I can't risk escorting you out of the fairgrounds. Do you think you can find your way out on your own?"

"Oh, no, don't leave me!"

"I must speak to them, it's a matter of duty."

"Then take me with you."

"There may be some unfortunate things back there. You already saw a head, who knows what else we might find?"

"I'll be all right. I see worse every day on the farm. It just… surprised me, that's all."

He shrugged. Most ladies he'd known would have died before admitting that they were exposed to farm drudgery and the less savory aspects of that life, but things – especially women, it seemed – were different in America. "Suit yourself."

As they crossed the final few yards separating them from the curtain, two large men emerged and stood beside the exit. They seemed, if not identical, then attempting to become so: both had bald, shiny pates, identical blue leotards, muscles upon muscles and were clean-shaven except for curling moustaches that caused Claude to gasp in grudging admiration.

"You can't go in there," the right-hand twin said in a voice much too high-pitched for one of his size. "It's private."

Claude looked them over. He was well-trained in the use violence of several sorts for the pursuit of the public good, but he preferred to indulge in it when he was in possession of a good, stout truncheon – or, better still, a pistol of some description – and the malefactor was unarmed. He suspected that not only would a scuffle with these two be unproductive, but it could conceivably ruin his clothes. A gentleman, of course, would never consider the fact that either of the two could likely tie him in knots with one hand tied behind his back.

"I am an officer of the law," he told them, addressing the one who'd spoken. "Please let me pass."

The two large men exchanged a glance. "I'll have to ask Mr. Peters." He ducked behind the curtain while his twin held the fort.

A few moments later, he reappeared, and held the curtain aside for them to pass.

Claude and Abby found themselves in a space whose walls were made of the canvas of adjacent tents. Essentially, the circus had created another room by roofing an unused area with dark tent cloth.

It was dark. Lit only by the light that came in through the cloth, the space seemed shrouded in eternal twilight – and the smell of lions and elephants and bears and horses seemed to be fighting for animal primacy. A large pile of dung had been shoveled off to one side and reclined against the circus tent.

The man in the top hat awaited. "So, you're police officers? I'm Peters."

"I am," Claude said. "The young lady is merely here as my companion."

Peters looked them over, taking Claude in at a glance, and spending more time assessing Abigail. "I didn't see you at the sheriff's office when we set up all our permits."

"I am visiting here, but I can assure you that the local constabulary would want me to look into what I've seen." That, of course, was a little white lie: policemen, as a rule, would prefer for other policemen not to poke their noses into affairs outside of their jurisdiction. But he didn't want to confuse his host with unimportant details.

"And what, pray, have you seen?"

"I think you know exactly what I saw. And I think you know what it means." He looked Peters in the eye. "In a word: murder."

"That will be mighty hard to prove."

"It is very easy to prove. My interest, however, is why the murder was committed, and by whom?"

Peters raised an eyebrow. "I think there's one thing you need to tell me first: who is your supposed victim?"

"Why, the Great Morindo, of course. Someone cut him into pieces in his cannon."

The ringmaster laughed. "The Great Morindo is an invention. A different man climbs into that cannon every performance. Sometimes it's a girl, and she's The Great Morinda. If that is all you have, ask around. You'll find us all here and accounted for."

"Then whose head and arms did I see?"

"Do you have them with you?"

"No."

"Then you I can't help you identify them, can I?"

Claude was about to respond that there was an arm sitting

out in the middle of the ring, but stopped himself. He was certain that someone in the troop would have noticed it while he was talking to the ringmaster. He cursed himself for his stupidity.

"I suppose you can't," he replied, and led Abby towards the exit. To his great relief, the big men let him out with nothing more than a smirk.

*****

Claude knew that he'd been outmaneuvered and, to make the sensation even worse, he could feel Abby's condescension, even though she walked silently alongside, only stealing an occasional glance. It was hard to believe that he could have been so easily beaten back by a group of savage circus-men, but consoled himself with the thought that he'd done it to avoid allowing Abby to get hurt if things got rough.

He didn't say this aloud, however. It sounded extraordinarily weak, even to him.

"Are you just going to let them get away with it?" she suddenly asked.

Claude nearly jumped. He wasn't expecting Abby to speak at all. In Europe, when a man was publicly shamed, it was customary for him to accompany any lady present to her home, and not subject her to any unwelcome conversations. It was unthinkable that the girl in question would commit a breach of that protocol. But, once again, his assessment of this friend of his family's as somewhat less than a lady seemed correct.

Or, he told himself, perhaps this was another case of America being different.

He stopped, and she did, too. "What do you expect me to do? I can't go to the sheriff without any evidence. He would ask me why no one else saw anything. Then he'd laugh and probably advise me to avoid drink that is too strong for me."

Abby thought about that for a moment. "Yes. I suppose so. And he wouldn't believe me either. He's convinced I stole a pie from Mrs. Percival's window. Nothing I say is going to help you."

"How awful. Why would he think that?"

"Because a lot of people saw me do it, I guess."

"Oh." Yes. Definitely different in America. "The only thing I can think of is to see what they do with the corpse. They'll have to do that at night. It's not something one can do in broad daylight."

"It will be dark in an hour. Walk me home so I can come with you."

"I'm sorry?"

"Just trust me."

When they arrived at Abby's house – a wooden building on a main road – she instructed him to wait for her. Then, she went inside, announced that she wasn't feeling well, and that she would go to bed immediately. An older female voice of the infirm type answered something that might or might not have been "Yes, dear." Five minutes later, a scuffling noise drew Claude to the side of the house, where Abby had just finished climbing down the drainpipe, oil lantern in hand.

"Are those men's trousers?" he asked her.

She blushed. "I wasn't going to wear them, but dresses are just useless for this kind of thing."

Claude wondered just how much experience the girl had in that kind of thing, and especially in what kind of thing it was exactly, but judged it best to keep his mouth firmly shut.

"So where are we going?"

"I think the logical place to start would be to see what our friends at the circus are up to. If we see anyone leaving with a heavy, that is probably important."

Or they could remove the pieces in smaller sacks, I guess."

"Yes, that's possible."

They retraced their steps back to the fairground. Claude felt pessimistic about their chances of seeing anything. It would take some distressingly unimaginative criminals to simply walk out with bulky sacks.

But that turned out to be exactly what they did. The two large twins and the big man in the top hat – now dressed in a worn brown suit that made him look like a common laborer – left the silent circus ground accompanied by two women.

As night fell, Claude and Abby followed them past the city limits and into the countryside, staying well behind to avoid being spotted.

Eventually, they came over a rise to find that the group ahead had vanished. Trees surrounded the road on both sides, but there was no one on it. Even in the twilight, they could see for hundreds of yards ahead."

"Oh. I was afraid they might be coming here," Abby said.

"Why? There isn't anything here."

"Yes, there is. There's an old chapel down a path between the trees. It was put there by the first family that settled in these parts, because they had their farm on these lands, but the town stopped using it after we built the new church. I haven't been here since I was a little girl."

The path was somewhat overgrown, but that fact that it existed at all showed that it still got some use. But even that couldn't disguise the fact that it was surrounded by trees. As soon as they taken a few steps onto the path, what seemed like pitch blackness enveloped them. Abby put her hand in his.

"Should we light the lantern?"

"We don't have a choice. I just hope they won't see us. Here, I have matches."

They proceeded carefully down the path until the trees suddenly ended and the soft light of the moonlit night reappeared.

Claude put the lamp out and they watched a small group huddled on a hill in the distance.

"That's the graveyard," Abby told him.

"I could tell."

Five forms were silhouetted against the sky: the four they'd been following, and one more. The new arrival was a gangling figure, scarecrow-like and wearing a hat. The sacks were emptied into a hole in the center of the group and the fifth man began to read from a book. Three of the other four held lanterns.

"That's a priest. Come on, we can catch them red-handed and use the preacher's testimony to get the sheriff to act."

"No, wait…"

But Claude wasn't in the mood for Abby to begin acting

like a woman right now. She'd been bold – irresponsibly so, as her reputation would be in tatters if anyone found out that they'd been out alone, at night, unchaperoned – so far. This wasn't the time for the natural timidity of her sex to reassert itself.

Using the inadequate moonlight as a guide, the young inspector crashed through the grass to arrive at the graveside.

"Father, you must testify. These people are getting away with murder."

The priest was a gaunt man with sunken eyes lost in the shadows cast by the flickering lantern light. He smiled faintly at Claude and responded in a tattered voice similar to that of the old drunks begging alms around Notre Dame. "I'm afraid I'm not your father, young man."

Claude felt the unmistakable sensation of the wrong end of a revolver pressing into his back.

"I thought you might pop up again," Peters said. "This time, perhaps, you'll be joining the man in there."

A struggling Abby was dragged up to the grave, hissing and spitting at the two bald musclemen. As Claude watched, aghast, she succeeded in biting one of their hands, only for the other man to twist her arm painfully behind her.

Thus immobilized, she gave Claude a dark look. "If you'd only stopped to listen, I could have told you that priests don't bury people at night around here. Especially not on unhallowed ground."

"I thought you said this was the graveyard."

"It was. It isn't anymore."

Claude sighed. He'd let his enthusiasm get the better of

him, just like his instructors always said he would.

It was probably too late to make up for it now because his captors would surely just shoot him and deposit him in the already open grave. But he was determined to stop embarrassing his teachers and begin to use his training for a change. He began by observing the single member of the group other than the priest that he could see: the woman.

Under other circumstances, she would probably have been beautiful. A full head of jet-black hair framed a face with delicate features and eyes that were pools of ink in her milk-white complexion. But the most notable thing about her is that she was crying and repeating the words "Oh Giorgio, Giorgio" over and over again. As Claude watched, she fell to her knees at the edge of the grave and sobbed until one of the big men pulled her back.

Sensing movement behind him, he began to turn, but a massive blow to the head staggered him. A second blow turned the lights out completely.

*****

Upon waking, the first thing he noticed was the pain in his head. Whoever had hit him had been serious about the endeavor. Opening his eyes was something that would require some building up to.

Nevertheless, he was able to acquire certain information about his surroundings. He concluded that he was in a stable: the warm air and the cloying but unmistakable smell of dung hit him squarely.

About to open his eyes to verify his suspicions, he suddenly felt the world move and decided to rest a bit more as he was clearly not in a fit state to move around just yet.

A few minutes later, he felt a moistness on his face and a soft snorting, as if a dog were nuzzling him. He held up a hand to push it away and opened one eye slightly.

He found himself looking into a large yellow orb whose vertical pupil observed him curiously.

Claude reacted immediately. He crawled as fast as he could in the opposite direction until he collided with a wall of metal bars. He felt behind him for a corner, an opening, or any other way he could escape, but found nothing. He never took his eyes of the animal.

The lion, meanwhile, regarded him placidly and paced back and forth a few times before lying down in the straw.

"Don't worry. He isn't hungry," a voice behind him said.

Claude turned to find the woman who he'd last seen crying over The Great Morindo's grave sitting on a stool behind him. She'd stopped crying, but red rings around her eyes bore witness to recent tears.

His highly trained observation faculties also revealed that he wasn't in a stable at all, but inside a large cage that had been built into one end of a boxcar. There was another cage at the other end, and in between, an open area where the woman was seated. That explained the sensation of movement, at least.

Daylight filtered through cracks in the car's roof and air holes in its side. Claude felt the back of his head, where a painful lump was surrounded by matted, dried blood. "How long have I been unconscious?"

"I'd say just over ten hours. We weren't really sure you were going to wake at all, which is why we decided to load up the animals and get some distance between us and the town."

"And you brought me with you?"

"It was the easiest way to get rid of the evidence if you died on us. All we would have to do is stop feeding the cats for a couple of days. Immediate body disposal. It's much easier to toss out some gnawed bones than to dispose of a whole body."

"Then why didn't you do that with the great Morindo?"

The woman's eyes flashed. "Because he was one of us, no matter his transgressions. We don't just feed our own to the beasts."

She glared at him defiantly, and then broke down in tears.

He waited what he thought would be a prudent interval, and then asked her. "Now that you know I'm going to live, can I ask you to let me out?"

Her look was hostile. "No. Those lions should be getting hungry in another couple of hours."

The woman left the boxcar through the door in its side, by a curious method. She grabbed hold of something above the door and swung herself up. His highly trained mind concluded that she must have been one of the acrobats in the show.

Once she'd gone, he focused on the other cage – keeping one eye on the lion in his own enclosure at all times. There, looking back at him, was Abby. She was huddled in one corner, only a few yards away from where a second feline reposed and watched her.

"Abby!" he said. She showed no signs of having heard him, seemingly mesmerized by the beast in the cage with her. Finally, he succeeded in getting her attention. "I'm so glad that you're all right."

She turned to face him and her face clouded over. "Well, at least they won't have to kill me now for watching them murder you," she said.

"They said they'd kill you?"

She nodded. "And I believe them, too." Then she turned away and muttered something that sounded like it was her own fault for something. But he wasn't able to catch the rest.

"Don't worry. I won't let them harm you."

Her look turned to one of disbelief. "And how do you propose to manage that? I'm sorry if I sound a little critical, but you had the drop on them, watching from the darkness when they were thinking of something else, and all you managed was to get us caught." All the soft, ladylike qualities that mothers liked to hear from their girls seemed to have disappeared from her voice. At that moment, he had little difficulty imagining her on a farm, possibly cursing at cows.

She might be unrefined, but she had a point. His impulsive nature had gotten her into this, and it was his obligation as a gentleman to extricate her from the situation. She was, after all, completely dependent on him.

Claude was still working on the problem when the woman returned. She ignored the inspector and went straight to Abby's cage.

"Was it you?" she said. "The letter. Was it you?"

Abby stood. At first she looked afraid, but then returned the woman's gaze, defiant. "Yes. It was me."

The woman from the circus began to clutch at her hair. "You killed him. It was you. Why? Why couldn't you be like the rest, content to have him for a few hours and then move on? He was my husband, and I loved him even though I knew what he was like."

"Because I didn't want him for a few hours. I never had him and I never wanted him. I only wrote that letter because he groped me without any permission. In public, no less. Then he made an awful proposition. I simply had to write to the ringmaster to complain."

"Then you didn't…"

"Most certainly not!" Abigail replied, stamping her foot. "What do you take me for?"

The other woman was silent, but it lasted only for a moment. "The ringmaster is my father."

"Oh."

"The blacksmith who built the cannon is my brother. He used to work on real cannons in the war, so I suppose he could have modified this one to…" She paused to gather herself. "None of my family liked Giorgio, and I was always afraid they'd do something to him. They were afraid of hurting me." She sat on the stool and held her face in her hands. "But with your letter… they had no choice."

Peters himself climbed into the boxcar. "It is true, we had no choice. He was tearing you apart, and I could never allow him to continue. I love you too much for that." He placed a hand gently on the woman's shoulder, and then let it fall away. The woman left, a trail of sobs in her wake as she swung out and away.

"But now, we do have a choice." He looked at Claude and Abby in turn. "Well, at least you do. I have no desire to kill anyone, but you two are a problem. If I let you go, I will hang, and so will my sons and many of my best friends.

"Killing you seems terrible, so how about this? If you can think of a way to convince me that by letting you go, I won't lose my circus and my life, I'll open the gates. If you take too long, the lions will get hungry… and the problem will take care of itself."

Claude knew it was his moment to shine. Surely, his word as a gentleman would speak for itself. Now that he knew the facts of the case, he was inclined to be lenient, and could surely convince a man such as this that he was in no danger.

He sat in his cage putting the words in the right order, knowing how much those who spoke English valued rhetoric and organization. The speech would not only serve to save his life, but also to ennoble him in the eyes of the young lady. She was disappointed in him now, but would certainly see him as the hero he was once he saved her life.

"I have an idea." Claude looked up, his composition interrupted. He had never expected Abby to speak. "If you let me out of here, I'll shoot him myself."

"Shoot him?" the man asked.

"Yes. That way, if we're ever discovered, I'd hang right along with you. You could let me go without any fear of me telling anyone. But I have one condition."

Claude spluttered, but was too overcome with rage to put his thoughts into words. The ringmaster had his back to the inspector, and he wished he could see his face as the silence stretched on.

"What's your condition?"

"You have to let me join the circus. I've always wanted to."

"Can you do anything?"

"You can teach me."

Suddenly, Peters moved. He took two steps to the right, pulled a metal key off a peg and grasped a whip from a shelf. He opened the door and motioned Abby to step out, whip in hand. The lion paid them almost no heed, however.

"Come here," he told her, as he pulled a revolver out of his pocket. "I'll aim, you pull the trigger. I'm not going to risk you taking this away from me."

She shrugged and put her hand over the weapon.

Claude looked into her eyes, wondering if she was telling the truth, or had some kind of plan. Surely this was a country girl's brave but simple attempt to save a man who'd completely knocked her off her feet. He was about to tell her not to worry, that he had the situation in hand.

She returned his gaze without emotion and his words died on his lips.

His last thought was that things were even more different in America than he'd believed.

Where There's Love
Michael Wiley

Sam Kelson and DeMarcus Rodman stood in an alcove off the Cannella Jewelers showroom. Midnight had passed, and the store was dark except for pulsing green lights on the silent alarm box.

During business hours, Mrs. Cannella would stand in the middle of a circular glass case displaying engagement rings, gold necklaces, and ruby earrings. A chandelier hung from the ceiling. An open stairway rose to a second level, where a staff of jewelers with headband magnifiers worked in tiny rooms and a large safe occupied a room of its own. Mr. and Mrs. Cannella replaced the downstairs carpet twice a year so the lustrous pile made buyers feel they were floating into a rarefied space where the limits on their regular spending applied no more than gravity would a million miles from earth.

"Enough to give me a migraine," Kelson said.

"Hush." Years ago, Rodman had scored at the top of his class of police recruits. Then his little brother died at a cop's hands, and Rodman quit the academy. Now he went from one hustle to another, with sharper eyes than any cop on the beat. He seemed to know everyone and everything, from who scored big with three-card monte on the sidewalk outside Wrigley Field to who opened a Southside chop shop to strip apart stolen Mercedes-Benzes.

"Why should I hush?" Kelson said. "No one's here."

"Practice," Rodman said. "Pretend it's happening."

"You know that'll do no good."

"Pretend to pretend."

"You can't confuse me into being quiet." That was true. Ever since a coke dealer shot Kelson in the head three years earlier, he talked compulsively, especially when he was nervous. He was nervous now. "This job feels like a setup."

"Why would it be?"

"Insurance fraud?" When Mr. Cannella hired Kelson to provide overnight security, the request felt funny. *Why did Cannella want him for only one night? Why did he want him at all?*

"A shipment's coming in the afternoon and going out the next morning," the jeweler said, gazing at him over the top of his wire-rimmed glasses. "We're taking this one as a distributor, reselling parcels to other stores. A lot of people in the city will know we have the stones."

"Why not lock them up with the rest of your jewelry?"

The man's lips curled. "Last week, my grandson was playing upstairs. He managed to change the combination on the safe."

"Huh. Smart kid."

"A little rat. The safe is useless until we get a technician here. So we need a night watchman."

"Your voice sounds expensive," Kelson said.

"I'm sorry?"

"Couldn't you hire a guard from a security firm?"

The jeweler said he'd read a newspaper article about Kelson—a former undercover cop, shot during a bust-gone-bad, now struggling to reinvent himself as a PI—and was moved.

"I don't do pity jobs," Kelson said.

Cannella said he understood and wanted to hire him for his skillset.

Kelson heard irony. "I talk a lot, but I'm good at my job," he said.

"I'm sure you are." The jeweler's smile made Kelson think he believed that, with the frontal lobe damage, Kelson would have the skillset of a hamster.

"I'm not a hamster," he said.

"I would never mistake you for one," Cannella said. "Look, you can hang out and collect your check. Bring a book if you want. But no guns—I don't like weapons in the shop. This is a simple job."

Too simple. Kelson Googled Cannella Jewelers and discovered that, three years earlier, the store had settled a claim that it sold a ruby brooch with an inflated appraisal. Two years before that, Mr. Cannella's name appeared on an industry list of jewelers under investigation for illegally sourcing gemstones. So Kelson invited Rodman to keep him company. Rodman was six foot eight and weighed almost three hundred pounds—better than a gun.

"I don't trust this guy," Kelson told him.

Rodman said, "Why would he hire security if he wants to rob himself?"

"He has a low opinion of me. If a burglar robbed the store after the owner hired a guard, no insurance company could fight the claim."

"Did he show you the paperwork for the shipment?"

"Paperwork?"

"At a fancy place like this, you should always know what they've got you on the hook for."

"I'm just a hired body."

Rodman leaned against the alcove wall. "Well, I'm guessing we'll have a quiet night."

"I'm guessing you're forgetting who you came with."

So Rodman put on a pair of earbuds and listened to his music while Kelson talked nonstop about Mrs. Cannella, who wore her artificially whitened smile like it was shiny jewelry, then about how strange it was that oysters made pearls.

*****

A half hour later, Kelson yanked the earbuds from Rodman's ears. Rodman had closed his eyes in the dark, and, though he stood upright, he was breathing deep and slow, nearly snoring.

"Upstairs," Kelson said.

Rodman opened his eyes.

Upstairs—no, up higher, up on the roof—there were footsteps. Almost too quiet to be heard, but definitely footsteps.

"Hmm," Rodman said.

166

Then something thudded on the roof.

"Is there a ceiling hatch?" Rodman asked.

Kelson moved from the alcove into the showroom. "I didn't notice." He started up the stairs.

"Where's the crate?" Rodman said.

"Right."

Mr. Cannella had showed Kelson a wooden crate in a closet at the back of the alcove. "This is why we need you," he'd said.

Kelson came down the steps. He and Rodman moved back into the alcove and waited.

Rusty hinges stretched and screeched upstairs. Someone thumped lightly to the floor, followed by a second, heavier thump.

Kelson glanced into the dark showroom. The lights on the silent alarm had turned solid red. "Amateurs," he said.

"*Shh*," Rodman said.

"*Shh* yourself," Kelson said.

Footsteps crossed the floor above them. An upstairs light went on, casting a glow down to the showroom, then went off again.

"Idiots," Kelson said.

"*Shh.*"

The footsteps came to the top of the stairway. Then two people came down, silent, slow.

"That's more like it," Kelson said.

"*Shh.*"

The burglars—one of them tall and thick-shouldered, the

other short and thin, both wearing cheap cloth masks—went to the display case and circled it. They shined penlights through the glass, paused, moved on. They whispered to each other like anxious shoppers. They passed a necklace with a sapphire pendant, passed an emerald-encrusted bracelet, and came to the ring display. Then, with startling speed, the short thief sprang over the case, vaulting into the space where Mrs. Cannella stood during store hours.

"Whoa," Kelson yelled.

The burglars swung around and aimed their flashlights at the alcove.

"Who's there?" the tall burglar said.

Rodman tried to silence Kelson.

"Sam Kelson," Kelson said.

The tall burglar fumbled at his waistband and found a black pistol. "Come out of there."

"Why?" Kelson said.

"I'll shoot you if you don't."

"You won't be the first." Kelson stepped from the alcove.

"What are you doing here?" the burglar said.

"Waiting for you. For a while I didn't think you were coming. DeMarcus thought we'd have a quiet night."

The burglar wiggled his pistol at him. "Who's DeMarcus?"

"You don't want to meet him. You've got a gun, but DeMarcus has something else. You could call it his skillset. The truth is, he's the gentlest man I know—and a real sucker for love— but he's huge and most people think he must be—"

"*Enough*," the burglar said.

168

"Probably not." Kelson glanced at the alcove. "Hey, DeMarcus."

Rodman sighed. "*Shh.*"

The burglars aimed their penlights at the alcove again. "DeMarcus is *here*?" the tall one said.

"You don't talk?" Kelson asked the little one.

Rodman hit a switch in the alcove, turning on the chandelier, then stepped into the bright showroom. He raised his hands to show he meant no harm, but the pose made him look like a grizzly working up an appetite.

"Holy crap," the tall burglar said.

"Told you," Kelson said.

But the little one vaulted over the display case as if to confront the enormous man.

"You don't want to do that," Rodman said, and lowered his hands.

Outside, a siren whined.

"Dammit," the little one said—with a girl's voice—and pulled off her mask. She looked about eighteen. Blond hair fell to her shoulders. She shook it to clear it from her face.

"Huh," Kelson said.

She went to the display case. "That one." She tapped a forefinger on the glass.

"Yes, ma'am," the tall burglar said, and smashed the glass top with his gun butt. He took a diamond ring from the display and offered it to her. "Will you?" he said, as a second siren and then a third joined the first.

"You're going to do this with the mask on?" she said.

"Oh." He pulled off his mask. He had the wide eyes and flat face of a kindly bulldog. He might've been twenty. "Will you?"

She smiled. "I thought you'd never ask."

"Aww," Kelson said.

"Aww," Rodman said.

The tall one slipped the ring onto the little one's finger, and the little one kissed him. "Let's split," she said.

They ran for the stairs.

"You're not taking the stones?" Kelson said.

The tall one stopped on the first step. "What stones?"

"In the closet."

"Shut up, Sam," Rodman said.

"What closet?" the tall one asked.

"In the—"

"*Shut up*," Rodman said.

The tall burglar came back down.

The little one, halfway up the stairs, said, "Don't be stupid, Lucky."

"Really?" Kelson said. "*Lucky?*"

"Listen to her, Lucky," Rodman said. "The cops will be here in about a second. If you want to get away, now's the time."

"Too late," Kelson said. "You're on video."

The tall burglar glanced around the store. A camera pointed back at him from the ceiling. He went to it and hit it with his gun butt. The casing could take more than that. So he shot it.

The girl on the stairs screamed. So did Kelson.

The tall burglar went to Rodman and pointed his pistol at his nose. "What stones?"

"Put down the gun," Rodman said, gentle.

"What closet?" the burglar asked.

"In the alcove," Kelson said.

The tall burglar lowered his pistol. "Check the closet, honey."

"Let's get out of here," she said.

"She's your smarter half, Lucky," Rodman said.

But the tall burglar went to the alcove and returned with the Cannellas' crate. He set it on the display case and pried open the top. There were twenty-five envelopes inside. He removed one, tore it open, and poured a dozen diamonds onto the glass counter.

The girl whooped like a bull rider, skipped down the steps, and scooped up a handful. She stood on her tiptoes and kissed Lucky again.

Outside the store, three police cars skidded to a stop, emergency lights flashing. More sirens approached.

"Uh-oh," Lucky said.

"Now Lucky's talking sense," Kelson said.

Rodman said, "Do you know how hard it is to get rid of hot diamonds?"

The girl said, "You ever heard of pawn shops?" She pulled another envelope from the crate and tore it open. She scooped a glinting handful.

Outside, a speaker crackled to life on one of the police cars, and an officer said, "Put your hands up and come out."

The girl yelled back through the display window, telling the officer what he could do with *his* hands.

"Technically, that's impossible," Kelson said. "I mean, biologically."

Rodman said, "You know that pawn shops give the cops daily reports of everything they buy? The reports include driver's license numbers."

"DeMarcus knows about this kind of thing," Kelson told the burglars. "He's an expert on stolen goods."

Officers climbed from their cars, drew their service pistols, and crouched behind their open doors. The man on the speaker repeated his demand. "Come out now."

Lucky looked confused, then said, "eBay."

Rodman said, "Because cops can't check eBay? You could make easier money shoplifting."

"That's how we met," the girl said. "He was coming out of electronics, and I was in the underwear aisle."

Another police car slid to a stop outside.

Rodman said, "Robbing a jewelry store's a loser score unless you have a fence."

"Maybe we *have* a fence," Lucky said.

Kelson snorted. "You're too dumb to have a fence."

"Who're you calling dumb?" the girl said.

"Who broke into a jewelry store to steal an engagement ring?"

"Nothing dumb about love," she said.

"Who's going to spend her honeymoon in jail?"

She grabbed the pistol from her boyfriend and pointed it at Kelson.

"You don't want to rile her," Lucky said.

The man on the speaker warned the burglars to do as they were told.

The girl held the pistol to Kelson's ear, led him to the front window, and yelled, "We have hostages."

A gun fired, and the front window imploded.

The girl and Kelson screamed. She dragged him back to Lucky and Rodman. They squatted behind the display case.

The girl yelled to the front, "You can't do that."

"Sorry," said the cop on the speaker. "Rookie error."

"We have hostages," she yelled again.

"That's us," Kelson yelled.

"Won't happen again," the speaker voice said.

Then, for a while, everything outside went quiet.

Rodman asked the burglars, "You came just for a ring?"

The girl said, "We thought stealing it would be romantic."

"Candlelit dinners are also good," Kelson said.

"I wanted to give her something nice," the tall burglar said.

"Ah, love," Rodman said.

"Funny story about a wedding I went to," Kelson said. "The bride's uncle—this old guy from Albania—toasted the couple at the reception. He said, 'Where there's love—'"

"Not the time for it," Rodman said.

Outside, a tactical van pulled up beyond the squad cars. Four men in body armor jumped from a sliding side panel. A square-jawed woman in plainclothes climbed out after them with a megaphone. She stepped between the cars and into the open, switched on the megaphone, and identified herself as Sergeant Angela Nguyen. She asked the burglars for their names.

The girl yelled back what Angela Nguyen could do with her questions.

"Biologically possible," Kelson said, "but sort of abstract."

"Do you *ever* shut up?" Lucky said.

"Nope," Kelson said.

Sergeant Nguyen spoke over the megaphone. "What do you want in exchange for the hostages?"

The burglars glanced at each other. "A helicopter?" the boyfriend suggested.

Kelson snorted. "What're you going to do with a helicopter?"

The man looked stung. "Go... somewhere."

"I don't want to go anywhere," the girl said. "My grandma needs me."

"You have a grandma?" Kelson said.

The girl scowled at him. "*Everyone* has a grandma."

"She takes care of her," the tall burglar said.

The megaphone voice asked again, "What do you want in exchange?"

Kelson yelled back, "They're discussing it."

Then Lucky yelled, "A helicopter."

Kelson snorted again.

"Can't do a helicopter," said the megaphone.

The girl yelled, "We have hostages."

"No helicopter," said the megaphone.

The girl told the sergeant what she could do with the helicopter she wouldn't give them.

The sergeant asked, "Who am I talking to?"

Kelson yelled back, "His name is Lucky, believe it or not. Don't know about the girlfriend."

The girl shoved the pistol into Kelson's ribs. "If you don't shut up—"

"Cute couple," Kelson yelled. "Just got engaged."

"Put a cork in it, Sam," Rodman said.

"Lucky," the megaphone voice said, "what do you need to make this right? No helicopters. No jet packs or rocket-powered cars either. How do we do this so no one gets hurt?"

The girl and Lucky stared at each other again, as if hoping one of them would know.

"I just wanted to get married," she told him.

"That's all *I* wanted," Lucky said.

"Why'd you go back down the stairs?" she asked. "We could've been home by now."

Lucky glared at Kelson. "*He* started talking about stones."

"Don't blame *me*," Kelson said.

"I only wanted a ring," the girl said to her boyfriend.

"Yeah?" He mimicked her scooping up handfuls of diamonds and whooping like a bull rider.

"Kids, *kids*," Rodman said.

The couple looked despondent.

"We're screwed," the girl said.

"How'd you come in?" Rodman asked.

"Across the roof next door," the boyfriend said. "The 7-Eleven."

"Any reason you can't go back out the same way?"

The girl said, "They'll see us."

"They seem pretty focused on what's happening in this room right now," Rodman said.

The couple looked unconvinced.

"We'll distract them," Kelson said. "DeMarcus will go out."

"No thanks," Rodman said.

"If I go, I'll tell them what's happening," Kelson said. "They won't even need to ask."

"Ah, hell," Rodman said.

"Hostage coming out," Kelson shouted. "Heck of a good guy. He comes in peace. My only real friend—"

"Shut up, Sam," Rodman said.

He stood up behind the counter. He raised his hands over his head. He went to the front door, unlocked it, and stepped into the brilliant police lights. His shadow fell all the way back to the display case.

Sergeant Nguyen said over the megaphone, "Holy crap."

Another cop yelled, "Get down on the ground." Then all the cops were yelling—*On the ground—Get down—Now—Get down on the ground now.*

Rodman lowered to the pavement. Inside the store, Kelson

crawled from the display case to the alcove.

Two tactical cops with ballistic shields shuffled over to Rodman and patted him down from his ears to his toes. They told him to stand, and all three retreated behind the patrol cars.

In the alcove, Kelson switched off the chandelier.

"Hey," one of the cops yelled outside.

"Go," Kelson said.

The burglars sprinted up the stairs to the second floor.

The cops shouted to each other. The tactical squad officers shuffled double-time behind their ballistic shields toward an alley at the back of the store. Cops crouching behind open patrol car doors swept their gun barrels across the front. A spotlight mounted on the tactical van shined through the shattered display window into the showroom. Kelson yelled, "Where there's love, there's no sin." The Albanian uncle's wedding toast.

The burglars pulled themselves through the ceiling hatch onto the roof. All the noise and commotion below seemed to belong to another world.

The girl kissed her boyfriend. "I love you, Lucky."

He kissed her back. "Love you too."

They sprang from Cannella Jewelers to the 7-Eleven roof. They crawled and kept crawling. As the tactical squad men kicked in the back door to the jewelry store and charged into the showroom, the burglars lowered themselves from the roof next door and disappeared into the dark.

*****

An hour before dawn, Mr. Cannella arrived in a silver Audi. His wire-rimmed glasses glinted in the flashing lights of three remaining police cars. He ducked under the crime scene tape and went to a pop-up tent outside the jewelry store, where Kelson and Rodman were waiting for the robbery detectives to decide what to do with them. He thumped Kelson on the chest.

"I paid you to guard the store, and not only did you let *this* happen"—Cannella gestured at the shattered front window—"but the officer who called me said you let the thieves go."

"The best defense is a strong offense?" Rodman said.

Cannella gave him a confused look and turned back to Kelson. "*Why?*"

"They weren't much for thieves. Nice kids, in over their heads. Lovebirds."

Cannella said, "I'll have you arrested. For abetting."

Rodman said, "The trick is misdirection."

Cannella said, "Who are you?"

"DeMarcus Rodman." He extended an enormous hand. "Sam brought me along for the ride."

"DeMarcus kept the robbery from turning ugly," Kelson said. "No one hurt."

Cannella ignored the hand. His fury at Kelson was growing. "Did I tell you to bring a friend?"

"Distract and deflect," Rodman said.

"What are you talking about?" Cannella said.

"Ah, come on, we see through you," Rodman said.

Kelson said, "DeMarcus knows his stuff."

"I don't care what he knows. I hired you to—"

"Why?" Rodman said.

Cannella blinked at him. "Sorry?"

"Why did you hire Sam? He's good at finding missing people, snapping pictures through windows, that kind of job. But jewelry shop security?"

Cannella shook off the question. "I read a story about him in the paper. Ex-cop. Bullet in the head. I felt sorry for the guy. This seemed like something he could do."

Rodman said, "You hired an inexperienced guy to guard, what, a million bucks in diamonds?"

Cannella said, "If someone tried to take them, he just had to call the police."

Rodman said, "Where'd you get them?"

"I'm sorry?"

"Where's the paperwork? The... what do you call it—the certification."

Now Cannella smiled, as if Rodman was hitting with a broken bat. "We don't need any of that."

Rodman said, "If the stones are legal, you have papers."

"DeMarcus is an expert on stolen goods," Kelson said.

Cannella was sweating in his suit. "I don't *know* that they're illegal."

"I suppose the cops will be happy to hold the stones for a while as they figure everything out," Rodman said. "I suppose the news will be happy to run some stories about a jewelry store under investigation for dirty gems."

Cannella moved close. "What do you want?"

Rodman said, "You used to have a security camera in the store—"

"Used to?"

"You might be able to recover the recording. If you do, you'll see a couple of kids dressed up like Ninja turtles. Maybe that recording could disappear."

"No one's getting away with this," Cannella said.

"They're bonehead kids. Either they'll grow up and get smart or they'll stay boneheads and get caught."

"Why would you want to help them?" the jeweler said.

Kelson was eager to answer. "DeMarcus looks tough, but he's a sucker for love."

Cannella was trying hard to swallow his fury. He stared at the shattered front window. "I guess insurance could cover this."

"Or not," Rodman said.

"The adjustor will want to talk to me," Kelson said. "That might not work out so well for you."

"Maybe you could suck up the pain," Rodman told the man.

Cannella started to argue—but stopped when Rodman leaned over him. "That's it then?" he said. He looked as if he might cry. "You let the thieves get away. You wreck my store. You threaten me. Are you sure you don't want to torch the place before you go?"

"What do you think, Sam?" Rodman said. "Are we done here?"

"Almost," Kelson said.

"Ah, of course."

"What?" Cannella barely kept from whining.

"You can write Sam his check."

Cannella wrote the check.

The Wait

Peter W. J. Hayes

David wrote poetry and talked about the folds of longing and loss in our lives. Ruger was large boned, brutal-looking, a weapon. The few times he talked, it was about fairy tales and mythical beings. And me, I was the opportunist, happy to follow them, to be swept along.

I should have known better, of course, but we were young.

I don't offer this as an excuse. David used to say life was easy, but in truth we'd never known hardship. We believed anything was possible, then again, we'd never been caught.

David would cup my cheek in his hand and say, "We are weightless."

But I wasn't. And one night, his weight pinning me to our bed, I noticed his eyes were closed. My first bite of the apple. He was teaching only himself to be weightless, I realized, no one else.

Knowledge is the curse that sets us free.

We lived together in a one-bedroom walk-up, each contributing money in our own way. I was badger game bait. Skirt hem high, neckline low, I'd sit at hotel bar until a mark approached. A shared drink or two, a few well-placed laughs, and I'd suggest a nightcap in my room. I had four minutes to slip off his pants before David and Ruger burst in. David would rage he was my husband while Ruger leaned over the man—his phone recording—and tell him it was ATM time.

The problem, I saw in time, was that we could only run the scam once a month. Upscale hotel bars are few, people talk. Bartenders especially. Several times I suggested cutting a barkeep in on it, but David wouldn't hear of it.

My second bite of the apple.

David held our money and was cheap. His weightlessness, I saw, improved or declined with the amount of money stored in his strongbox under our bed.

David contributed by cheating at poker, but Ruger was the real money maker. Sometimes when money was short, near midnight Ruger would shoulder into his windbreaker and slip out. David always took me to bed soon afterward. He was rougher with me those nights, as if he needed to prove something to me, or himself.

We would wake to a stack of bills on the kitchen table and Ruger asleep on his workout mat under the living room windows, his face marred by bruises and swelling. We spoke in whispers not to wake him.

I often wondered what he did on those nights. It had to be some kind of fighting, but he never answered my questions. I was left with guesswork, until one evening I didn't fall asleep after David was finished with me.

I heard Ruger return about three-thirty, his usual light step now a shuffle. When the kitchen faucet started, I stole from David's bed.

A stack of bills waited on the kitchen table. Ruger was bent over the sink, shirtless, taking water in his big hands and splashing it on his face. He didn't hear me come in. Ruger did things one-at-a-time, and he was nursing himself. I had never seen him shirtless, despite how closely we all lived together.

I couldn't take my eyes off him.

Muscles flickered along his side and down a wide slab of meat on his back. On the arm nearest to me, a muscle like a croquet ball tightened and loosened between his shoulder and elbow. His skin was littered with purple marks edged in red.

He sensed me, straightened and turned. We stared at each other across the kitchen. The six muscular squares of his belly were covered with red welts and bruises. On his face, a line of blood stretched from a cut above his eye. Seeing his body made me keenly aware of my own. Despite the long t-shirt I wore to bed, I felt naked in front of him.

I wanted to be naked in front of him.

My third bite of the apple.

If he saw my reaction, or sensed the hot blood in my veins, he didn't say anything. He turned off the water, crossed to the table and slid a bill from the bottom of the money pile. Held it out to me.

One hundred dollars.

I looked up at him. He pressed a finger to his lips to stay silent. He leaned toward me, his mouth close to my ear, and I smelled sweat and musk.

"Buy something good for yourself," he whispered. "Or keep it for when you need it."

He straightened, and I took the bill. He flexed the fingers on his swollen right hand and I felt the same movement inside me. He turned through the doorway into the darkness of the living room.

Just like that, he and I were subversives. A revolutionary cell in the center of David's fist. The largest bite of the apple so far.

The feeling was potent, dizzying.

Yet, the next day, everything was the same. Flush with Ruger's cash, David sat at the kitchen table with his notebook and a chewed pen, writing poetry. Ruger slept until noon and didn't glance at me when he woke. As he showered, I wondered about his body, and watched him settle stiffly into the living room armchair. He chose between his only two books, a Brothers Grimm collection of fairy tales and a children's encyclopedia of folklore heroes. Soon Johnny Appleseed, Joe Magarac and Paul Bunyan had his attention.

Confused, I retreated into the bedroom and checked behind the lining of my purse for Ruger's hundred-dollar bill. It was still there.

Sitting on the bed, I wondered what had happened to me. I'd arrived in the city and climbed off the bus, still anger-blind at my mother and uncle. Standing in the waiting room, wondering what to do, David had sidled up, an easy smile on his face, and offered to buy me breakfast. Hungry, I accepted. At a nearby diner, Ruger's bulk opposite me, David asked if I could help them.

A perfect lightning strike.

As he'd said the words, I realized how desperately I wanted to be part of something, to feel needed. And as I ate those syrup-soaked pancakes, another thought came to me. I saw that—through them—if I played it right, in a few years I could go home with money in my pocket, confident. Tell my uncle and his wandering hands—and my mother who pretended not to notice—that I was better than them. How my father's death had actually made me stronger.

Now, eighteen months later, all I had was a one-hundred-dollar bill given to me in secret, by a man who thrilled and scared me at the same time.

I've forgotten what I did for the remainder of that day, or the rest of that week. I just remember feeling pared down, laid bare to the core.

The following week, as if David sensed my thinking, he began to say we needed new ways to make money. The poker tables were closed to him now, following a lucky escape after someone caught him cheating. But I knew there was more to it. He wanted a larger place to live, to eat in restaurants. That was David, I decided, the poet of greed.

A day or two later, David said we needed a badger game. I told him no. I don't remember who said what, but a vicious argument followed, only ending when David slammed the door on his way out of the apartment.

He returned two hours later, all sugar and honey. From shopping bags, he offered me skirts and tops. When he presented me with a gold necklace, I fell for it. I was blinded by his apologies, too young to know they often hid a straight razor.

That evening, feeling exposed in a new scoop-neck top, I perched on one of the stools in a Madison Avenue hotel bar. I knew the clothing David bought wasn't right. We chose upscale bars where men expected thoughtful, well-turned women, not trashy shows of cleavage. I was right. For half the night I nursed a single drink, and wasn't approached by anyone. It was nearly eleven before two men arrived, flushed and loud, and the paunchiest of the two spotted me. A few minutes later he lurched over. He had twenty years on me, but liquor has a way of making men believe age differences don't matter.

I played along, drank what he bought me, and avoided the concerned glances of the bartender. It was almost too easy.

I suggested my room.

What happened next blurs. I remember undressing him, his shirt off, his swollen stomach white as a fish belly. He pawed me, his hands down the front of my scoop-neck. I willed the door to crash open, for David and Ruger, but nothing. A hard push and I was on my back on the bed. The man's hot breath in my face, his weight crushing me. I rose out of myself, disappeared.

Ruger's voice brought me back. He kept saying my name. "Kelly. Kelly."

He came into focus, leaning over me. "Kelly." His eyes searched my face. "Get dressed. Can you get dressed?"

I looked about. The man from the bar was on all fours, his pants around his ankles, blood dripping from his face onto the carpet. I tried to speak and nothing came.

Ruger straightened. "We have to go." He gently pulled my top down from around my neck. I straightened my skirt and struggled upright, numb. Ruger circled the room, grabbing my things. I tried to stand but my legs quivered and I sagged back onto the bed.

"That's everything," Ruger said. The next moment his arms were under my shoulders and knees. He lifted me and held me to his chest, my strap sandals swinging from his teeth. We hurried down the hallway. In the elevator he lowered me to my feet and handed me the sandals. I wavered, caught my balance.

"Where were you?" The words came out in a strangle. I

slugged him on the chest as hard as I could. "Where were you?" A scream, this time, and I hit him again. Tears rushed down my cheeks.

He stood unmoved. He didn't try to avoid the punches.

When I calmed, he pulled out the bottom of his t-shirt and offered it as a towel. I rubbed it into my face.

"Where were you?" I panted, pulling away from him.

The doors opened and Ruger took my arm. We stopped halfway across the lobby so I could put on my sandals. It was then he said, "David told me he would handle it." I rose and followed him through the revolving door onto the street. The air and city hum slapped me in the face. I stopped and turned to him. Waited.

"I was at the apartment," Ruger mumbled. "I thought it was taking too long. I came here and saw you go upstairs with the guy. David was walking out. I stopped him, made him give me the key."

"He left me?" I wiped at my face, anger blossoming inside me. "How could he do that? Do you know what happened to me?"

He wouldn't meet my gaze.

We stood on the sidewalk, people sweeping around us. I gathered myself. This was David's revenge for our fight. I knew it. "I'm sorry, Ruger." I touched his chest. "Thank you."

He shrugged. "Where do you want to go?"

And there it was. I had nowhere I *could* go. My one hundred dollars was at our apartment, and it wouldn't last me two days. I touched my neck. My gold chain was missing. "To the apartment," I said softly.

I had no choice.

Ruger turned. I walked beside him, my anger strangled by frustration. At my circumstances. At myself.

David was passed out drunk when we got back. I stood in the semi-darkness of the bedroom staring at him, hating him, before taking a long shower. I took the blanket from his bed and slept on the couch.

The next morning, I stayed in the living room. Near noon, David leaned against the kitchen doorway and looked right at me.

"Where's the money from last night?" A half smile lurked on his face.

"Screw you," I said.

Ruger was on his knees on his workout mat, doing a side-to-side twisting motion while holding forty pounds of weights. Without missing a twist, he said "There isn't any. Hard enough to get her out."

David watched Ruger's back and forth motion. "Yeah, that's my point. That's why you guys need me. People can't pull their weight, I have to fix it." To Ruger, he added, "When you're done. I have an idea. Real money. Not this piddling shit we've been doing."

Ruger swung the weight one more time and lowered it to the mat. He was breathing hard, a vein pulsing in his bull neck. I wanted to place my hand on it, to calm him.

"I'm listening." Ruger stared at him.

David glanced at me and turned into the kitchen. Ruger rose, wiping his head with a small towel, and followed him.

They said little to me over the next few days. Ruger disappeared each afternoon and conferred with David at the kitchen table when he returned. My anger seethed. I was still sleeping on the couch and David seemed unconcerned about it, which angered me more.

It was a Friday night, I remember, and Ruger and David were at the kitchen table. David called into the living room and asked me join them.

I sat down, my knees together, taking up as little of the chair as I could. "Here's the plan," David said. "You know GuardDog, right? The band?"

I didn't want to nod, but I did.

"Okay. They have this thing about ticket brokers. They say ticketing companies rip off fans by selling tickets to corporations and scalpers, that kind of thing, right?" David didn't wait for my reaction, he just kept talking. "They're trying this new thing. Their show tomorrow night, tickets are only sold at the gate, cash, seventy-five dollars each. No pre-purchases. They're saying it's for their fans."

"It's at the park coliseum," Ruger added. He watched me closely. "Seats three thousand. I've been checking it out. One building sells the tickets. Couple of ways in and out."

"Two hundred and twenty-five thousand dollars. Cash." David wore the same look that used to come over him when he saw me naked. I hadn't seen it in months.

"We won't get that," Ruger said quickly. "They'll be moving money into a safe as it stacks up. A bit of luck, maybe one-hundred and fifty thousand."

I was interested, now. Not in the money, but how we would

do it. "But they'll have guards. Cameras."

Ruger nodded. He seemed pleased at my question. "Yeah. That's why we need you. The electrical comes into the building in conduit down the back. Cut that and the cameras and alarms go out, we hop the cashier windows and take the money." He took out his phone and showed me a photo of the back of the building, the line of conduit a silver ribbon. "I'm going back tonight," Ruger said. "I'll put cuts in the conduit here, all you need to do is open it up and snip the wires."

I realized, slowly, that David had come up with the idea, but the detailed planning belonged to Ruger. "Will I get shocked?"

"Don't worry about it," David said quickly.

"I'll insulate your wire cutters." Ruger said gently. "Just don't touch any of the wires once you're done."

I thought I saw the trace of a smile on his lips, as if he liked how engaged I was. The conversation then turned to escaping after the robbery. Today, I don't remember those details. What I can't forget is this: at midnight Ruger left to make his cuts. And David, who had been drinking for most of the night, collapsed next to me on the couch and reached for me.

I told him I wasn't interested.

He threw up his hands, slurring something about my body, lurched upright and staggered into the bedroom. He slept until noon the next day. An hour after picking at breakfast, he started on me, needling. He remembered the night before. He wasn't going to let me forget it.

It started slowly enough, but within an hour we were shouting at one another. I couldn't control my rage. Again and again I accused him of leaving me in the hotel room. He blamed me for disagreeing with him earlier that same day.

At three o'clock, sick of the noise, Ruger slipped out. I have no idea where he went. David and I kept at it for another forty-five minutes, until David disappeared into the bedroom. He came back carrying something and raised his arm. A small revolver. I scuttled backwards, my calves hitting the couch. I sat heavily. He pressed the barrel into my forehead.

I couldn't breathe.

"Shut up," he hissed, his face flushed, eyes burning. "You do what I say, or after tonight I'll put a goddamned bullet in your brain."

I couldn't speak. I didn't even know he owned a gun.

He lifted the barrel from my forehead. "And when I tell you it's time for bed. You go to bed." He dropped his arm.

I didn't say a word after that, I just seethed. When Ruger returned he looked from me to David and back again, but didn't say anything.

We rode the subway to the concert in silence. I sat as far from David as I could, but my gaze kept wandering back to him in anger.

I wanted to hurt him. Physically hurt him. I'd never felt anything like it before.

When we arrived, David and Ruger joined the line to the ticket window. I walked to a cluster of women next to the ticket building, near the flow of people into the building and out a side door into the amphitheater. I was in a bubble, everyone's laughter and friendliness washing over me. The wire cutters in my back pocket were a dead weight.

David and Ruger came into view, and when I saw David my hands shook with anger. Just before they stepped into the building, he phoned me.

"Cut the line" he hissed. "Screw it up and you can find somewhere else to sleep."

I stepped behind the building and found Ruger's 'x' cut in the conduit exactly where he promised it would be. Using the wire cutters, I grabbed the point of the triangle where the cuts crossed. I lifted and peeled back. Inside was a thick grey wire and two thin ones. I breathed to steady my hands, nudged the wire cutter around the thickest one and squeezed. Snip. I cut the others lower down and rejoined the crowd, David's words ringing in my ears.

Fifteen yards away, two police officers sauntered along the line, keeping order.

I don't know why I did it. I was so glazed with anger I couldn't think straight. I wanted to make David pay. When I reached the cops, the younger one glanced down my shirt. I looked right at the older one. "Someone's robbing the ticket office. Right now."

He blinked, his brown eyes sharp. "How do you know?"

"I saw them, one has a gun."

He reached for the radio mike on his shoulder and said something like 'Security check,' adding a string of numbers. No one answered. He slapped the younger man on the shoulder and started for the ticket office, talking urgently into his mike. I faded along the path, stopping at the top of a rise.

The two police officers positioned themselves outside the ticket office doors. Two other cops hurried past me. David forced his way out of the doors, revolver in hand, Ruger on his heels. The police officers raised their weapons, shouting. David stumbled back and dropped his gun like he'd been burned. Ruger shifted to his left, the small knapsack he'd brought to hold the money in his right hand. David sank to his knees, arms raised. Ruger stared at the officers.

I thought I was going to vomit. Ruger. I'd been so focused on David I hadn't thought about Ruger.

The two cops who passed me reached Ruger. One pointed a blunt-looking weapon at him, shouting. Something flashed in the air. Ruger started shaking and dropped the bag. He grabbed at his chest and pulled. Another officer fired a similar weapon and Ruger shook harder. He sank to his knees.

Tears streaming from my eyes, I turned and ran.

I reached our apartment an hour later and found David's strongbox. I stood it lock side up on Ruger's workout mat, grabbed one of his free weights and slammed it down on the lock. The box sprang open and five hundred dollars scattered across the mat. I added it to the one hundred dollars Ruger had given me, threw clothes into a knapsack and took the subway to the train station. I bought a ticket on the first train leaving the state.

Forty minutes later, moving into twilight, I was on my way to Miami.

*****

If knowledge is the curse that sets us free, then freedom is cursed by knowledge.

I sat up the entire night. I had come to believe, I realized, that no one could bring Ruger to his knees. But I had done it, through my blind anger at David.

Ruger had saved me, and I had betrayed him. I hated myself for it. I'd eaten the apple down to the core and had nowhere to put the seeds.

I knew David would come for revenge, and I guessed Ruger would too. David would bring a gun, but Ruger scared me more. I knew what Ruger could do with his hands, what it would mean for my body and face.

From Miami I kept moving south. I slept in a cheap motel and ate next to nothing for two days. I wandered, trying to decide what to do. Somehow, I ended up on a road to a state park on Biscayne Bay. Near the entrance I passed a restaurant and marina. A small sign on the door advertised for a waitress.

Inside, I sat on a barstool and asked the bartender about the job. He brought over the owner, a deeply tanned man in his fifties with skin cancer scars on his bald head.

He looked me up and down. "Experience?"

The only waitress, a hefty, plodding woman in her mid-forties, passed on her way to a table of sunburned young men. I shifted sideways, something I'd learned running the badger game, and gave him a look at my profile. From the corner of my eye I saw him look at my chest, then follow my line of sight to the waitress. When I was sure the comparison was made, I turned back to him.

"None. But I can learn. And I would be good with tables like that." I nodded at the young men.

"Hell," he said after a moment. "As long as you hustle you should be fine. Ellie can show you what to do. I'll give you a two-day trial. It's three dollars an hour plus tips, and one free meal per shift."

Three days later I was full time lunch and dinner, six days a week.

Ellie let me stay on her couch for a few days, until Mike, the owner, mentioned he had an efficiency apartment available above the restaurant.

I took it.

And just like that, five years disappeared. I didn't mind. Mike was easy-going and lived to run his restaurant. He'd sneak glances at my chest sometimes, but kept his hands to himself. Ellie was raising a young boy on her own. We got along, and in time she stopped asking why I didn't have a boyfriend. I bought a cheap second-hand car and filled a large coffee can with my tips, and then a second.

When the tension of waiting for Ruger or David to show up weighed too much, I picked out a customer and asked him the name of his boat. After work I would cross to the marina, find the boat and suggest a nightcap.

I learned that David's lovemaking had been limited, and that some men took more time with women than for themselves. But I knew what I was doing. These men spent their day soaked in sun and their evening drenched in beer. It muted their instincts and smudged their responses. Softened them. It gave me a measure of control, and somehow, at that time, I needed that. It also reminded me that nothing we did was real.

The only real thing was the revenge I had coming.

It came sooner than expected, but can you really prepare for it?

The Wait

I remember a cloudless night and a full moon, the whisper of surf from Biscayne Bay. I woke at some point and stared through the open window. Something felt off in the room, a displacement of the air, somehow. I sat up and pressed my back to the wall.

My eyes adjusted to the dark. My efficiency was small, just a twin bed and a bistro table and two chairs near the kitchen. I saw a black mass in one of the two chairs, and my breath left me. Something moved, an arm, and the dim light above the stove clicked on.

"Ruger," I managed to say.

"Kelly," he replied, tightly.

He was as big as I remembered. His eyes looked deeper set and there were more lines on his face, but that might have been the low light. Neither of us spoke. The surf was god's breath being drawn and released.

"I knew you'd find me," I said, finally. Despite the warmth of the night I was chilled through. I pulled my legs to my chest and wrapped my arms around them. "I've been waiting."

"You got a Florida driver's license. Has this address on it."

I nodded. "I needed to buy a car."

He shifted on the chair. "Back when I was fighting, I went a few rounds with this cop. He's a private investigator now. When I got out, I went to see him. He found you before we finished talking about the old days. Didn't even charge me."

I tried to calm the quiver in me. "I'm sorry, Ruger. I never meant to hurt you. I was just so mad at David. I wanted to hurt him. I forgot I was doing it to you as well."

He didn't say anything for so long I started to sweat, despite how cold I felt.

"Yeah," he said finally. "Something like that."

I desperately wanted to change the subject. "Are you out for good?"

"A year ago, but I couldn't leave the state." He looked around the apartment. "I can now."

"Is David free? I don't want to ever see him again. But if he's free he'll want to find me. I mean if you can find me…"

He brought his dark eyes back to me. "He and jail didn't get along. He got in a lot of fights, by that I mean he got beat up a lot. About a year ago he tried to shiv someone, but the guy took it away and cut his throat."

I couldn't breathe. "He's dead?"

"Yeah. I found out from our mother."

I was confused, and it must have shown. "Foster mother," he supplied. "That's how David and I met. We fostered together in high school. Then went to the city."

I was stunned. I had never asked how they met, what made them stick together. "I didn't know. I'm sorry," I said slowly. "I thought you guys were just friends."

"Closest thing to a brother I ever had." As he rose from the chair that statement sank through me like an icicle. In the shadows he loomed larger than I remembered. My mouth tasted like I had crushed an apple seed in my teeth: it was the bitterness of fear. He took a step toward me.

"How did you get in here?" I heard desperation in my voice. Anything to delay him.

He stopped. "I've been watching the place for a couple of

days. Wasn't hard. I read everything I could in the jail library. Even books on locksmithing. Funny, huh? Teaching crooks how to pick a lock." His smile was grim.

I was gripping my legs so tightly my knees hurt and arms ached. He took another step and blotted out the moon. I closed my eyes. "Just do it," I whispered. "I deserve it. I know that."

Silence, even the surf seemed to have stopped. I waited for the jarring thump, the electricity of pain. Nothing. I opened my eyes.

He gazed at me, concentrating, a light frown on his face.

"I sent you to jail," I managed to whisper. "I've been waiting."

"What did you think I was going to do?" He gently reached out and hooked a strand of my hair behind my ear. "I came to tell you I'm going to the islands. St. John. Start a business."

I couldn't process the words. "I thought you came to get even." The words caught in my throat.

He sat on the edge of the bed, searching my eyes. "I would never hurt you."

"But I put you in jail."

"Yeah, but that's on me." He looked through the window, the moonlight bathing his face. "I made a deal. That night when David left you in the hotel? I told him if he ever touched you again, I would break him. Told him I was leaving. But he brought up the robbery, played every card he could about how we were brothers. How we'd always looked out for each other. And I needed money, because I wanted to ask you to go with me. So I agreed."

Something released in me, five years of it, and tears streamed down my face. My arms felt rubbery. I slid my legs out in front of me and stared at his face, the large bones under his cheeks. I saw his neck, and wanted to touch it. "All this time," I said slowly, "I've been waiting for you or David to show up. Take it out on me."

"No," he said gently. "Like I said, I had a lot of time to think. I decided…you know that Johnny Appleseed story? How he crossed the country planting apple trees? Thousands of them? I decided he had it wrong. Me, I just want to plant maybe two or three. And then watch 'em like crazy. Take care of them. Make sure they grow strong. Be there. That's the one thing I didn't have when I was growing up. I took every class I could take in jail. Got a chef's certification, been cooking since I got out. Now I'm going to the islands. Find a place of my own. Just breakfast and lunch. Put those seeds in the ground." He looked at me, and the moonlight was silver on his face. "I was hoping maybe in a year you might want to come down. See what I'm doing. Hang out or something."

"No," I whispered. A laugh welled up in me. I got to my knees, facing him. "I'm not waiting a year. I'm going with you now." I put a hand on each side of his neck.

His warmth shot down my arms into my chest, and I kissed him.

Ariadne's Skein of Thread
Michael Anthony Dioguardi

From: Skein of Thread
[skeinofthreadariadne@protonicmail.com]
To: Dionysus [godofwine@protonicmail.com]
Date: July 18, 2019, 8:39 PM
Subject: Encryption guarantee

You're the second-best alternative. I need reliability. I need guaranteed digital encryption and minimal competition. We want what's best for both of us, right?

Your initial concern about the quality of my product is unfounded. That customer complaint about bunk blotter tabs? It's bullshit. There are only six guys in the world that are manufacturing right now and I know one of them. That customer is trying to wrangle back his money. If this was SR, I'd hire someone to scare him straight, but I know you want to keep this place clean.

Olympus? That's a good one—selling the divine. Let me know what your thoughts are on my proposal. No suspicious packages, no duds. Just pure, clean tears and cubensis. Maybe later I'll branch out.

Ariadne's Skein of Thread

From: Dionysus [godofwine@protonicmail.com]

To: Skein of Thread

[Skeinofthreadariadne@protonicmail.com]

Date: July 20, 2019, 11:35 PM

Subject: RE: Encryption guarantee

I've told you several times now. This is a closed circuit. The likelihood of anybody unearthing these conversations is insanely low.

Clean is the idea. I want to avoid the mistakes that SR made, with the intention being to keep Mt. Olympus up and running for as long as possible.

It's just me over here—no one else. And I'm sorry, I'll have to open up to competition. If there's a problem with your product, the site will need an alternative. But that won't be an issue with you. Like you said, you'd hire a *cleaner* under normal circumstances, and that's enough evidence for me to turn you away. So, you want to sell? You want to make money? Let's lay off the threats.

From: Ralmuto [ralmuto@protonicmail.com]

To: Dionysus [godofwine@protonicmail.com]

Date: July 30, 2019, 8:49 AM

Subject: Lebanese Blonde Shipment

The Amazon boxes worked. This is starting to look pretty good. I just transferred over ฿ .12. Let me know if everything checks out on your end.

In the meantime, I recently established a birria connect. I

know in our initial correspondences you were apprehensive regarding opioids, but they're in demand. If not Mt. Olympus, then who? If you become the most trusted vendor, then we'd both have a large slice of the pie.

I'm telling you though—I'm already starting to see it— you're adding new vendors daily; it's a bad idea. We don't step on each other's toes in the business. I've been running since you were shitting yourself. Be careful who you associate with. I've given you results. Happy customers—and more importantly—returning customers. Don't fuck this up. I can tell you're just some kid. Programming ain't dealing. You want this birria. Folks want it. Be smart.

Regards,

Ralmuto

From: Skein of Thread [Skeinofthreadariadne@protonicmail.com]

To: Dionysus [godofwine@protonicmail.com]

Date: Aug. 2, 2019, 5:46 PM

Subject: RE: Encryption guarantee

Attachment: image 0238.jpg

I tried your Amazon box idea and it still got picked up by USPS. See attached. The recipient got this slip in his PO box. You're running a real house of cards here.

From: Gotlieb [jgotlieb_49@protonicmail.com]

To: Dionysus [godofwine@protonicmail.com]

Date: Aug. 15, 2019, 9:01 PM

Subject: First shipment

I'll be good by Monday. Put up my posting. Pleasure doing business with you.

From: Dionysus [godofwine@protonicmail.com]

To: Gotlieb [jgotlieb_49@protonicmail.com]

Date: Aug. 15, 2019, 10:30 PM

Subject: RE: First shipment

Good news. Let me know how it goes.

From: Dionysus [godofwine@protonicmail.com]

To: Skein of Thread

[Skeinofthreadariadne@protonicmail.com]

Date: Aug. 15, 2019, 10:49 PM

Subject: RE: Encryption guarantee

Post problems are on you. I provide the platform—nothing else. If you can't make it happen then I'm sorry but there are plenty of other people lined up waiting to have their postings made public. Get your shit together.

From: Dionysus [godofwine@protonicmail.com]

To: Ralmuto [ralmuto@protonicmail.com]

Date: Aug. 28, 2019, 7:46 AM

Subject: RE: Lebanese Blonde Shipment

Your tough talk has no effect on how I run Mt. Olympus. If you're looking for a better cut, or you'd like to comment on how I run my business, you might as well find another place.

We'll go ahead with the birria and whatever other narcotics you feel comfortable shipping internationally. I'm starting to realize that they are in demand, like you mentioned.

When you're ready to move your shipment, send me an email.

From: Dionysus [godofwine@protonicmail.com]

To: Cheryl Pitcher [c_pitcher@geemail.com]

Date: Sept. 1, 2019, 9:45 AM

Subject: Online mental health check in

Hi Cheryl,

My name is James. I'm reaching out to you because I saw you do online consultation. I'd like to begin an email correspondence with you as that looked appealing on your website. I need help. I'm working a stressful job right now and I need somebody to talk to.

I look forward to hearing back from you.

Thanks,

James

From: Skein of Thread [Skeinofthreadariadne@protonicmail.com]

To: Dionysus [godofwine@protonicmail.com]

Date: Sept. 2, 2019, 11:28 PM

Subject: Success

Dionysus! The eagle has landed! I've had over 30 orders in

the last 24 hours!

From: Dionysus [godofwine@protonicmail.com]

To: Skein of Thread

[Skeinofthreadariadne @protonicmail.com]

Date: Sept. 2, 2019, 11:31 PM

Subject: RE: Success

That's what I like to hear. Now, if you have any issues, I'd advise that you contact me as a last resort. Basically, less contact=less paper trail.

From: Gotlieb [jgotlieb_49@protonicmail.com]

To: Dionysus [godofwine@protonicmail.com]

Date: Sept. 4, 2019, 2:41 AM

Subject: RE: First shipment

Something happened in Toronto. There's going to be a delay. I'm on it.

From: Skein of Thread

[Skeinofthreadariadne@protonicmail.com]

To: Dionysus [godofwine@protonicmail.com]

Date: Sept. 4, 2019, 3:08 AM

Subject: Delay

Hate to break your rule so early, but my connect just hit me up saying he doesn't have anything. Stand by.

From: Cheryl Pitcher [c_pitcher@geemail.com]

To: Dionysus [godofwine@protonicmail.com]

Date: Sept. 5, 2019, 12:13 PM

Subject: RE: Online mental health check in

Hi James,

Thanks for reaching out! We can start right away. Have you ever been to therapy before? What do you do for a living? Do you live with family?

Just some questions to get us started off. One last thing, do you have an insurance card you can fax me?

Sincerely,

Dr. Cheryl Pitcher

From: Dionysus [godofwine@protonicmail.com]

To: Skein of Thread
[Skeinofthreadariadne@protonicmail.com]

Date: Sept. 9, 2019, 11:34 PM

Subject: RE: Delay

That's all right. No rush. I have to take the site down probably this weekend for maintenance. It's already exceeded the initial bandwidth and it's starting to get all wonky.

Also, I'm using my own personal server (for obvious security reasons), so that doesn't help either. I hope this doesn't affect your livelihood.

From: Dionysus [godofwine@protonicmail.com]

To: Gotlieb [jgotlieb_49@protonicmail.com]

Date: Sept. 12, 2019, 4:31 PM

Subject: RE: First shipment

Any word on that delay?

From: Dionysus [godofwine@protonicmail.com]

To: Cheryl Pitcher [c_pitcher@geemail.com]

Date: Sept. 14, 2019, 6:38 PM

Subject: RE: Online mental health check in

Hi Cheryl,

No insurance unfortunately, my employer doesn't exactly provide anything. Never been to therapy before—never thought I'd need it. I guess I'm just feeling scared. I graduated college last spring. I have a coding degree and I'm freelancing at the moment, but I still find it super stressful.

I shiver sometimes I get so anxious. I sit all day in front of the screen and just hope everything turns out ok.

James

From: Ralmuto [ralmuto@protonicmail.com]

To: Dionysus [godofwine@protonicmail.com]

Date: Sept. 15, 2019, 4:30 AM

Subject: RE: Lebanese Blonde Shipment

Attachments: image_02398.jpg,   image_02399, image_02400

Take a good hard look at those pictures.

Not only are my associates dead, but they were fucking dismembered. Bite marks and everything. I've never seen anything like this. Intestines ripped out. And you know what was spelled with their own fucking blood?

Olympus…

I'm out, it's over.

From: Skein of Thread [Skeinofthreadariadne@protonicmail.com]

To: Dionysus [godofwine@protonicmail.com]

Date: Sept. 15, 2019, 4:35 AM

Subject: RE: Delay

Hey! Everything's good. Just checked in with my connect. Should have my next few batches here before the end of this week.

I'm sorry too, for coming on strong. I realize you're probably just some nerd (no offense). And this is your risqué pet project. Sometimes I don't even know why I'm into this stuff either. I'm probably the only drug-slinging girl in the whole state.

From: Gotlieb [jgotlieb_49@protonicmail.com]

To: Dionysus [godofwine@protonicmail.com]

Date: Sept. 17, 2019, 6:23 PM

Subject: RE: First shipment

We're rolling again. Something went down. I'm not sure what though. Regardless, the shipment is here and I'd like to add a couple of items to your posting:

- 1. Oz. White Rhino ฿3.92
- ICE / 1 Point (0.1G) ฿2.33
- 50x MDMA / 1gr pure ฿2.12

More to come. Thanks.

From: Dionysus [godofwine@protonicmail.com]

To: Ralmuto [ralmuto@protonicmail.com]

Date: Sept. 19, 2019, 7:30 PM

Subject: RE: Lebanese Blonde Shipment

Attachments: image_02398.jpg, image_02399, image_02400

Destroy everything. Whatever device you took those photos on, your hard drives, anything that has any evidence at all on it. I can't have this trace back to me. I want no involvement. Before you go, just reply so I know we're on the same page.

From: Dionysus [godofwine@protonicmail.com]

To: Skein of Thread
[Skeinofthreadariadne@protonicmail.com]

Date: Sept. 21, 2019, 8:59 PM

Subject: RE: Delay

It's been a wild ride this week. Not sure if the site will be up for much longer. Not sure I want to even keep it up at this point.

On a side note, with consideration for online anonymity, I have my doubts that anything you are saying is actually true. You know how it goes: there's no such thing as a girl on the Internet ☺

From Cheryl Pitcher [c_pitcher@geemail.com]

To: Dionysus [godofwine@protonicmail.com]

Date: Sept 24, 2019, 9:05 PM

Subject: RE: Online mental health check in

Hi James,

I understand how you feel. Sometimes stress can just get to us. But it's also up to us to know where our stress comes from, so we can isolate it and manage ourselves effectively. Anxiety is self-made, but influenced by external factors. My job here is to equip you with a pathway toward your own self-fulfillment, but only you can travel down that path. In other words, *you are responsible for you.*

Have you looked into other career paths that may be less stressful? This may be a beneficial exercise for your long-term mental health. A lot of folks are rejecting the 9-to-5 behind-a-screen life, you know?

Dr. Pitcher

From: Dionysus [godofwine@protonicmail.com]

To: Gotlieb [jgotlieb_49@protonicmail.com]

Date: Sept. 30, 2019, 5:56 PM

Subject: RE: First shipment

That's an impressive selection you have there. Looks like you've opened up quite a bit. One of my other vendors just pulled out so you're the man for now.

From: Hera [wifeofgods@protonicmail.com]

To: Dionysus [godofwine@protonicmail.com]

Date: Oct. 4, 2019, 6:34 AM

Subject: none

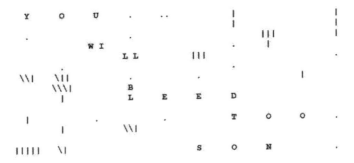

From: Dionysus [godofwine@protonicmail.com]

To: Cheryl Pitcher [c_pitcher@geemail.com]

Date: Oct, 7, 2019, 2:14 AM

Subject: RE: Online mental health check in

Hi Cheryl,

I'm really feeling isolated. Everything just got worse this week. I feel like I'm on the verge of breaking, but so many people are relying on me. If I told you the amount of moving parts there were in my profession, you'd call me liar. I know it sounds crazy, but the nature of what I do puts people's lives on the line and I think I may have indirectly caused the death of one of my clients. I don't know what to do. I don't know where to turn. Please help.

Sincerely,

James

From Cheryl Pitcher [c_pitcher@geemail.com]

To: Dionysus [godofwine@protonicmail.com]

Date: Oct, 9, 2019, 8:34 AM

Subject: RE: Online mental health check in

James,

It sounds like you're under a lot of stress. I'd like you to take a breath and try to find some inner calm. If you are feeling like you may harm yourself or others, I ask that you call 1-800-SUICIDE as an immediate resource.

I think I can help you, but our consultations would then move beyond a standard check-in and I would need to start billing you.

I know you mentioned you didn't have an insurance card, and my rates are not exactly cheap. I'm willing to work out a payment plan with you. To get that started, you will need to provide your residential address so I can get started on a file and generate a quote.

Look over the quote and see if it can work for you. The next step would be an assessment, which is best done in-person due to its intimate nature. While the information you've provided to me has been eye-opening and deeply personal, it is not sufficient to provide a proper diagnosis.

But to keep the ball rolling, can you go into more depth about what you do? I don't know much about programming; I don't know how you would be responsible for another's death.

If at any time you'd like to text or call, please reach out to work phone with any questions: 917-555-7148.

Sincerely,

Dr. Pitcher

From: Skein of Thread

[Skeinofthreadariadne@protonicmail.com]

To: Dionysus [godofwine@protonicmail.com]

Date: Oct. 12, 2019, 7:23 PM

Subject: RE: Delay

Attachment: image_9087.jpg

Pics or shens? I feel like I'm posting on a forum. I actually studied programming, in addition to my, uh, "day job." If you're even looking for a second in command so-to-speak, I think I'd make a competent counterpart. So, do I get to see what the mysterious god of wine looks like? I'm imagining a scrawny, scraggly ghost boy who lives off Monsters and Cheetos ☺

From: Hera [wifeofgods@protonicmail.com]

To: Dionysus [godofwine@protonicmail.com]

Date: Oct, 19, 2019, 5:00 PM

Subject: none

James,

You were easy to find. Apparently my first message wasn't enough. How about a little visit soon? If you thought what I did to Ralmuto's guys was bad, just wait and find out what I'm going to do with you...

From: Dionysus [godofwine@protonicmail.com]

To: Gotlieb [jgotlieb_49@protonicmail.com]

Date: Oct, 23, 2019 7:08 PM

Subject: Favor

I need a favor. Let's talk services here. I mean, beyond the standard rocks and pills you're shipping all over the place, what else can you offer?

I'll make this short, so I don't waste your time. I need someone to be taken care of. I'm being threatened. And if I'm being threatened, Mt. Olympus is too. That's your livelihood.

I don't care about how it gets done. I'll figure out where they are and give you and your people solid intel. What's your price?

From: Dionysus [godofwine@protonicmail.com]

To: Skein of Thread

[Skeinofthreadariadne@protonicmail.com]

Date: Oct. 24, 2019, 8:04 PM

Subject: RE: Delay

Attachment: image_1478.jpg, image_1479.jpg

You nailed it to an extent. Sometimes I wish I wasn't so damn tall, but for the most part it's been my positive aspect of my life.

For the record, this felt weird in the beginning, like talking this way with one of my clients. But it feels natural with you all of a sudden. Shit's been getting real on my end, and it's nice to have someone actually be nice to me for a change!

If things keep going the way they're going with Mt. Olympus I might need to hire some help. I was planning on just grabbing someone local. Like a dweeb who I know would keep his mouth shut, but a remote programmer? I'd have to think about that one.

From: Dionysus [godofwine@protonicmail.com]

To: Cheryl Pitcher [c_pitcher@geemail.com]

Date: Oct. 24, 2019 6:58 PM

Subject: RE: Online mental health check in

Hi Dr. Pitcher,

Thanks for being so supportive. I've been getting some harassing emails as of late. Some sickos out there are just into scaring folks, I guess. But I'm getting by – I think I might've found a solution to my current problems, but we'll have to wait and see.

As per my address, I live in my parent's basement. (I know, how typical?)

1316 E. 89th St.

Elmhurst Park, NJ

11758-13850

Like I mentioned in our prior correspondences, I don't have any insurance because I am self-employed. I could ask my parents if they're willing to cover me, but then they'd be suspicious as to why I'm reaching out to mental health professional. So, I'd rather keep this under control and pay out-of-pocket.

You asked about what I do. Well, it's hard to describe, but I essentially run an online retailer that sells everything. And sometimes the nature of a product requires special attention and covert confidentiality. There are instances in which I can't guarantee what my clients are looking for, and the consequences can get violent.

I'm thinking about hiring an assistant soon to take some of the load off my shoulders. But, again, that too is up in the air.

In general, this week was an overall improvement from last week. I'm feeling a little better, and I think I might have even met a potential girlfriend. I've started emailing someone back and forth and they seem nice. Will keep you posted. I look forward to hearing back from you again.

Thanks,

James

From: Gotlieb [jgotlieb_49@protonicmail.com]

To: Dionysus [godofwine@protonicmail.com]

Date: Oct. 30, 2019, 3:42 PM

Subject: RE: Favor

All right, here's the deal. $15,000 up front, and $15,000 once we're done. I don't know how much that is in ₿, but that's what I'd charge someone in person. Most folks turn around at that price. There's no negotiating; we do a clean job.

I need a name if you got one, but the best thing would be a workplace or home address. Also, one more thing—if you can—make it a listing. SR used to offer it and folks would avoid them, the feds don't keep up with our terminology. Any *decorator* worth his salt knows how to distinguish himself from the federal honey bucket. With your blessing, it'll be up and you'll receive your cut as well each time the service is used.

From: Skein of Thread

[Skeinofthreadariadne@protonicmail.com]

To: Dionysus [godofwine@protonicmail.com]

Date: Nov. 3, 2019, 5:46 PM

Subject: RE: Delay

Attachments: image_9254.jpg,   image_9255.jpg, image_9256.jpg

More pics! ☺

Hope you're having better days. I see you added *gun for hire* to Mt. Olympus. Had a change of heart? You're starting to look a lot like the early 2000s Tor portal sites. Now you're deep in the shitter. I might have to rescind my job application to the *Mount.*

Idle question: Have you ever tried any psychedelics? I have to stop myself sometimes from blowing through my whole stash!

Be careful, my little god of wine 😊

From: Dionysus [godofwine@protonicmail.com]

To: Gotlieb [jgotlieb_49@protonicmail.com]

Date: Nov. 5, 2019 7:08 PM

Subject: RE: Favor

Attachment: image_7897.jpg

Done. I just transferred over 1.49 ₿. I managed to get through protonicmail's security. I geolocated the IP to a bunch of warehouses outside Jersey City. It's on the water. The image I attached has the Google Maps coordinates. They're abandoned, so you'll have to follow the wires.

From: Gotlieb [jgotlieb_49@protonicmail.com]

To: Dionysus [godofwine@protonicmail.com]

Date: Nov. 7, 2019 9:09 PM

Subject: RE: Favor

I need a name and a location.

From: Dionysus [godofwine@protonicmail.com]

To: Gotlieb [jgotlieb_49@protonicmail.com]

Date: Nov. 8, 2019, 10:15 PM

Subject: RE: Favor

1.5 ฿ transferred your way. I'm serious about this. It's the best I can do. I expect to hear back from you soon.

From Cheryl Pitcher [c_pitcher@geemail.com]

To: Dionysus [godofwine@protonicmail.com]

Date: Nov. 10, 2019, 9:27 AM

Subject: RE: Online mental health check in

Hi James,

I'm happy to hear you're staying positive.

If you're in a particularly stressful line of work, despite the money you may be receiving, it would be best to look for employment elsewhere. This shouldn't be difficult for a person of your skill level. Programmers are always in demand. I'm sure you can find a company to work for where you don't feel so threatened on a daily basis.

I've mailed you the quote. Are you sure you don't want to use insurance?

Regarding the potential girlfriend, finding that special someone always will always give you that spark of excitement! I hope everything works out. I'd really like to hear back from you with that same positive outlook! All things will pass, James.

From: Hera [wifeofgods@protonicmail.com]

To: Dionysus [godofwine@protonicmail.com]

Date: Nov. 12, 2019, 6:07 PM

Subject: none

You're a god, boy.

Why don't you behave like one?

Elmhurst Park...I know where that is...

From: Gotlieb [jgotlieb_49@protonicmail.com]

To: Dionysus [godofwine@protonicmail.com]

Date: Nov. 14, 2019, 6:30 PM

Subject: RE: Favor

Wire checks out. We're taking care of it tonight. Stand by.

From: Skein of Thread
[Skeinofthreadariadne@protonicmail.com]

To: Dionysus [godofwine@protonicmail.com]

Date: Nov. 14, 2019 8:02 PM

Subject: RE: Delay

Hi Mr. Dionysus! I'm going to be in your neck of the woods
tonight ☺

From: Dionysus [godofwine@protonicmail.com]

To: Skein of Thread

[Skeinofthreadariadne@protonicmail.com]

Date: Nov. 14, 2019 9:00 PM

Subject: RE: Delay

And where would that be?

From: Dionysus [godofwine@protonicmail.com]

To: Dionysus [godofwine@protonicmail.com]

Date: Nov. 15, 2019 2:30 AM

Subject: none

I am writing this because I'm scared. I don't know what will happen tonight. I thought it would be easy, that I could run this website, my Mt. Olympus and be hands off—let the clients and sellers handle their business. But I was wrong, and now I will be responsible for killing someone tonight.

I've spent more money than most people make in a year to murder another human being. Although my hands will be clean, my mind is bathed in blood.

I have to see the deed complete. It has dawned on me that perhaps this is a trap. That maybe I am the one that may be killed tonight. I worry things won't go over well; that I might die.

If I don't return, hopefully someone will find this message. If not, it'll just come off like sophomoric poetry. I was never any good at writing anyway.

I love you Mom. I love you Dad.

James

From: Hera [wifeofgods@protonicmail.com]

To: Dionysus [godofwine@protonicmail.com]

Date: Nov. 15, 2019, 2:35 AM

Subject: none

Δολοφονήστε τον μεθυσμένο

C R

E A T E

I

M B I B E

M Y   M O U N T A I N

AUTOPSY REPORT

ME NO.: 789-09

CASE TITLE: FONTANETTE, JAMES

DECEASED: NOVEMBER 15, 2019   **SEX:** M   **AGE:** 20

DATE AND HOUR OF DEATH: NOVEMBER 15, 2019, 3:30 AM

DATE AND HOUR OF AUTOPSY: NOVEMBER 15, 2019, 7:30 AM

PATHOLOGIST: DR. AITA CEBERO

FINAL DIAGNOSES:

Tracheal exsanguination

Jugular exsanguination

Carotid exsanguination

CAUSE OF DEATH

Stab wounds, skin punctures, skin removal.

I. Fontanette was found face down in a pool of his own blood.

II. "PROUD GOD" carved into the victim's back. Puncture size matches dimensions of human nails. Over 275 stab wounds across back, chest, and face. Face partially ripped off, from the victim's jawline to his clavicle.

III. Toxicology: The victim tested positive for CI-581, ketamine, 70kg. Drug was administered shortly before his death.

IV. Additional notes:

a. INTERNAL EXAMINATION: See section III

b. HEAD: The subcutaneous scalp and soft tissues are partially removed from bone—all parts recovered. The calvarium is exposed, as is the dura mater. Cerebrospinal fluid has drained from the skull. Coronal sections demonstrate effective mingling of white and grey matter, severe hemorrhaging. The ventricles are punctured, with what appears to be teeth marks.

I-768 (Rev. 3-24-20)
U.S. Department of Justice
Federal Bureau of Investigation

Clarksburg, WV 26306

Dear Director ▮▮▮▮▮▮▮▮▮▮▮▮

Enclosed you will find documents related to our progress in the "Mt. Olympus" investigation. In short, the operation has switched helms. After a brief hiatus, the site has been recovered—even expanding the bandwidth to sizes previously unseen on the *onion* network. Their inventory has expanded rapidly as well, with a surge in arms sales, prostitution, and home bomb kits. Please note bureau intelligence poses as "Dr. Cheryl Pitcher," throughout the correspondences, a social worker, to whom our subject unknowingly divulges much of his pertinent details.

Local authorities in New Jersey have confirmed that James Fontanette, "Dionysus," was the man found dead earlier this month. He owned and operated the website alone through a private server in Elmhurst Park. The DOJ has named one suspect, but the information herein is not public. The details are in the email correspondences attached to this memo, dating back to July of 2019.

Rachel Emile: known by several aliases, primarily "Skein of Thread," but also, "Hera." She used fake email addresses to obtain information from Fontanette, which ultimately lead to his murder and the consequent high-jacking of his website.

We have evidence to suspect she had planned from the beginning to use Fontanette to initially advertise her own drugs on the platform. She then managed to obtain his address and photographs.

Perhaps the most cold-blooded aspect of this whole investigation is the nature of their alleged relationship. Although not legally tenable, it would be in our best interest to look further into any other correspondences between Fontanette and Emile. At one point, Fontanette nearly viewed her as his "girlfriend." With consideration for the photos she sent, I don't doubt the feeling was mutual. Why else would she send him actual photographs of herself? An adept tracker and hunter, but a criminal—well, she has some things to learn.

Hera reunites with Dionysus. It could only happen in such a vile corner of the Internet.

Olympus stands for now.

Regards,

██████████████

Love and Divorce
Robert Petyo

Bret knew the type.

She overdid the makeup with blackened lashes that curled almost an inch away from her lids. Mascara darkened the skin under her eyes like a goth tattoo. Her dress was too tight, corseting and hefting her bosom, and the black spiked heels she wore made her strut as she walked into his office.

She was the kind of woman he dealt with professionally but always ignored personally. She was all about sexual conquests, the kind of woman no intelligent man would marry since it was obvious she wouldn't be faithful.

Yet, many men succumbed. And that's what kept Bret in business.

"Afternoon," he said, after his secretary left the office and closed the door behind her. "How can I help you?"

"Missy sent me."

Missy. In college they had dated a few times, but both moved on, he to law school, she to a bad marriage. He had represented Missy in her divorce, and it hadn't gone well for her, so he always paid when they met for dinner. He even let her do some filing in his office, and cover for Stephanie when necessary, for some extra cash. "How do you know Missy?" He gestured for her to sit.

She struggled into the chair, making no effort to stop the dress from crawling up her thighs. "We went to school together. She says you're a good lawyer."

He twitched at the bogus compliment. He knew Missy didn't think much of his lawyering talents. She blamed him for her botched divorce settlement, even though it was her own scheming and lies that the opposing lawyer had turned into a treasure chest for his client. "What can I do for you?" He would much rather represent her poor husband, but his client list was light at the moment.

She crossed her legs, hiking the dress up even more. "I want to sue Angelo Phillips, my wedding photographer."

"Oh? Why?"

"He did a terrible job with the pictures of my wedding."

"By terrible, you mean?" he prompted her.

"He didn't listen to anything I said. He did everything his way, and he botched it all. I'm the bride. He's supposed to listen to me. If I wanted a picture of my mom dancing with her ex, then he should take the picture." Her voice grew higher in pitch as she ranted until she chirped like a bird and he barely understood her. "And I know something about wedding photography."

"You do?"

She sifted through her clutch purse and leaned forward to hand him a card across the desk.

On it was a tiny black and white image of a wedding couple standing under a rainbow of words. "Daria Fellanchetto,

Wedding Visions." He held up the card. "You're a professional photographer?"

"That's right? Heard of me?"

He hadn't, but he said nothing as he slipped the card into the breast pocket of his shirt. "I'll tell you right now that a lot of people are unhappy with the pictures their photographer takes. Just as a lot of people are disappointed with any kind of work they've contracted for. But unless there was something criminal in his behavior, there are really no grounds for a lawsuit."

"The pictures he took were criminal." She sat upright in the chair, and leaned forward. "I should know."

"Yes." He looked away from her cleavage as he tapped the card in his pocket. "You're a photographer."

"One of the best." She switched legs, crossing the left over the right, again making no effort to adjust her dress. "And I know a slipshod job when I see one. That man should be out of business. I'm going to do whatever I can to ruin him."

He took a deep breath to smother his sigh as he imagined the pressure her wedding photographer faced. It would be like his handling the divorce of another divorce lawyer. The client would question his every move. "I'm sorry. I can't help you. I guess Missy didn't make it clear. I'm strictly a divorce lawyer."

Her face hardened and the long lashes hovered in an excruciatingly long blink. "No. She didn't say that. I told her I wanted to see a lawyer. She recommended you."

"I could refer you to someone if you wish. But I really think you should reconsider. How long ago were these pictures taken?"

"I've been married six months. And I've been arguing with Phillips since the wedding. I hoped he would make things right."

"A lawsuit because you're unhappy with the way a job turned out is very difficult to pursue."

"The pictures were deplorable."

"Being unhappy with their artistic qualities is not really grounds for a suit."

"The lighting on the picture of us cutting the cake was atrocious. I would be embarrassed if I presented such pictures to a client. People have to be told what kind of jerk he is."

Bret realized any logical legal arguments were pointless. He rose. "Let me give you a card." He paged through a book he kept on top of the file cabinet behind his desk and found a card for a lawyer he was not particularly fond of. He would never refer this arrogant woman to someone he respected.

"Attorney Ashton handles these kinds of cases." He held out the card. "I would suggest you call his office."

After a few seconds, she clambered out of the chair and tugged her skirt down. "Fine." She snatched the card. "Thanks for all your help," she sneered as she sauntered out of the office as quickly as her tight skirt allowed.

He dreaded tomorrow's dinner with Missy. It wasn't going to go well.

*****

Missy was late. Bret sat at the hotel lobby bar sipping a glass of ice water, and was about to leave, when a balding man moved next to his stool and bumped him as he tried to get the barmaid's attention. "Sorry," he said in a clipped tone.

"No problem," Bret said, shifting a bit to allow him more space. He watched him rapping chubby fingers on the bar, breath spraying from his pouting lips as he stared at the slender woman who was busy preparing a mixed drink. He started to snort like a bull preparing to charge.

He was the kind of demanding man who would drive his wife crazy. Bret turned away and tried to calm himself. He had dealt with too many divorces, too many unhappy couples. In fifteen years, he had seen it all, and it dominated his interactions with people.

It was why he had never been able to establish a relationship of his own, let alone get married. He was resigned to live the single life.

"Excuse me," the man finally shouted across the bar.

Bret felt sorry for the barmaid.

"Sorry, honey," she said as she strode to him.

"I've been standing here for five minutes."

A blatant lie.

The barmaid shrugged. "What can I get you, sweetie?"

He rapped the bar. "I'm not your sweetie."

"Sorry. What'll it be?"

He glanced at Bret as if expecting him to agree that she was a bitch. After a few seconds, he huffed and spun away. "Never mind. I'll take my business elsewhere." He stormed off.

The barmaid tilted her head and tightened her lips as she looked at Bret.

"He was kind of impatient," Bret said.

"That was Willy."

"You know him?"

"He's my ex."

Bret slid off the stool and grabbed the bar for support. "Well, I can see why, considering the way he treated you."

She looked up and down the bar to confirm that no one was waiting for service before leaning toward Bret. "I wasn't the greatest wife, either. Kinda expected too much of him. And then I started—" She stopped and looked up and down the bar again.

"Has your divorce been finalized?" Bret asked, his hand slipping toward his jacket pocket as he sensed she might need a lawyer. But before she answered, Bret heard someone call his name. Turning, he saw Missy standing inside the entrance waving her arms like she was flagging a taxi.

"Are you okay?" He asked when he saw the fright on her face. "You're late."

"Sorry." Trembling, she leaned against the bar for support. "I was at your office."

"What for?" Steph left early today, but Missy had a key. "You know we meet here first Thursday."

"I'm upset. Not thinking straight."

"What's wrong?"

Her cheeks wobbled like she was struggling to control her tears. "Daria."

"That friend of yours. What about her?"

She pressed fingertips against her cheek. "She's dead."

"What?"

She stumbled toward one of the circular tables scattered

around the floor. "The police are looking for her husband. Daria had filed for a protection order. That's why she went to see you. For a divorce."

He sat across from her. "That's not what she told me. She said she wanted to sue her wedding photographer."

"What? She told me she wanted a divorce."

"What exactly did she say?"

"We met for lunch the other day and all she did was complain about her husband. He beats her. A lot. She was thinking about a PFA. She said she needed a divorce. A couple minutes later she asked me if I knew any good lawyers and I gave her your name."

"Did she specifically say she was looking for a divorce lawyer?"

"No." She leaned toward him and lowered her voice. "But I thought." She stopped.

"Did she say anything to you about her wedding photographer? She seemed really worked up about him."

"No. She just talked about her husband." She sucked in a breath. "Chuck. That's who killed her."

"Let's back up. What exactly happened?"

"Neighbor found her dead on her front porch. Bruises all over her body. Someone beat her up real bad. She told me Chuck beat her all the time."

Bret stood. "When did this happen?"

"Yesterday afternoon." She reached for his arm. "As far as I can tell, not long after she talked to you."

"And the police have arrested the husband?"

"No. Not yet. The police are looking for him," she said. "He killed her. He must have."

He held out a hand. "Calm down. Let's not jump to conclusions."

"She was afraid of him. And now he probably knows I was trying to help her get a divorce." She slapped a hand to her cheek. "He might be after me now. Oh, my God. They've got to find him." She started to stand.

Bret caught her forearm and forced her back into the seat. "Take it easy." He checked his watch as he stepped away from the table. "Let me go to the police station and see what I can find out. Maybe Garfield's still there." Garfield Billings was a police detective. Bret had handled his divorce from his drug addicted wife.

*****

"Not my case." They sat in a cramped visitor's cubicle at the downtown police station. "It was assigned to Harrison."

"You know anything about it?"

He shrugged his knobby shoulders that threatened to burst out of his white dress shirt that was soggy with sweat. "I know the woman was beat to death. Though it looks like one blow to the head did the trick."

"Bare hands? Or a weapon?"

"A little bit of both as I hear it. They're looking for her husband. Neighbor said they fought a lot."

"What's his name?"

He stroked his stubbled chin. "Chuck Corcoran, I think. Listen, I could ask Harrison to talk to you, if you want."

"I can't stand Harrison."

That drew a smile. "Join the club."

He briefly explained his interest in the case and Daria Fellanchetto's visit to him yesterday. "I'm just curious. I'll check in with Harrison another time."

*****

He saw Harrison sooner than he expected.

The next morning, two police detectives sat in his secretary's outer room. She introduced them, though he knew them both, and said, "I insisted they wait out here for you."

Good for you, he thought. "Can I help you, gentlemen?"

Harrison, the older of the two, stood and gestured toward his office. "Are you Daria Fellanchetto's lawyer?"

He walked in and waited until both detectives were inside so he could close the door behind them. "No."

"Oh?" The younger one, Ferdinand, a thin athletic type with jet black hair, fumbled toward a chair. "We were told you were."

"Who told you that?" He looked at Harrison, who smoothed the dusting of gray hair atop his scalp.

"We'd rather not say," he said.

Bret moved behind his desk. "Okay. Let's not play any games. I know why you're here. Mrs. Fellanchetto was murdered. But I'm not her lawyer and don't have any information that might help your investigation. I never met her until yesterday." He briefly explained the reason for her visit and the reason he sent her away.

"Phillips." When Bret mentioned the photographer,

Harrison indicated for Ferdinand to make a note of the name. "Seems strange," Harrison said. "She came to see a divorce lawyer and she never mentioned anything about her husband who supposedly beats her. Are you sure?"

Bret tightened his biceps in an effort to control his anger. "I'm sure."

"Then there must have been a mix up." He stepped toward the door and jerked a thumb at Ferdinand. "Sorry to have bothered you."

Ferdinand realized that it was time to go and he stood.

"Thanks for your time," Harrison said as he took another step toward the door.

"I understand that her husband beat her to death," Bret said.

"Where did you hear that?"

"Is he in custody?"

"We've interviewed him."

"Really. You found him?"

Grunting, Harrison nudged Ferdinand toward the door.

Bret persisted. "Is he the one who told you I was her lawyer?"

Harrison turned.

"Because if he did, then that means he must have been following her. He saw her come to my office. And later that day she ends up dead. Sounds pretty clear cut to me."

"We're done here," Harrison said. "For now. We'll be in touch."

*****

The studio was a small building on the edge of the woods that crawled up Knob's Hill just outside of the city. It was set back a bit, barely visible from the road, and there was no sign broadcasting its presence, just a small plaque on the door, once Bret found it. There was no bell. He had to rap loudly before the door opened.

"Can I help you?" He was a thin man with a bent nose that caused a slightly nasal twang.

"Are you Mr. Phillips?"

"That's what it says on the door." He stepped back. "What can I do for you?"

Bret stepped inside the tiny outer room. The door that led into what he assumed was the photography studio was closed. "I want to ask you a few questions about Daria Fellanchetto."

"That bitch?" He tapped slender fingers against his lips. "Sorry."

Bret shrugged. "She's dead."

"What?"

"Someone beat her to death and left her body on her front porch."

"What's that got to do with me? Wait. You don't think?" He stopped and looked around the room as if seeking a place to sit. There were no chairs. Only a small table and a coat rack. And photographs filling the walls. "Who are you?"

He identified himself. "She came to me because she wanted to sue you."

"Why?"

"Because she thought you did a lousy job with the wedding

pictures."

He chuckled, then snorted like a bull and tugged at his crooked nose. "And now the cops think I killed her? Is that why you're here?"

"The police have interviewed her husband." It was the most non-committal phrasing he could manage.

"That bum? I'm sure he probably killed the bitch."

"You know him?"

"I was at their wedding, remember? Listen, what did she tell you about me?"

"Just that you're a lousy photographer."

He sneered again and considered his words. "You're sure she didn't hire you?"

"No. I'm a divorce lawyer."

His eyebrows arched for a moment at that. "She didn't give you anything?"

"No."

"You're not her lawyer?"

"No. How many times do I have to keep saying that?"

"Then what do you care that she's dead? Why are you bothering me?"

"I'm just wondering when you last saw her."

"That would be two weeks after her wedding when I delivered the pictures."

"You haven't seen her since?"

"No. Talked with her on the phone a few times. Exchanged some nasty emails. But, no, I haven't seen her." He pointed to the door. "Now, leave me alone."

*****

Bret called Garfield Billings who confirmed that Fellanchetto's husband was not in custody.

"Why not?"

"Don't worry. They're keeping tabs on him while they investigate."

"I think he's a violent man. She was getting a PFA against him. Believe me, I've handled enough bitter divorces. He fits the profile."

"No paperwork for a PFA was filed. But I'll tell Harrison of your concerns."

"Good luck with that."

*****

After a quick meal in the diner a half mile from his office, Bret returned to his building, parking in the small lot across the street from the four-story structure whose main tenant on the ground floor was a foot doctor. It was after hours and the outer door was locked. He went inside and took the stairs to his second-floor office.

He froze as soon as he went through the door into the hall. His outer office door was ajar. Stephanie had been here when he left, and she would never neglect to lock the door. Nor would she be here this late. He took a few deep breaths as he tried to decide on his course of action. He had no weapon on his person, though he did keep a handgun locked in a cabinet in the office.

He took out his cell and called Detective Billings. "Get a car to my office," he whispered. "There's someone inside." When Billings started to ask questions, he simply snapped, "Hurry," and disconnected.

He pushed in the door to Steph's outer office but stayed out in the hall. When there was no response from inside, he took another breath, and jumped into the room, quickly moving away from the door.

Still no reaction. No sound from his inner office, either. That door was also open. And the light was on.

He crept to Stephanie's desk and found her brass letter opener. It wasn't much of a weapon but it was the best he had. He figured his chances of getting to the gun cabinet in his office were pretty slim. It was behind his desk and he would probably never get to it if there was anyone inside. He clutched the opener like a dagger as he approached the door to his office.

"Who's there?" he shouted.

There was no response. No sound at all.

"The cops are on their way."

That brought an audible gasp and the sounds of a struggle.

And a woman's scream.

He surged through the door and saw Missy behind his desk struggling with a tall man for control of a handgun. He recognized Angelo Phillips as he hopped up on the desk and dove, crashing into them while still gripping the letter opener.

Missy kept screaming.

The three of them smashed against the high cabinet behind his desk, but thankfully, Phillips took the brunt of the collision, his neck and shoulders slamming the door shut with a nuclear bang. Missy fell away to the floor and Bret dropped to his knees. He heard the clatter of the gun but lost sight of it. From the floor Phillips lashed out with his foot, catching Bret in the shoulder. Phillips scrambled to his feet and shoved him away.

"Stop."

Phillips was scrambling around the desk when Missy shot him.

Bret used the desk for support as he struggled to his feet and he saw Phillips writhing on the floor. "Missy, no."

She was approaching him, the gun raised. "He was going to kill us," she said.

"The police will be here any second."

"He was looking for a letter. He thought I was your secretary. He thought I knew where it was."

"What kind of letter?"

"A letter he sent to Daria. A threatening letter. He knew it would lead the police to him."

Still gasping for breath, Phillips had managed to get on all fours, facing the door. He crawled one foot and gasped for breath, then another foot.

Missy raised the gun.

"No." Bret was able to catch her hand and the bullet went into the ceiling.

"Nobody move." Billings and a uniformed officer stood in the doorway.

*****

Missy was late again. Bret sat on a barstool and watched the balding man slap his hands on the bar. "Can I get some service?"

The young bartender seemed frightened as she rushed to him.

"I'm sorry," he said. "I thought you were Josie."

"She's off tonight." Her hands were shaking. "What can I get you?"

"Never mind. I'm fine." He turned and strolled away like it was just another day at the office.

Bret sipped his drink and wondered what kind of bizarre game he and his ex-wife were playing. With a shiver, he grabbed his glass and slid off the stool. Maybe it was time to find another line of work.

He went into the restaurant to wait for Missy.

Angelo Phillips had survived his wound but was still recovering in the hospital. His lawyer shielded him from the police while insisting that he had nothing to do with Daria Fellanchetto's murder. The threatening letter he wrote was found in her office. Harrison wouldn't let Bret see it but Billings told him that, though it was a direct threat of violence, it was clearly the ravings of a harmless blowhard.

Harrison was still considering an arrest, once Phillips got out of the hospital.

"Phillips won't be charged," Bret told Missy when she arrived. "He didn't kill her."

"I know." She slipped into the seat across from him. She puffed like she had just run a marathon and her hands trembled like leaves in the wind. "Her husband beat her to death. Everybody knows that. Phillips was just worried about that threatening letter because it would make him look bad. It might make the police check him out. I tried to tell him—" She stopped.

"Tell him what?"

She looked around for a few seconds, her eyes twirling like marbles. "He wanted that letter."

"You're not a good liar, Missy. You never were. That's why we had so much trouble with your divorce."

"I'm not lying."

"For starters, what were you doing in my office?" After she didn't respond, he continued. "You have a key. You let yourself in."

"I wanted to talk to you, so I went inside to wait."

"You lured him there by telling him I had the letter he was looking for."

"No." Her head sagged.

"You're playing a dangerous game."

"What?"

"I know you were hoping Phillips died in my office, right?"

She tapped her throat like she was fighting off a cough.

"You tried to kill him."

"No."

"But you're not a very good shot."

"I don't know what you're talking about."

"It was my gun."

"Yes. I took it out when I heard someone coming into the outer office."

"How did you know it wasn't me coming in?"

"I— I—"

"You said you were waiting for me, right?"

"I wasn't sure."

"You set the whole thing up. When I came in, all I saw was you two struggling over the gun. But you're the one who had it. It was a fake hostage situation where you planned to end up killing him. Then the police would have a dead suspect in the Fellanchetto murder. They'd pin it on him."

She started shaking her head. "You're not making any sense."

"But now that Phillips lived, you're back to blaming the husband."

"That's crazy."

"I'm not crazy when I tell you that you need a good lawyer. Phillips is going to survive. And he's going to tell the police what happened. You called him, didn't you? You said you were my secretary and told him I had the letter."

She kept shaking her head and popping her lips like she were trying to speak.

"You staged the whole thing."

"Bret."

"Once the police get the whole story out of Phillips about the gun and the supposed letter, they're going to figure out you're playing games."

"No."

"You killed her, didn't you?"

"I— I'm sorry." She started to ramble. "I hated her. I always hated her. Even back in school. And Chuck." She stopped and slapped her fingers to her lip.

"She wasn't seeking a PFA, was she? You just started that rumor."

Her head sagged.

"You planned all this. You're trying to pin a murder on him."

She smacked the table. "I loved him."

"What?"

"But he wouldn't divorce her. He said he wanted to work it out. He laughed at me."

Bret took a deep breath. Love and divorce. Fifteen years and he still couldn't understand it. "Like I said, you better get yourself a good lawyer." He stood.

She raised her head and gaped with wide eyes and pleading brows. "Will you help me?" she whispered. "Please."

"Sorry," he said. "I'm strictly a divorce lawyer."

One Night in a Barn in Montana

Sam Westcott

"Are you cold?" It was the first thing I'd said in thirty minutes. It was a cold evening and I expected her to nod. Checking my watch, I realised it was now morning and wondered if she was tired as well.

It was raining and windy, the wind blew the doors on the barn against their wooden frames and sounded like constant explosions. She jumped or attempted too whenever this happened. She was shivering and the roof on this old place wasn't secure. An old wooden barn wouldn't survive a swat team or the FBI, I only needed tonight. One night.

But the location was secure, that was the important thing. We were miles from everywhere in each direction, nothing but forests and grass. She could scream, howl and cry and it wouldn't make a difference. But she didn't make any noise, she jumped every time the wind blew and ignored the rain pouring from the sky outside.

She didn't respond to the situation. I guessed that she would have. She fought so hard when I put her in the van. I still have bruises on my legs, scratches on my arms. I grabbed her from the parking lot of a shopping mall when she finished her shift. I put a bag over her head and tied up her wrists. I thought this one would be a fighter, would at least continue fighting. But watching her from across this old wooden desk, there wasn't a fighter sat there. There was a scared girl. She was sat shivering, sometimes the odd tear and hard breathing now. Fear was setting in. Nothing except that, she didn't even look at me. Her eyes stared at the desk, stared at the marks and old varnish and mould.

"It's a nice uniform… Have you worked there long?" She was a security guard at the mall. She was easy to follow and easy to see when all her colleagues were men thirty years older.

She always smiled when she went around on patrol. Customers liked her, and shop workers enjoyed saying "hello." Her popularity made her easy to track and easy to snatch from the parking lot. I'd learnt her shifts in a week. But she never noticed me. I kept away from cameras, but behind her. I wore hats, wigs and sunglasses. It was a cliché, but I wasn't gonna get caught. I blend in, something the Army liked about me as well.

I blew out the smoke from my cigarette. Straight in her face and it disappeared. She coughed like I wanted her to, finally a reaction and she looked up at me. No response to the provocation aside from sad eyes and shock.

Her eyes were deep and brown, welcoming and warm. They looked familiar, made me remember something I'd tried to forget. For a minute I almost got lost in them, that's not an exaggeration. Around us the dark seemed somehow more encompassing now. The one little light in the centre of the desk shone, it made her look like an angel fallen to Earth.

I put the cigarette on the floor, stamped on it and she was still looking at me.

"What are you gonna do to me?" Her first words in the

barn. I felt satisfied, happy even. Her voice sounded smaller than I expected, childlike and vulnerable. We hadn't been formally introduced yet. She wasn't crying now but I could tell she didn't want to. She didn't wanna seem weak or scared, holding in the tears.

"Not what you think Gemma." I leant forward, hands on the table and my palms facing upward. Open body language, with a slight smile. I wasn't threatening, I wanted to talk.

"How do you know my name?" She was shaking, upset. I saw her holding back tears and I saw so much fragility, failing at it now. Traci wouldn't do that; she'd try and scratch my eyes out now. I could see why Gemma was known as the "butterfly" or "butter" in her family. A gust of wind could smash her into a tree. Was this a good idea?

"I knew your sister."

"My sister was murdered by her boyfriend... Before Thanksgiving." Gemma said that in a low voice, upset voice. "Look if you let me out of here, I'll do anything right now... I won't tell anybody about this and I mean it... I'll do anything."

"Oh Christ." I said that under my breath, but she still heard it. This had to have been a mistake. How can two people have the same parents and be so different? I stood up and walked back into the shadows contemplating my next move. I opened the barn door and behind me I left her in fear. It was a ten-minute walk in the pouring rain to the house I grew up in. I hoped the time away would give me an opportunity to see an answer.

For an hour I ate some of the supplies I had allocated for the week. I sat in the chair I always did at the kitchen table I grew up in. The generator for the house wasn't working so I had to settle for a battery powered flashlight.

I walked over to the barn again. The rain was still going on. I was wet and dishevelled, I looked like a hermit by the time I got there. It's what I've become anyway, wouldn't make a difference to the situation. My time away from the barn didn't give me an answer.

Gemma was still sat in the centre. Her eyes were closed now, and she seemed to be muttering something. "A prayer Gemma? Really?"

"There's nothing else I can do. Is there?" She opened her eyes as I sat down opposite her again. I passed her a bag of Cheetos I'd carried over.

"You can pray all you like, but trust me God doesn't exist, and he won't save you here…You must be hungry Gemma? I know you like Cheetos… I've been told you like them so much you kept some in your bedside cabinet well into high school for a midnight snack." I opened the packed and started chewing on a Cheeto.

"How do you know that? You're a stalker, right?" She looked at the Cheetos.

"A stalker? I'm at least ten years older than you, so you can drop the theory of me being a weird guy you went to high school with. I'm not a stalker and I'm not a killer… I'm not a rapist and I'm not a bad guy…" I stood up and walked over to her chair, she instinctively backed away. I leant forward and undid the rope around her hands, looked at the red marks on her wrists. Then she tried punching me. Yeah. This was Traci's sister.

"Let me fucking go then!"

I walked back and sat on the chair. I wasn't worried she'd escape; the chair was ninety pounds heavier than her and she'd never undo the rest of the ropes. "It wasn't a great punch Gemma..."

"Fuck you weirdo!" There's the attitude, something you expect from a security guard and something you expect from Traci's sister.

"I'm not a weirdo... Though I'm in need of a shower?" She didn't laugh, and I pulled on the beard I'd grown over the past six months. "I'm not a rapist and I'm not a stalker or killer like I said... Gemma I'm just a guy who wants justice and I need your help." She had her arms held up; the Cheetos were untouched. "Sergeant Tobias Stone at your service ma'am." I leant in and offered my hand.

For a second, she didn't move. She was completely silent, looking only at the desk and breathing hard. "You killed her... It was you wasn't it? Wasn't it?! You were her boyfriend!"

The chair scraped as she moved it, banged her fist on the table, probably hurting her more than the wood. "You killed my sister! You killed my sister you bastard!"

I let her get it all out. It had to happen. This wasn't grief, she was done with grief now. She had been for a long time, spent nights crying over the loss of her elder sister. She had lost a lifetime of shared secrets and bonds, arguments and making up. I didn't say a word and didn't even react when she threw the bag of Cheetos back at me. I picked one up actually and ate it, I preferred the apples at the house though.

"She loved you... She loved you, you bastard and you killed

253

her! You killed her… She even told me your name, said you were amazing and she could see a future with you." She started crying, small sobs like a wounded animal as her head hung down facing the floor. She was defeated, the wound was opened.

"I didn't kill Traci… I loved your sister Gemma; I was looking forward to meeting you over Thanksgiving and I was gonna propose as well… I didn't kill her… Butter, I didn't kill her."

"Don't you call me that! She called me that… You fucking murderer! You stole her…"

"Gemma if you calm down… I'll tell you why I didn't kill her." I tried to be calm, rational but I had to open this wound again and feel the pain. For six months I've been alone here in the farm. I've been contemplating, planning and brooding. I've hunted for food and bought supplies from the local store. I thought I wasn't human anymore but when I hear Gemma crying and shouting, calling me a murderer… I think I am. I'm a man. I'm a man who lost the woman I love. I'm a man who sees nothing ahead and behind all I know is a nightmare.

"You would say that… They've been looking for you for six months… God your face was on a billboard in town… It was in the news…You bastard! The second you let me out of here I am gonna kill you!" I understood her rage. I'd felt it myself.

"I didn't kill her Gemma… I remember that night as well! God, it never leaves me… Tell me, have you ever loved anyone Gemma?" She was silent, waiting. The rage had been silenced for a moment. I touched my head, stroked my beard. It was a reflex, a source of comfort as I opened memories I thought were long dead. "Because I loved her… It wasn't just the type of high school love where you write in a yearbook, get pregnant and get fat and resentful together. She was the other half of me Gemma… For six months I've lived as half a person and I won't do that anymore."

"Tell me what happened?" The question I never wanted to answer. But she wasn't shouting, wasn't threatening to kill me.

"I had been sent back from Iraq… I was tired, dirty and just wanted to get in a hole by the time I got back to the good old US of A…" I couldn't look at Gemma. Just keep talking I told myself. You've done it, opened the memories. Be brave. Come on soldier. "I was staying in a friend's apartment while they were spending the weekend with their parents… One night on a trip to an all-night corner shop run by a friendly Korean guy for a whisky run, I had a cake dropped on me…"

"She loved baking… And she was always clumsy… I used to love her lemon cheesecake, but you could make this up… You'll have to do better." Not a voice that believed.

"I had cream and icing and shit all over my clothes… She invited me up to her apartment, above the little Korean place to clean up… Yelled down to say sorry almost straight away… When I got up there it turns out she thought I was a vagrant alcoholic and kept a knife with her in case I got a bit to handsy… Then we started talking and we talked until four am… Then I never left, and we fell in love… thirty-three days later I was alone again." I could feel tears in the corner of my eyes, like little pieces of glass wanting to poke out. You're still human soldier. You've opened the wound now. Let it bleed.

"Tell me what her favourite book was?" Traci asked her question while I sat in silence.

"What?" That was surprising.

"What was her favourite book fucker?! She was doing a Masters in English Literature if you knew her, you'd know what it is…"

"It was "A Farewell to Arms" when she was with her family… Your Dad loved Hemingway, didn't he? Your Dad the Literature Professor would even give lectures when had more than a couple of glass of wine about how good a writer Hemingway was…" She looked surprised; I knew something only the family would know.

"But with friends and when she was with me… It was the sonnets; she had a well-worn book of every Shakespearian sonnet… Some even had notes on them." I smiled as I said that. I remembered every night I'd spent with her listening to her opinions about those beautiful sonnets. I miss you Traci.

"You did know her… But you could have still killed her."

"I know you think that and you're right… I could have still killed her… But ask yourself if I did do it… If I escaped from the Police and have been on the run for six months, what is the point of me coming here? I'm asking you to believe me… Look at the man in front of you Gemma…" My voice shook, I couldn't help it. "This is the man who found the woman he loved covered in blood… her eyes still open and the blood still flowing out of her…"

"Don't please don't say it… Don't." She was crying again, no passion behind the tears. There was sadness, like a poor pathetic mouse. Did I do the right thing? Will she help me.

"She had been stabbed… God too many times to count, her skirt had been ripped off and… I called the Police, they turned up... Just the one car though... I don't remember anything more than that.... Nothing from that night" I felt sick. I'd been honest, spoken more openly then I had in months.

Her quiet tears kept going. I didn't know if I could stop them. Mine were leaking too.

I felt empty inside, just a void. I had no heart or soul, that died in the blood. God that everlasting pool of blood. I'd seen death before of course. I'd caused death before. That was the reason I was sent home... I just never knew you could have that much blood in the human

I reached into my left jacket pocket and I let it drop onto the table.

Her tears stopped, only for a moment. On her face I could read surprise, joy and finally sadness. "That's Traci's sonnet book... It is, isn't it?"

"Yes, it is Gemma... It's all I have left, I'll never let it go... I didn't kill Traci; I hope you believe that now Gemma?" She nodded, slowly. There was a wariness there that I knew would never leave her. "I was sent home from the middle east because I killed a civilian and I couldn't get over it... Not all the counsellors and psychiatrists in the world helped... I promised myself that I would never kill again... Not even a bug on the sidewalk." I smirked silently, she kept listening though. "I didn't kill Traci, but I think I know who did Gemma... For six months I've been the most wanted man in the state and probably top ten on the Federal list, but I know who killed her and when I find him... I'm gonna break my promise." Now the question I had to ask, the only reason she was here. "Will you help me Traci?"

Traci watched me with wet eyes. I stared back trying to hold back own tears. Around us was silence and darkness. The rain hadn't stopped. It was five am, almost sunrise.

I had nothing left, if I let her go and she didn't agree to help then I'd be in prison before tomorrow night. But then she said in a quiet voice, not shaking or nervous just one word. She said, confidently, "yes."

I nodded back.

Oh Babylon

Bryn Fortey

Rain, rain, go away, come again another day. It's not been raining for 40 days and 40 nights. It just seems like it...

I guess being black and named Marvin Bone, so therefore called Boney by the other kids, it was sort of inevitable that I would dig into the back catalogue of that old German-based disco group. I, after all, was M. Bone, and they were Boney M. I loved all their stuff, but *Rivers of Babylon* was my favourite. One of the biggest selling UK singles ever, so the record books say.

Being big as well as black, and not the quickest pupil in the class, my future prospects seemed limited by both my situation and my inclinations. On the one hand, a life of crime beckoned -muscle being an always useful commodity. On the other, the possibility of a sporting career -something the young me excelled at in general. I still hold the area school-age shotput record, to this day.

Paul Mulligan could have been an academic success.

He had the brains. Could have passed exams, gone to university, qualified as whatever he wanted; skinny little white-arsed honky rebel. Trouble was, he only had eyes for the gangs. School, when he bothered to turn up, was just an amusement.

Some of the kids took the piss out of me, often with a racial element, and I usually flattened them. When Paul Mulligan took the piss I generally saw the joke and laughed along with it. His barbs were never about my colour. In that strange way of opposites attracting, we got along okay.

I sometimes wondered if I was named after Marvin Hagler, *Marvellous* Marvin Hagler, one-time Middle-weight Champion of the World. According to my Mum, my father chose the name and I couldn't ask him since he did a runner before my first birthday. I hoped it was after Hagler though, because I was well into boxing myself.

Marvin's fight with Tommy *Hitman* Hearns was short, brutal, and an absolute epic, which he won. He was either dumb or too cocky when he lost to Sugar Ray Leonard, letting them talk him down from fifteen rounds to twelve. Sugar Ray, after a good first half, was tiring towards the end while Hagler was coming on strong. Another three rounds and he might well have been the winner.

I won some schoolboy titles and joined the local Amateur Boxing Club, moving through the weights as I grew into the heavies. I wasn't very scientific but was able to bludgeon my way to building up a reasonable record with a good percentage of wins against my name.

Paul Mulligan, meanwhile, had worked his way through the small-time hoodlum ranks. He aimed to make his mark and move up with the big boys, and in our neck of the woods that meant Olly Roxborough. Our local Big Cheese, with legit business interests as well as all the illegal ones. He dabbled in boxing as a small-hall promoter and manager, owning a gym which was situated over a pub, which he also owned.

"Don't go with Roxborough," was the advice given to any budding talent at my Amateur Club. "None of his fighters have good careers." But when I came to Roxborough's attention he had my old school friend whispering in his ear, and it was Paul who made the approach.

"They say he don't look after his boys," I said.

"I can't comment on the past," said Paul, dismissing it with an expressive shrug, "but I'm on board now and I'll make sure that everyone gets a fair crack, especially my old mucker."

"My trainer says I should be okay to go for the ABA's in a year or two."

"Why wait? You might get injured, you might get beat. Then it's a couple of years wasted. Turn pro now, Marvin. Get some money in your pocket. I'll make sure Olly Roxborough treats you right."

I listened to him then, just as I had at Merton Hill Comprehensive. I should have remembered that Paul often got me into trouble back in our schooldays.

If I ever asked about my father, Mum would usually laugh and say he had been a Haitian Warlock. I guess she wasn't too cut up at his vanishing act since I had a succession of "uncles" and even a step-dad or two. She was a survivor, my mother, and always made sure there was someone able to put food on our plates.

But a Haitian Warlock?

More chance of my dad being from Birmingham, and if he

had been from Haiti he would've been a Voodoo Priest rather than a Warlock. I knew that much. I might have been slow in the classroom but that didn't mean stupid. Things would click into place eventually but by the time they did the teacher had already moved on to something else.

So I signed a contract with Olly Roxborough and embarked upon a boxing career. My new home-from-home, the gym over the pub, was Spartan in comparison to my old Amateur Club, but it did have Bob Jenkinson as Head Trainer. Old, yes, with a walnut face and not much hair left, but still trim at not much more than the featherweight limit. He had briefly held the British Title, though his best remembered fight was losing an all-out battle against Baby Mendoza, before the Spaniard went on to win one of the World Belts.

Those were the best of times, my early pro career; working and learning under Bob's tutelage while putting together an unbeaten run of twelve fights. Six and then eight rounds on paper but none of them went the distance. One was stopped because the guy was badly cut; on three occasions the ref stepped in to save a helpless opponent from further punishment; and the other eight were straight kayos.

"Don't run before you can walk," Bob would council me in husky tones that were maybe an early warning of the throat cancer that would put him down for the full count only a few years later. "The bums and no-hopers are okay for your learning curve but you aren't ready for the big boys yet."

I look out at the rain, now, coming down in sheets, like the world is going to flood. Is there a new Noah somewhere?

Building a new Ark? Could be that we humans are not worth saving though...

Twelve straight inside-the-distance wins and I had become something of a local celebrity, making the sporting pages of the press. Even the nationals were tipping me as a prospect of note, building me up as a future champion.

"Easy does it, Marvin," warned Bob Jenkinson. "The papers will knock you down as quick as they build you up."

"You could be British Champion tomorrow," claimed my pal Paul. "None of them could stand up to your punching power."

"I look at your muscles and I go weak," said Tiffany Burrows, and I flipped the record so Boney M were singing "Brown Girl in the Ring".

Tiffany was a mixed-race beauty and an aspiring model. Like I keep stressing: slow but not stupid. I knew she would never have glanced in my direction if I'd been stacking shelves in a supermarket. Tiffany wanted to go places and was willing to hitch a lift with anyone who could help, and being seen on the arm of British boxing's new heavyweight hope wouldn't hurt. I knew it but didn't care. Me, with a girl like Tiffany! It was barely credible.

"You dog!" laughed Paul. "You lucky, lucky dog!" "Don't let your love-life interfere with training," snapped Bob Jenkinson.

"Come here, baby," purred Tiffany.

Then Olly Roxborough, local villain and my promoter/manager, announced my first ten rounder, a final eliminator against Alan "Pitbull" Pope, the winner to challenge for the British title. My trainer was not pleased. It was the first time I had seen anyone stand up to Mr Roxborough, but Bob Jenkinson insisted on having his say. Basically, he did not think I was ready to mix it with likes of Pope, a roughhouse slugger and former champion who was looking to get his title back.

The boss left it to Paul Mulligan to put the trainer in his place. Did Bob like his job looking after the Roxborough stable of fighters? Did he want to keep that job? If he did, then it was time to button up and concentrate on keeping them in good shape. Match-making was not his concern.

As for myself, with an unbeaten dozen stretching out behind me and Tiffany making me feel like a king, my attitude was: you line 'em up and I'll knock 'em down. I was going to the top; my girl was certain of it.

It's Biblical, this rainfall. Been pouring down for weeks and there have been news reports of flooding all over the country. No-one could remember the last time our river had burst its banks. I look out with my one good eye, and it's like seeing a shimmering curtain of wet.

I trained hard for the eliminator, skipping and punching to the rhythms of Boney M; though maybe I should have concentrated more on the biblical lyrics of "Rivers of Babylon" rather than the Tiffany-linked "Brown Girl in the Ring". Bob Jenkinson tried to give me a crash course in defensive strategies. I listened to him, out of respect, but I was confident that my punching power would get the job done.

"Pope has a good chin. He takes punishment well," said Bob.

Not punching like mine, I thought.

"And he's got a big overarm right hand."

I've got a left and a right, and a knockout in both.

"They don't call him 'Pitbull' for nothing. If he spots a weakness he's all over it like a rash and doesn't let go." Weakness? What weakness!

Was I overconfident? Well it's no good climbing into the ring if you don't think you can win. You see the worry lines and nervous expressions on boxers who know they are on a hiding to nothing. You see their hesitant actions as they are manoeuvred into positions that the other guy dictates.

"How are you feeling, Marvin?"

"Just fine, Mr Roxborough, fine and dandy."

"Good lad. Win this one and you'll be going for the title."

Two fights and I would be British Champion, with European and maybe World title fights to come. It all spread out before me, and Tiffany was part and parcel of the whole thing, maybe even as Mrs Bone. But first I had to get passed the Pitbull.

My thirteenth bout! Unlucky for some but I wasn't superstitious. Maybe I should have been.

Bone versus Pope was a contender for "Fight of the Year".

No, it wasn't a fight, it was more like a war. He might have been nearing the veteran stage but he still had ambitions. I had youth but he had experience.

We went at each-other straight from the opening bell, both

of us determined to land the killer blows that would win us the fight. Never mind fancy footwork and building up the points, neither of us planned on it going to the scorecards.

Was Pitbull a dirty fighter? Of course he was, but clever with it. He knew how to do the majority of the rough stuff on the blind side where the referee couldn't see it. I was too raw and when I retaliated I would be pulled up and warned.

For three rounds we went toe-to-toe. His chin was as good as Bob had said, but so was mine, and we hit one another with punches strong enough to stun a bull. The crowd was going wild.

"Where's your defence?" Bob was snapping into my ear between rounds. "He's suckering you into his sort of fight. Stand off him and move. Make him work." But all I was thinking of was landing the big one and seeing Pitbull flat on his back.

Halfway through the fourth I threw a big right hook, timed to perfection and as hard as I could. Sensing what was coming, Pope leant towards me as he tried to duck and I hit the top of his shaven skull. The hurt that shot up my arm told me that the damage was serious. Pitbull was staggered, but his skull was thick and he grabbed me into a clinch while his head cleared. I dug a gentle right into his ribs and nearly cried out with the pain. It turned out later that I had broken bones in my wrist, but all I knew at the time was that I would be throwing no more big right handers that night.

Backing off I tried to switch from slugger to orthodox, keeping him at bay with straight lefts. Suddenly I was wishing I had paid more attention to Bob's attempts at improving my defence. The bell was a welcome relief but there was little Bob could do during the interval. I admitted to having hurt my hand but played down the full extent of the damage. Bob wanted to retire me there and then but I insisted on a few rounds more to see if I could nail him with a big left.

Alan Pope was canny enough to realise something was wrong and upped the pressure, giving me no respite as he stormed forward. Over the next four rounds he gradually dismantled me, handing out quite a beating in the process. A more experienced individual would either have gone down and taken the ten count, or have retired hurt as Bob wanted; but I kept demanding one round more, hoping against hope that I could still land a knockout.

Come the ninth and Pope was concentrating on a cut on my left eyebrow. He backed me onto the ropes and while the referee tried to break up our mauling he thumbed me hard in the already bloodied eye. I dropped to my knees, Bob threw in the towel, and the referee stopped the contest. Pitbull had won on a technical knockout.

My wrist healed fine, no problem. But the eye, oh man, my left eye. Detached retina, burst blood vessels, and goodness knew what else. I came out with twenty-five percent vision, and lucky to have that, which ended my boxing career. One-eyed fighters don't cut it.

I'm stuck here, now, in Paul's house, looking at the deluge with my one good eye.

I don't think Pitbull tried to blind me deliberately. He was probably after the cut, hoping to worsen it enough to cause a stoppage, and his thumb slipped down into the eye. Though the ref missed it, television cameras caught the incident quite clearly. The British Boxing Board of Control withheld Pope's purse money, eventually declared the fight "No Contest", and offered me a rematch, but the full extent of my injury made that impossible.

In the end another heavyweight was nominated to replace me in the eliminator and was easily defeated. Pitbull went on the challenge for the title but a cagey champion kept him at bay for a decisive points victory. As for me, my license was revoked; Marvin Bone, ex-boxer.

Tiffany came to see me twice in hospital, then her visits tailed off. Paul dropped by occasionally. He was sorry the way things had worked out but when I was ready I could become one of Bob Jenkinson's assistant trainers at the gym. The old guy seemed to be ailing, he said, so eventually the Head Trainer position would be up for grabs.

His last visit hit me as hard as any of Alan Pope's punches. "Someone's going to tell you, so I guess it had better be me," said Paul, my friend since schooldays. "Tiffany has moved into my place. We are an item, now.

Oh, Babylon! The river that splits you rises to swallow you whole. Babylon! Babylon! Was it you who sinned so badly, or am I mixing it with Sodom and Gomorrah? Either way, destruction was the cure.

I'd thought Tiffany was Boney M's *Brown Girl in the Ring*, my magnificent mulatto. But no, she turned out to be the Whore of Babylon. God would punish her one day, of that I was sure.

And still the rains pour down.

A man has to eat, and all I really knew was boxing so when the doctors finished with me I joined the staff at Roxborough's gym, under the direction of Bob Jen-kinson. The boss would drop in now and then, talk to Bob and usually pat me on the back: "Always a job for you here, Marvin."

Paul Mulligan rarely showed his face. He had moved up and no longer concerned himself with the boxing side of things. Word had it that he was Olly Roxborough's right hand man now. On the odd occasion he had to visit the gym we both behaved as if we were strangers, staying as far apart as possible. He pulled a few strings and got Tiffany some catalogue assignments. Her coffee-coloured skin looked sen-sational in snowy white underwear. Well I thought so anyway. Bitch!

Without going into it too deeply, I have always considered myself a Christian, especially the Old Testament variety. An eye for an eye, tooth for a tooth, and I saw nothing wrong with mixing in any other belief system that offered a possible answer. After all, my Mum had always named my father as a Haitian Warlock, whatever that might have meant.

So I fashioned an eight-inch Voodoo Doll and scrawled the name *PAUL* across its body with an indelible marker. I stuck needles and nails into it and tried to send damaging thoughts in his direction. Maybe this would be the prompt God needed to bring down His wrath and lay it at the sinner's door. Not long after I started doing this, Paul accompanied Olly

Roxborough on a visit to the gym and I overheard him complaining of bad indigestion that he couldn't seem to get rid of.

Indigestion! Or black magic? Could that little figure back in my apartment be working?

Bob Jenkinson's health continued to deteriorate and by the time he got himself checked out the throat cancer was terminal and the Sisters of Mercy were soon caring for him as the end approached. I didn't get the Head Trainer position -there were others better qualified than me but I remained on the team.

The last time I saw him he was as talkative as ever, though obviously with great difficulty. "Come close so you can hear me, Marvin," he instructed hoarsely.

"Be cool, Bob," I said. "Don't strain yourself."

"Shut up and listen. There's things I should have told you before. You knew at the time that I wasn't happy when they matched you with Alan Pope."

"And you were right."

"You put up a marvellous show of pure guts, Marvin."

"Marvellous Marvin," I said with a chuckle, trying to keep it light.

"But it was three or four fights too early. The papers had built you up though, looking for a new young hope, and even the bookies were taken in by your twelve straight wins. You were the betting favourite and there were good odds on offer if you wanted to back the old Pitbull."

"What are you saying, Bob?"

"'Olly Roxborough, for all his faults, knows a bit about the fight game. He knew you were still too raw and inexperienced for a roughhouse nutter like Pope."

"So?" I asked, beginning to suspect where this was leading.

"So your pal Mulligan spread the bets out and about. A bit here, a bit there, until Olly had laid out really big money, and all on Pope to win."

"Are you sure about this?"

"I wouldn't be telling you otherwise. Nobody knew how it would end, mind. You were supposed to just take a beating and then Olly would look to get your career back on track again. Nobody foresaw the injuries you would suffer, or the 'No Contest' verdict."

"If I hadn't broken my bloody wrist I would've beaten him." "You might well have, Marvin, you might well have ..."

Bob's voice was barely a whisper and I could see how much the conversation had taken out of him. "At least all bets were cancelled, spoiling their plans. Ask the nurse to come, please, Marvin. Me! Addicted to morphine. Who would have thought it?"

He died the following week.

I kept what Bob told me to myself. I'd been warned that Olly Roxborough didn't look after his boys. I'd been told that his boxers didn't have good careers. My mistake had been in thinking that Paul Mulligan would look after me; I couldn't plead ignorance.

I turned up at the gym and did my job. I was polite to Mr Roxborough when the occasion arose. My continued blanking of Paul was put down to the Tiffany situation, which was partly right. I made a second doll and wrote OLLY on it. I stuck pins in them both, and when the boss man complained of rheumatic pains I smiled to myself. God moved in mysterious ways and if He wanted to use a bit of Voodoo help, that was fine by me.

Oh, didn't it rain, children. Forty days and forty nights! It seemed longer this time. I bumped into Tiffany in the High Street and she was brazen enough to stop and talk.

"Want a coffee?" she asked.

Anything to get out of that non-stop rain so we dodged into a nearby cafe.

"I'm sorry the way things turned out, Marvin."

I just grunted.

"I know you must think me shallow and mercenary, and maybe I am, but I'm also ambitious -you knew that -and I need a partner who can match those ambitions; maybe even help them. We had some good times though, didn't we?"

"Sure, good times," I agreed.

"Maybe the timing wasn't good but I had to move on. I wasn't cut out for the dutiful little woman looking after her injured man."

"I guess not."

Tiffany finished her coffee. "I'm glad we've had this little chat," she said. "Paul tells me the two of you don't speak, like a pair of kids. You really should shake hands and start afresh."

"Maybe one day," I mumbled, "but not yet."

"Bye-bye, Marvin."

I stayed in the cafe, playing with my empty mug and watched as she put up her umbrella and strode out into the rain: statuesque, regal, the Whore of Babylon. But had I detected a tinge of regret in her manner? Could it be that, deep down where she didn't fully realise it herself, she wished that she was still with me?

My apartment, which I could ill afford now on Assistant Trainer wages, was on the fourth floor. Whatever the flooding situation, which seemed destined to reach our corner sooner or later, I would be okay. Paul, however, was looking a bit dodgy. Moving up, he had bought a detached residence in a new housing project. Nice place, well suited to someone getting on, but it nestled in a substantial dip. He obviously hadn't considered the possibility that God's punishment might again be by water.

I had heard him mouthing off, that last time he'd come to the gym, when the subject of potential flooding came up. "I'll not leave my property unguarded for the looters," he'd declared. "I'm well prepared for a long stay."

Cocky bastard!

That evening I let his Voodoo Doll lie in a bowl and turned on the tap. The waters were building up and Babylon would sink beneath the waves. I imagined a little stream of bubbles leaving the doll's mouth and racing to the surface. Drown, Mulligan, fill your lungs with the Lord's holy water.

But what about Tiffany?

Was she a whore or just deluded? In spite of all that had happened I couldn't erase the memories of my hands on her perfect skin, back when she lay beside me. Was I right in suspecting that she still harboured feelings in my direction? Did I want her to drown too?

Things went from bad to worse right across the country. A State of Emergency was declared and the Army was belatedly put on sand-bagging duties, but not even Governments can control the weather and there were no dry spells in the forecast. Locally, the river was swollen with all the excess liquid pouring into it, and the next high tide was awaited with horror. People living in the low parts of town had been advised to evacuate their homes, but I knew my one-time friend had said he wouldn't do it.

It came to me, then, what I had to do. It wasn't about Paul anymore, or about me. It was about Tiffany, trapped in a house that was likely to be flooded. It was about that beautiful brown-skinned girl waiting to be rescued; waiting for me to rescue her.

She would be so grateful, and would see Paul for the treacherous rat he really was. "Take me home, Marvin," she would whisper, throwing her arms around my neck. "Take me away from this terrible man."

Drenched from the moment I stepped outside, I ran all the way to his part of town. The wind howled and the rain beat down. Sodden, I hammered at his front door. Paul opened it and I pushed him aside before his surprise could be translated into speech. "Tiff any?" I called. "Where are you, girl? I'm going to take you to safety."

"She's safe here," retorted Paul.

"When it floods?"

"Sure, up in the attic. It won't reach that high. She's up there now, making it cosy. We've got plenty of food and bottled water, and whatever else I could carry up. Your knight in shining armour act is wasted here."

I just stood there, clenching and unclenching my hands. Not sure what to say or do.

"It's about time you stopped carrying a torch for her.

Tiffany is mine! End of story."

"It's not just about her though, is it?" I snarled, anger rising through me.

"What else?"

"How about me being overmatched against Pope, just so you and Roxborough could bet against me, expecting me to lose!"

"It was just business, Marvin. You weren't supposed to be so badly injured."

"What's going on?" asked a new voice.

We both turned towards Tiffany as she entered the room. "I heard voices," she said. "Marvin has come to rescue you from the floods, and from me."

"My apartment will be safer than this house," I explained, trying to ignore the sarcasm in Mulligan's voice.

"Don't be silly, Marvin," she said. "Paul is my blue-eyed soul boy and he's going to manage my modelling career. This house will be just fine."

"Get back up the attic, Tiff. High tide is nearly upon us. I'll join you shortly."

"Yes, Paul," she said, ignoring me completely.

"You've got your answer, Marvin," he said after she had left the room.

"We were such good friends, Paul, all through our school years. Why did it go wrong?"

He laughed, nastily. "I was the runt, easy to beat, but who was going to touch me when the hardest kid around was my pal? We were never really friends, Marvin, but you were useful."

Two things happened next, in quick succession. Firstly, I hit him with all the pent-up rage that had been building within me, and Paul dropped like a lead weight. Secondly, there was a terrific roar which could only mean that our river had burst its banks and was reaching out to submerge the town. I heard Tiffany scream, up above me in the attic. Then the tidal wave struck the house; flowing, surrounding, finding its way into the ground floor.

Stepping forward as the water swirled at knee height and rising, I placed a foot on Paul's unconscious body. In a repeat of the scene I had played out with the Voodoo Doll I watched real air bubbles rise from his mouth. I didn't remove my foot until those bubbles had stopped.

Wading through the water, which had by then reached over my waist, I went looking for the stairs. Up higher would be the means to reach the attic. What was it Paul had said? Food, bottled water, all they would need for a long stay? Well he wouldn't need it any longer -but I was still alive.

Glancing down, as I stand here now, it looks as if the downstairs rooms are almost totally submerged. Above me Tiffany is in the attic, crying. "Paul?" she keeps calling. "Paul? What's happening? Where are you...?"

I grip the sides of the metal ladder and place my foot on the first rung. The Whore of Babylon waits above me and when I join her I will pull up the ladder and close the trap door. We will be snug and safe until the Lord's vengeance starts to subside, though I think it will be a long wait.

I start to climb the ladder...

The Usual Unusual Suspects

Steve Sneyd sadly passed away mid-2018, and will be greatly missed, not only as a poet, a publisher, an essayist and commentator, but also as a friend to many in the large & small press communities alike. It would be impossible to completely catalogue his appearances – well into the thousands - but http://www.isfdb.org/cgi-bin/ea.cgi?11125 has a very creditable swing at his SFnal material.

Wil A. Emerson has been on the writing path for approximately fifteen years. While not fresh out of college to write the Best Seller, she spent her early years as a Registered Nurse. Now on the fringe of being overlooked due to the inconvenient late start, she's successfully published in anthologies and has one novel under her belt. ***Taking Rosie's Arm***, a Five Star, Thorndike publication, recounts the story of an elderly woman who befriends a troubled, but determined young girl. Writer, artist, traveler, cook: soup's on.
Wil's recent work is mainly mystery and women's fiction. Also a struggling artist, her art can be viewed on her website. www.wilemerson.com

Matthew Wilson has been published repeatedly in *Star*Line*, *Night to Dawn Magazine, Zimbell House Publishing* and many others. He is currently editing his first novel and can be found

Russell Richardson has published many short stories, illustrated a book of poetry, and created children's books to benefit kids with cancer. His YA novel, **Level Up and Die!** (www.levelupanddie.com) was released in April 2021. He lives with his wife and sons in Binghamton, NY, the carousel capital of the world. Learn more about him at http://russellrichardson.org.

Ange Morrissey says she writes for pleasure. 'That's my addiction, which I have no desire to dismiss. Guinness is my other drug of choice, preferably enjoyed in a pub which doesn't do food, apart from crisps and peanuts. My favourites have all survived. Oh, cheese and onion rolls and pork pies are also acceptable.'
Apart from her small but extremely satisfying family, she feels her life is 'blessedly unexceptional, it needs to be, my imagination is peopled with an ever changing, often less than salubrious, cast of characters in quiet turmoil, or noisy disarray. There are dragons there too.'
She also has STRANGESIDE - The Book of Hands: Volume 1 – a fantasy/horror novel on Kindle
(https://www.amazon.co.uk/STRANGESIDE-Book-Hands-Ange-Morrissey/dp/1500790028/)
and is presently working on new full length material.

James Roth is an American, who likes to say he was "Made in Japan" during the U.S. occupation of that country. He lived there for many years. China as well. But now he divides his time between Zimbabwe, South Africa, and the U.S., places where it never snows. He writes fiction and nonfiction in a variety of genres and recently completed a historical mystery/noir novel set in Meiji era Yokohama.

Twitter handle: @Tweet_JRoth 2

Brandon Barrows is the author of the novels *Burn Me Out, This Rough Old World, Nervosa*, and has had over seventy published stories, a selection of which are collected in the books *The Alter In The Hills* and *The Castle-Town Tragedy*. He is an active member of Private Eye Writers of America and International Thriller Writers, and lives in Vermont by a big lake with a patient wife and two impatient cats.

His short story, *Don't You See?* appears in *Crimeucopia – As In Funny Ha-Ha, Or Just Peculiar.*

He can be found at http://www.brandonbarrowscomics.com

On Twitter @Brandon Barrows

Bern Sy Moss has had short mystery fiction in anthologies and in *Mystery Tribune, Woman's World, Spinetingler Magazine, Mysterical-E*, Akashic Books' Nior Series: *Mondays are Murder*, and *Kings River Life.*

Gustavo Bondoni is a novelist and short story writer, a member of *Codex* and an Active Member of *SFWA*. His debut novel, *Siege* was published in 2016, and he has since published two more science fiction novels, one comic fantasy, three monster novels and a thriller. On the short fiction side, he has had over three hundred short stories published in fifteen countries. They have been translated into eight languages. My writing has appeared in *Future Science Fiction Digest, The*

Grantville Gazette, *DreamForge*, *Pearson's Texas STAAR English Test* cycle and many others.

In 2019, he was awarded second place in the *Jim Baen Memorial Contest* and was also a *Writers of the Future* Finalist. In 2018, he received a Judges' Commendation (and second place) in *The James White Award*.

Gustavo has also published two reprint collections, *Tenth Orbit and Other Faraway Places* (2010) and *Virtuoso and Other Stories* (2011). My website is at

www.gustavobondoni.com.

He can be reached at gbondoni@hotmail.com.

Michael Wiley is the Shamus Award-winning writer of two series of PI novels: the Joe Kozmarski mysteries (*St. Martin's/Minotaur*) and the Kelson mysteries (*Severn House*), as well as four non-PI novels. Sam Kelson short stories have appeared in *Ellery Queen* and elsewhere.

Peter W. J. Hayes was born in Newcastle upon Tyne, but his family emigrated to the U.S. many years ago. He has in the past worked as a journalist, advertising copywriter and marketing executive before turning to mystery and crime writing.

He's the author of the Silver Falchion-nominated *Pittsburgh Trilogy*, a police procedural series published by *Level Best Books*, and a Derringer-nominated author of more than a dozen short stories. His short work has appeared in *Black Cat Mystery Magazine*, *Mystery Weekly*, *Pulp Modern* and various anthologies, including two *Malice Domestic* collections and *The Best New England Crime Stories*. Peter has also been short listed for the *Crime Writers Association* Debut Dagger Award.

Michael Anthony Dioguardi teaches and writes in upstate New York. Links to more of his published work can be found here: https://michaeldioguardisciencefiction.tumblr.com/

Robert Petyo's most recent stories have been published in the anthologies: *EconoClash Review*, *COLP: Big*, *Hardboiled*, *Suspense Unimagined*, *Transcendent*, *Serial Magazine*, *Classics Remixed*, *Thuggish Itch*, *Flash Bang Mysteries*, *The Black Beacon Book of Mystery*, and *COLP: Treasure*. His short story – *Legacies* – appeared in CRIMEUCOPIA – We're All Animals Under The Skin.

Sam Westcott has never been published before and **One Night in a Barn** is his first to make it to the printed page.
"I love books and have loved them for as long as I remember. I like literature that evokes a reaction and am a great fan especially of Dashiell Hammet, Patricia Highsmith and Jeff Lindsay. I've always been attracted to stories of people outside of society's rules, not necessarily good people by any stretch of the imagination but people who can be understood. I really enjoy writing, for me it's therapeutic and enjoyable.

Bryn Fortey (1937 – 2021) sadly passed away 21st July 2021. I had known him off and on since the late 1970s both as a writer and poet. Over the years his writing output came and went, though his more recent output can be found in **Merry-Go-Round And Other Words** – and – **Compromising The Truth** (both published by The Alchemy Press https://alchemypress.wordpress.com/alchemy-publications/alchemy-collections/.

He will always be remembered with fondness, and sadness that, after sending me **Mahogany Halls**, and an adjusted reprint of **Oh Babylon**, he would finally depart for good.

Vicky LaPerso (original name Mariana Fuego de Cunha LaPerso) was born in Patagonia on February 29th 1936. Little is known or has been documented about her childhood *("I ain't saying nuthin' about any of that!" - Stone Rolling Magazine interview, 1959)* except that she believes her vocal range of 4 ¾ octaves was instrumental in her ability to call alpacas down off nearby mountains so she could comb them for their wool.

Then, in 1954, she was kidnapped by the Bolivian cell of the Yma Sumac International Appreciation Society, and with the aid of the Mexican contingent of the Carmen Miranda Fan Club, Vicky was successfully smuggled into the United States – eventually ending up in Los Angeles where she was immediately signed to a 5 album deal by legendary producer, Nicky Nakolides, for his Irish based record label, Nic-Nak's Paddy Wax.

Now, at 85, she is one of the leading lights in the Bueno Visa Anti-Social Club revival, with her Greatest Hit – **Good Love Gone Bad** b/w **Strong Poison** – being retro-pressed as a 10-inch 78rpm shellac.

16 stories ranging from the 14th to the 21st Century, all from women authors whose forte is crime.

Featuring *Karen Skinner, Hilary Davidson, Pauline Gostling, Linda Kerr, Kate Miller, Tiffany Lindfield, Lena Ng, Ginny Swart, Sandrine Bergèss, Michelle Ann King, Amanda Steel, Kelly Lewis, Paulene Turner, Claire Leng, Madeleine McDonald and Joan Hall Hovey.*

Paperback Edition ISBN:
9781909498198
eBook Edition ISBN:
9781909498204

CRIMEUCOPIA

We're All Animals Under The Skin

Featuring: John Gerard Fagan, Nick Boldock, Weldon Burge, Chris Phillips, Dan Meyers, Jeff Dosser, Eve Fisher, Emilian Wojnowski, Fabiyas M V, Lamont A. Turner, Edward Ahern, Robert Petyo, Al Hagan, Caroline Tuohey, Steve Carr, Bobby Mathews, Michael Bracken, and June Lorraine Roberts

18 authors take time to look under the skin of the people who sometimes inhabit their heads, and put what they find down on paper.

Featuring John Gerard Fagan, Nick Boldock, Weldon Burge, Chris Phillips, Dan Meyers, Jeff Dosser, Eve Fisher, Emilian Wojnowski, Fabiyas M V, Lamont A. Turner, Edward Ahern, Robert Petyo, Al Hagan, Caroline Tuohey, Steve Carr, Bobby Mathews, Michael Bracken, and June Lorraine Roberts.

Paperback Edition ISBN:
9781909498235
eBook Edition ISBN:
9781909498228

A Crimeucopia Family Gathering

17 writers take us on Cosy journeys - some more traditional, while others are very much up to date.

Eve Fisher, Alexander Frew, Tom Johnstone, John M.Floyd, Andrew Humphrey, Joan Leotta, Gary Thomson, Eamonn Murphey, Matias Travieso-Diaz, Madeline McEwen, Lyn Fraser, Ella Moon, Gina L. Grandi, Louise Taylor, Judy Penz Sheluk, Joan Hall Hovey and Judy Upton.

**Paperback Edition ISBN:
9781909498242
eBook Edition ISBN:
9781909498259**

CRIMEUCOPIA

As In Funny Ha-Ha

Or Just Peculiar

**Putting the Outré back into
OMG are**

*Jesse Hilson, Gabriel Stevenson,
Maddi Davidson, Brandon Barrows,
Robb T. White, Regina Clarke,
Martin Zeigler, K. G. Anderson,
Andrew Hook, Ed Nobody,
Jody Smith, Michael Grimala,
W. T. Paterson, James Blakey,
Emilian Wojnowski,
Andrew Darlington,
Lawrence Allan, Ricky Sprague,
Bethany Maines, John M. Floyd and
Julie Richards*

**Paperback Edition ISBN:
9781909498266
eBook Edition ISBN:
9781909498273**

The five writers here have very respectable track records in the Western genre, and are old hands when it comes to telling compelling stories.

So join
John M. Floyd
Alexander Frew
Jim Doherty
Bruce Harris
and
Brandon Barrows

and let them take you back to a time of six-guns an' whiskey, an' wild, wild fiction.

Paperback Edition ISBN:
9781909498266
eBook Edition ISBN:
9781909498273

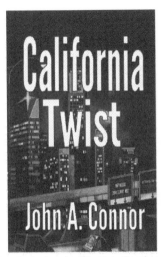

Being dumped sucks. Big time. So when Harry
Rhimes helps Lindsey Fairfax walk into his office, and
she drops a runaway fiancé case in front of him,
Harry knows exactly what's driving her to look for
Preston Llyle.

And that's where the problems start.

What should have been a simple hide-and-go-seek
missing persons case explodes into a rolling life and
death situation as Harry becomes more and more
involved with murders – old, new, and some yet to
happen – old family money, even older malignant
greed, calculating siblings, the city police, hot IT
specialists, cold relationships, college football, drugs,
Californian girl gangs, the Richardsons' dog, and not
forgetting a sadistic killer who has a taste for opera.

But that's just one week in the slightly surreal world
of American born, but British bred, ex-Army major
turned Californian Private Investigator, Harry
Rhimes.

California Twist sees the start of a new series of
novels featuring the life and times of Harry Rhimes, a
Private Investigator who likes to think he's funny – as
in ha-ha, rather than just peculiar...

Paperback ISBN: 9781909498174
Electronic ISBN: 9781909498181

Printed in Great Britain
by Amazon